MW01234554

Starting Over in Sedona

Sedona Silver Romance Book 1

LYNNE M. SPREEN

Silver Life Press

ALSO BY LYNNE M. SPREEN

Silver Life Press

To my sweet husband, Bill, always and forever.

Starting Over in Sedona

Sedona Silver Romance Book 1

LYNNE M. SPREEN

Silver Life Press

Chapter One

Fleeing the Fourth of July party, Sue Weston drove through the sprawling senior community, squinting at the sun as it dropped into the Central Valley haze. The cookie-cutter houses rolled past, streets deserted but for a solitary jogger. Sue waved, but the woman didn't look up.

She drove into her spotless garage, roomier now without Mike's truck. Custom cabinets held dozens of plastic storage containers, all precisely labeled and lined up in alphabetical order. Brooms, dusters, and mops hung on the wall in order from tall to short. The garage smelled faintly of insecticide. Everything was squared-away.

She rolled forward until the windshield kissed the bobbing yellow tennis ball hung from the rafters. Then she shut off the motor and sat in silence, dreading the thought of going inside. For all the humans living in Golden Era, the place was a ghost town. Residents drove inside their garages and disappeared. Except for morning and evening dog-walking, all activity centered at the clubhouse, and it was there Sue had tried to make new friends.

Mike was the one who'd wanted to retire to Visalia after a lifetime of moving around the country. He said it would be like coming home. His roots were here.

Hers were not.

But three years had passed since he died. Wasn't that time enough to be stuck?

Shoving open the door to the kitchen, the stench hit Sue immediately. In a blur of silver-brown, a tiny Yorkie skittered across the beige tile, making a beeline to the living room where she dove behind the couch.

Muttering a curse, Sue went back into the garage for cleaning products.

In his last days, Mike told her to make a life for herself, and she was trying. She socialized. She exercised. She did not eat dinner standing over the kitchen sink. And she resisted the dead weight of loneliness that settled over her like a soggy wool blanket every time she entered her quiet house alone.

Which was why she had stupidly adopted the dog. Gypsy was crazy, a fact the workers at the pet adoption center had minimized. When Sue went there to see what was available, they'd matched her with the Yorkie, no doubt assuming the two old girls would hit it off. Over the past month, Sue had tried everything possible to help the dog feel safe, with no success.

Heaving a sigh, she cleaned up the spot, then peeled off the disposable gloves, and washed her hands. Tomorrow, she would return the dog to the shelter.

At the patio door, the dog trembled, her tail tucked, spine rounded. When Sue slid it open, Gypsy shot past, racing down the hall to the guest room.

"Oh no, you don't." Sue followed and sat on the floor in front of the closet. "I'm not going to let you poop in my shoes. Come on out."

Quaking, Gypsy peered from behind a rack of boots. Despite her misgivings, Sue's heart softened.

"Come here. You'll be okay. You're safe with me." Sue lay on her side, propped on an elbow. "Come on."

Gypsy yawned, a little whine escaping.

"Come on, girl. You can do it."

Ears plastered against her head, the frightened animal crept toward Sue, who lay still until the dog leaned against her chest.

"That's better." Sue scooped her close.

The two of them lay quietly on the carpet, Sue wishing the dog could have settled in and been happy.

They both needed it.

When Mike died, at first, she'd been numb. Then she attended a grief group, and that was helpful. In the past year, discouraged about not healing more quickly, she read everything she could about grief. Viktor Frankl once told a widower that by being the survivor, he had saved his wife the agony. In this way, the man was heroic. Sue found comfort in this interpretation, but at times, she couldn't imagine moving forward. The future looked like a wall of dense fog.

Sometimes she'd awaken in the middle of the night, heart pounding, wondering what set her off, and if something happened to her, who would know? But she was too proud to get one of those medical alert bracelets, and anyway, she was healthy as a horse.

What Sue needed was a loneliness alert bracelet. She could press the button and a friendly voice, probably that of a sympathetic older woman, would come over the loudspeaker.

Sue? Did you call? Everything okay?

I feel anxious, Sue would answer, sitting up in the dark. It's hard to be alone.

I know how that is.

And then the woman would talk companionably, perhaps jabbering about her grandchildren or a pie she baked earlier. Or, depending on your answers to the intake questionnaire, she might remind you that the philosopher Nietzsche was famous for saying a person could survive any "what" if they just knew the "why."

If they only knew what their purpose was.

But Sue didn't know anymore. She crooked her elbow and rested her head on her arm. For the past forty years, her purpose had been family, but the kids were grown and gone, and Mike was—

She squeezed her eyes shut. *Stop it*, she told herself. *Just stop.*

She rearranged her arm over the warm ball of fur that was her new rescue pup. Gypsy had stopped trembling, and her small body was a comfort. Maybe Sue could do more research about house-training a nervous Yorkie. She might give it another week.

An hour later, she awoke to the sound of exploding fireworks and car alarms and a panicked little dog trying to burrow into her armpit. Holding Gypsy tight, they rode out the celebration. When it ended, Sue clambered to her feet, sore from lying on the floor. Sue carried the dog to her bed in the kitchen, made a cup of chamomile tea, opened her laptop, and waded through social media, sucked in by videos of cute baby animals.

What a roller coaster. What a waste of time. This was stupid. She needed to get a grip. Mike was gone. She needed to start living.

She needed sleep.

Checking her email one last time, she spotted the shocking new message.

Roseanne?

Blinking to clear her vision, Sue stared at the bolded header, not trusting the words on the screen.

Emailing me?

How had she even found Sue after all these years? Decades. The last time they spoke, email didn't exist. Since then, the only time Sue had tried to approach her ill sister, she'd been thwarted by a vicious dog, chained near the door of their childhood home. The home Roseanne had extorted at their mother's deathbed.

Fingers trembling, Sue clicked on the link. The message loaded. Biting her lip, she scrolled down to read her sister's words.

Hey, Sis. Long time no talk to. You should come for a visit. Sedona's pretty in the summer and I'm dying.

Chapter Two

Rafael Palacios cut into a perfectly grilled steak and pretended to be interested in the inane patter from the couple sitting across from him. Stifling a sigh, he resigned himself to another hour at the trendiest restaurant in Sedona.

He was getting too old for this.

At least the food was good.

The woman, platinum blond with chrome talons, kept waving her hands around, her many bracelets clanking. The man, a sweaty toad wearing pinky rings, shoveled mashed potatoes into his maw. Rafael controlled his revulsion because the couple, movie people from LA, had money, and they were poised to commit a significant amount of it to his bank account.

"When will you show us the Mesa?" The woman leaned back, martini in hand, silver loop earrings flashing in the candlelight.

"That particular property will not be available for a few days, but I have others," he said.

"Wait, you're not going to let us walk the one you told us about? But I want to see it."

"And you will, just as soon as the lumberjacks are finished cleaning up the remaining logs and lumber from the perimeter."

"Lumberjacks?" The woman all but salivated.

The toad squinted a cynical smile. "In Arizona?"

Rafael nodded. "Absolutamente. There is a forest on adjacent land, and the piñon pines have grown large. I have a crew of men clearing them." Men from the county jail, working off DUIs. Less lumberjack, more failed accountant on a bender. But Rafael didn't have to tell them that.

"I want to see them," she said. "I mean it. The land."

"And you will, just as soon as it is perfect and not a second before." He locked eyes with her. "It is a matter of pride."

"Fine." She threw her head back and raked her nails through long blond hair. "Tell me again about the view, how beautiful it is."

Rafael allowed her a lingering gaze that seemed to convey promise, all part of the dance. It amused him how people fell under the spell of the town and its surroundings. Sedona was beautiful, but it didn't compel him. Certainly not in a spiritual sense. In that, he knew he was alone. He had established his business here solely for commercial reasons, his success testifying to the wisdom of that move.

Gazing across the flickering candle at the center of the table, he adopted a faraway look. "The first thing you notice is the light, especially in the early evening, when the sun is

at such an angle as, hmm, perhaps just before twilight." He
rotated the stem of his wineglass back and forth, feeling her
eyes on him. "Down below the Mesa, the canyon is in
shadow, but on the other side, every spire, every butte is
turning from red to gold to purple. It is—it is—" He paused
to motion with his hands, a gesture meant to signal futility.
"It is indescribable."

The woman licked her lips.

Rafael flashed a self-deprecating smile. "It is easy to be
carried away."

"Sounds nice." The man reached for his woman's hand.

She pulled it back. "And we get to see it when?"

"Soon." That was a lie. The property was a landfill.

But it had potential, and what a score the sale would be.
With the money from this transaction, Rafael would finally
have the cushion to feel secure, to stop running so hard. Of
course, he shouldn't feel this way, but old wounds still
festered. The only thing he trusted now was money.

The check arrived. Rafael paid it and made his escape
before the woman developed greater expectations.

Gunning the Corvette up 89A into the mountains
overlooking Sedona, he missed the early days. Back then,
when he built a modest home here, a minor strip mall
there, the transactions seemed cleaner, more honest. Now,
when the clients planned to hand over multimillions of
dollars for a property, the dream—the seduction—was
expected as part of the deal.

He scowled, sick and tired of the routine, but this would
be the last one. After the sale of Roseanne's property, he
would be able to breathe. Not retire. Never that. He would

always work; he loved work. But he could afford to be more selective. Only do the projects that interested him.

An opossum waddled into the road in front of him. Rafael swerved across the center line and back. An oncoming truck blared its horn at him.

Breathing hard, Rafael swore. He loved living up the mountain, but the highway was narrow, and he didn't like driving after dark. To change his mood, he tried to conjure up the beautiful face of the woman with whom he'd spent the last several nights. But he couldn't. Faces came and went, circling around in his memory like a carousel, nothing sticking, no one woman standing out.

He switched on satellite radio to his favorite jazz station.

Rafael loved women, all women. Their varying shapes and movement, the pitch or depth of their voices, the costumes they chose to wear, the way they performed for him. It was a dance, and he loved to dance, but when the music ended, he always went home alone, no matter how late, always saying goodbye, never sneaking out. The women would protest, but he would not stay, and he did not invite women to his house. He lived in solitude, and that was the way he preferred it.

The sports car growled through the curves and switchbacks toward home.

Rehashing the dinner meeting with his potential buyers, he felt both pride and boredom. What a great performance. And yet, how routine. Not challenging. Not even, to be truthful, that interesting. At this point, he could do this work in his sleep.

He drove up the mountain, speeding through the curves and enjoying the car's performance. He would sell

Roseanne's property as quickly as possible and tuck his fortune into a safe investment. At this point in his life, it wasn't necessary to realize significant growth. No, what Rafael wanted was the security of a big, fat bank account.

Beyond that? He could put John or Matt in charge, take a few months off, and head for Argentina. His contacts told him she would be there. He would reconnect, make amends, and then? Well, he wasn't sure what came next. Maybe he would live in another country part of the time.

He'd been working like a dog for decades, and he loved to be busy, but what might it feel like to stop? To sit on a beach somewhere, sipping a cold beer and watching the women parade around in scraps of fabric?

But that would never happen. Rafael lived to work. In a few more years, he'd drop dead at his desk, and that would be it. Until then, he would mine paradise.

He put on his blinker and turned off the highway. At the end of a narrow lane through the trees, he stopped at a gate, tapped in his code, and continued down a private driveway. Sensors in the driveway, hidden cameras, and infrared alarms activated after he passed. No one could approach his home without his knowledge. He slept well, knowing he would never again be surprised in the darkness.

A muted glow emanated from the windows, the lights having switched on when the sun went down. Soft music would start the moment he stepped through the door. Below a certain temperature, his fireplace would activate, casting a blue glow from clear stones in the glass firebox. His pantry was stocked, his kitchen held only the finest equipment and utensils, and his wine cellar was extensive.

Everything in Rafael's life was arranged exactly the way he wanted it.

As he rounded the last curve leading to his house, the garage door, sensing his presence, rose to welcome him home.

Chapter Three

Driving toward the canyon past the towering red rock bluffs, Sue felt the whisper of ghosts. A shiver of anticipation ran up her spine. From earliest childhood, she'd hiked near cliff dwellings abandoned by the Sinagua. She'd felt the power and wonder of the vortices. In her lifetime, multitudes had come to enjoy the magic of Sedona, but for Sue, the magic had persisted since her childhood.

And now she was almost home, perhaps to right a wrong. She'd been away too long. What happened wasn't fair, but Roseanne was going to fix it, at long last, because she was dying and wanted to put things right.

At least, that's what she'd hinted at. Sue had been fooled many times before, but the stakes were too high this time. She had no choice but to come, clutching the dream in her mind like an unscratched lottery ticket, knowing it was probably worthless but daring to hope.

Up ahead, the highway split, and she headed east. An early monsoon had refreshed the desert, and the ocotillos were blooming, their ghostly stalks decorated with red blossoms the size of silver dollars. Along the shoulder, the bright pink and yellow blooms of prickly pear called out for a camera, but Sue couldn't stop.

She was so fired up, she found herself speeding until the specter of Roseanne's terminal illness hit her again, and with it, the guilt. They'd emailed back and forth a few more times. Roseanne was typically cryptic. Her liver was shot. Her body was shutting down. It was time to make things right.

On the one hand, Sue had compassion. On the other, Roseanne's gift would rectify a grievous wrong.

All the way here from Visalia, Sue imagined what she might do with a property whose glorified images were burnished by time. The cool, thick adobe walls and wooden beams across the ceilings. The ranch-sized kitchen and dining room, big enough to seat all the hands at once. Her parents' bedroom with French doors opening to the front of the house and that spectacular view of the canyon and Mesa beyond. The original adobe brick fireplaces, native stone foundation, and log walls in the common areas. The central courtyard draped with bougainvillea and jasmine. The front acreage that, in her youth, held corrals, a stable, and a bunkhouse.

Coyotes calling in the night; cactus wrens rasping out their greetings in the day. Quail darting across the open areas, their babies chasing behind in a straight line.

She couldn't wait to see it again. She had so many plans. She wondered how much of it still stood.

Sue dreamed of rehabbing the old hacienda with its herb and rose gardens and enjoying breakfast on the front patio. She would feel the presence of her mother and father and finally begin to grow roots after all the transfers and moving over the years with Mike's military career.

She would paint and invite others to join her. Soon, the Mesa would become a gathering place for the Sedona creative community. She would invite her old friends from so many postings around the country, offering a place to relax and get caught up. She would make new friends and a rich new life on her own terms.

She could start over.

Coming into town, she slowed for the traffic and tourists. It had been years, and the amount of congestion surprised her. Everyone wanted to enjoy Sedona. She waited while another herd of tourists swarmed into the crosswalk. She couldn't wait to be home. Couldn't wait to see the site where her dreams would come true.

Turning off the highway, she drove through piñon pines and chaparral. The powdered red earth provided a backdrop for the manzanitas' gray-green leaves and burgundy branches. She rolled down her window and inhaled the familiar fragrance of the land—sunbaked pine needles, sage, and dust.

The blacktop changed from smooth to cracked, and Sue steered around increasing numbers of potholes. The pavement ended at the forest, a dirt road branching off to the left. Twin posts sagged, two halves of a broken metal chain hanging from each. A rural mailbox lay on the ground, crushed as if someone had smashed into it, backed up, and run over it again. The replacement, a metal washtub, contained flyers and junk mail floating in an inch of rainwater.

Sue turned up the road leading to her family home. The SUV bounced down the rutted path, barely avoiding the overgrown scrub that reached out to claw its paint. When she was a kid, her dad would order a couple truckloads of gravel delivered every few years to even out the roadway. Now it was ridged and pitted, so she drove slowly. Fast-food wrappers and plastic trash bags clung to branches. That was bad enough. As she neared the house, Sue's eyebrows lifted, and her mouth dropped open.

She'd expected poor maintenance. It was Roseanne, after all.

What she hadn't expected were the discarded mattresses or the broken-down sofa. The rusting appliances. The mound of concrete rubble. Garbage had been left here as if it were the city dump. No wonder there had been a chain across the road. But the chain broke and was left broken, and this was the result.

At the end of the lane, a corral-type gate hung at an angle, no longer functioning to keep livestock in or out. Up the drive a ways, a pickup was parked near the house, but before she could wonder who it belonged to, the view through her windshield stopped her breath. She stared at the homesite in horror.

The Mesa, as long and wide as two football fields, lay buried under trash. The front entrance to the house was barricaded by an old sofa, shelving components, and a roll of fencing. Two station wagons, lacking tires, sat rusting on wooden blocks. Scrap wood, plastic barrels, and electronic waste lay baking and rotting in the sun.

Sue's jaw tightened as she scanned the scene. She'd spent the entire day fantasizing about justice and reconciliation, but now, she felt only fury.

Gypsy gave one impatient bark. They'd been on the road for hours and the old girl wanted out.

Sue parked and opened the door.

Her inheritance was a literal dump. Roseanne's joke to the very end: the old homestead was a hoarder's paradise. The mess was appalling. The front door of the house was blocked. She'd probably have to go around back. She dreaded seeing the inside.

How did anyone live here?

Sue reached into the kennel, snapped on Gypsy's leash, and lifted the dog to the ground. Rubbing her back, she studied the house.

At the sound of a cough, she spun around.

* * * * *

A FEW MINUTES EARLIER, Rafael had been sitting on the bunkhouse steps at the edge of the Mesa, gazing across the canyon to the tablelands on the far side, where the afternoon sun turned the rock formations to shades of burgundy, chocolate, and gold. A person couldn't help but sense the richness of life here, good and bad. Sedona was famous for its vortices, the door between this world and another dimension. He didn't believe it, but his buyers did.

Which was good for business.

He had sat for a long time, both troubled and excited. The property was sensational. Nothing like it had come on the market in years. Besides the views, it stood near the heart of Sedona. The Mesa would be a gold mine for

Palacios Development. Rafael would scrape the house and build a showplace. It would be his biggest score in years.

The thought bothered him a little. He loved the house, with its tile roof, front courtyard, and the vigas poking out from under the roofline. In its day, the house would have matched anything he could build on this hilltop. But its time was past. Too bad to lose all that history, but he had a business to run.

A vehicle approached, crunching across the gravel and dirt toward the house. He stood and went to investigate. No doubt a lost tourist looking for a vortex to experience or a place to take a picture of Sedona's famous red rocks. He would give the driver directions, help them turn the vehicle around, and go back into the house to check on Roseanne.

But the SUV parked, the door opened, and a woman stepped out. She had shoulder-length silver hair and a fine ass, not that he was looking, but he noticed as she bent to gather a dog from the kennel in the back. The woman let the dog down and straightened, rubbing her back. She stared at the house as if trying to decide whether to approach.

He cleared his throat, and she startled, turning toward him in alarm.

Rafael's breath caught.

She was Roseanne, except she was still beautiful. With posture erect, shoulders thrown back, she was imperious in spite of her size and those faded jeans that fit so snugly over her curves. The woman stared back, radiating strength and determination, and just for a moment, the steel vault around his heart threatened to crack open. But no. He'd gone the last thirty years not letting that vault open even the smallest bit, and it wasn't going to happen now. Especially not for this beautiful stranger with cold eyes, the relative of the one inside.

"Can I help you?" he asked.

"I'm looking for my sister." Her voice was deep. Her gaze was level, unafraid. "Who are you?"

"I am—"

And then he realized why she was there. After all these years, it could be for one reason only.

She had come for the land.

Chapter Four

Gypsy gave out a yip and a growl. Sue shaded her eyes to see the man standing in the sun's blinding path. He was brawny with brown skin and black hair swept back from a high forehead. Reflective aviators hid his eyes. His mustache was shot through with silver. A braided metal bracelet encircled one thick wrist. He held himself like a guard, quietly containing power in his braced legs and clenched jaw. He was only a few inches taller than her but seemed to tower. Was he a friend? Private security?

"Can I help you?" His voice was soft, threatening. He had an air about him. Protective.

She stifled a smirk. What was he protecting? The piles of shit in the front yard?

They stared at each other, both on guard.

His lip twitched. "She told us you were dead."

"And yet, here I am."

"This is funny?" he asked.

"Do you see me laughing?" She grimaced. "Sorry. I'm just shocked. I wasn't expecting all this."

The man didn't react. With his dark eyebrows and mustache, eyes hidden, he exuded territoriality.

Let him be imperious all he wanted, she thought. She had come a long way, and she was tired. Not to mention it was her family homestead, and her sister waited inside.

He folded his arms. "Does she know?"

"That I'm here? She should. She invited me." Sue pulled on the leash to keep Gypsy from disappearing into an old oil barrel. "And you are?"

"I am her friend, Rafael Palacios. Some of us have been helping her as she has become less capable recently." He reached out his hand to shake hers. When they touched, a spark zapped their skin. Both of them flinched.

"The desert," he said. "It is very dry here." Rafael stuck his hands in his pockets. His forearms were dusted with dark hair, and the silver bracelet on his left wrist seemed all the more masculine.

"It rained all the way here," Sue said.

The summer monsoons were kicking up, frightening but beautiful. The entire homestead was damp.

Gypsy sniffed at a one-handled wheelbarrow tilted on its side in the weeds. Its tire was flat. Sue tightened the leash. "I need to let my dog walk. We drove a long way today."

"The walkway is clear from here to the edge of the Mesa, if you like."

"Thank you." Sue took off down the path, surprised when Rafael joined her. The trail was narrow, nearby junk and garbage having been shoved aside to create access to the bunkhouse. As she walked, Sue took silent inventory. The stable looked to be in good shape still, but the smokehouse and tool shed were collapsing on themselves. Her mother's pottery studio was intact, as was the greenhouse's frame, but the gardens and fountains in the center of the yard were buried under rubble.

She sighed. What an absolute mess. She'd need heavy equipment and a sizable crew to make this place habitable again. But she would do it, and revel in the work, because regardless of its junkyard condition, from the moment she stepped out of the car and inhaled the familiar fragrance of chaparral and pine, she felt a sense of sanctuary. Regardless of Roseanne's corruption, and the agony she'd brought to the family, Sue felt her parents' presence here. The property was home.

But at the moment, it was a hellscape. "How did it happen?"

"She fell in with a man who had a recycling scheme. I tried to dissuade her, but she wouldn't listen. When the friend moved on, she continued collecting items she thought were valuable. As the piles grew, local citizens began dumping trash on the premises. Over time, the refuse accumulated."

Sue squinted at him. "You're not from around here, are you?"

His mustache twitched. He didn't answer.

She resumed walking. "Surely she could have stopped it from going this far."

"By a certain point, she wasn't entirely rational."

Sue jerked on Gypsy's leash as the dog tried to disappear into a spider's nest of rusted metal. "My sister was never entirely rational."

"Perhaps, but in addition, she had become ill and lacked the energy to object. Also, money was a factor. She had few resources."

"Except the land. I guess I should be happy she never sold it."

They reached the edge of the Mesa where the old bunkhouse, now boarded up, stood with a rustic wood porch and a million-dollar view. Shadows began to outline the red rocks and purple sage as the summer sun moved westward. Rafael pointed at the red rocks across the canyon. In the far distance, hikers were ascending a peak.

"The Prism," Sue said. She hadn't been to that vortex in years. Local lore said it was good for receiving insights into the future, particularly with regard to human relationships. Maybe she should have gotten a hotel room in town and hiked there in the morning instead of barreling straight to the old homestead. Maybe then she would have been better prepared.

She turned to see herself reflected in his glasses, her hair wild and windblown from the drive. She glanced away, feeling ambushed. Although she'd adapted to life as a widow, the appraisal of a handsome man took her by surprise.

She tugged Gypsy's leash. "I'd like to see my sister now."

He inclined his head, and they turned back. "Her request for a transplant was denied."

"I'm sorry to hear that."

"You didn't know?" His tone was curious, as if he were trying to figure her out.

"We didn't communicate. Haven't for years. She didn't want me here. I've respected her wishes."

Sue wouldn't explain further. She must look like a vulture, circling the property on black wings, waiting to sail downward and claim a big prize. She looked away. Who was this man to judge her? And what was she supposed to do, burst into tears over Roseanne's imminent death?

She couldn't. It wasn't in her anymore. She just felt sad. For Roseanne, for her parents, for their ancestors who'd settled here with such big dreams.

When they reached the house, Rafael scooped up Gypsy and tucked her under his arm. "You wouldn't want her stepping in broken glass."

"I can't believe this." Sue gaped at the audacious move and the fact that Gypsy hadn't turned into a snarling, squirming demon. "She never lets anyone else touch her."

"Animals love me." He scratched Gypsy behind one ear. "We need to go around to the back."

He led the way around the side of the house, along a debris-strewn pathway under a jungle of oleander bushes. Sue stepped carefully, avoiding the glitter of broken glass. She wanted to watch him walk, all broad shoulders and confident movement, but the path was treacherous, so she tore her eyes away from his retreating backside.

The backyard was just as awful as the front, with two more abandoned vehicles and an overflowing dumpster. The patio was covered in piles of old furniture and clothing. Sue swore silently.

At the back door, he set Gypsy down and handed over the leash. "Prepare yourself."

Sue wrapped the leash around her hand, keeping the dog close. From what she'd already seen, the inside couldn't be good.

He pushed the door open, shoving it with one foot. It creaked. He paused on the threshold, stuck his sunglasses in a breast pocket, and called out. "Rosie? I'm back."

Rosie? Nobody ever called her sister that and lived.

Sue waited for Rafael to get moving so she could see the interior of her old family home for the first time in so many years.

He turned to look at her, his eyes deep-set and shadowed, so dark she couldn't see his pupils. "She has been ill for a long time. You should keep that in mind."

"Fine, fine. Let's go." She tried to look around him, but his shoulders were blocking her.

"All right. We go."

When she saw, her stomach turned over. "What on earth is this?"

"As I warned you, she has not been able to care for the place."

From the back of the house to the front, every square foot was covered with junk. Shoes, clothing, magazines. A couple of radios, an ironing board, folding tables groaning under the weight of small appliances, photo albums, lamps, vases, and gardening tools. Newspapers were stacked waist-high in places. The front door was blocked by a folding table on which stood a tool chest. Underneath it stood a television in its cabinet, the console strangely antique yet shockingly familiar. Amid the garbage and clutter, she caught glimpses of the home she remembered from childhood. The door to the sunroom through the dining room was now blocked by a weight bench covered in boxes. The breakfast bar in the kitchen was now covered with containers and boxes. The fireplace mantel bench, where empty flower pots and bricks were stacked. Everything was buried in junk.

"Holy shit," said Sue.

For a long moment, they stood without speaking, strangers united in the horror of their surroundings.

His eyes were sad. Kind.

"Let's go." Rafael's voice was gentle.

She followed him down a narrow walkway through the den to the hall, where they turned right. In front of Sue's old bedroom door stood a clothing rack full of shirts and slacks. Next to it stood two chairs buried by black trash bags stuffed with plastic housewares. There was hardly any room to walk.

Stunned by the sheer volume of garbage, she followed Rafael to the bedroom at the end of the hall, still Roseanne's room. In their youth, she preferred it because she could climb out the window without anyone in the house realizing it.

"Rosie, I'm here with a surprise visitor." His voice was vaguely accusing, and Sue wondered how close the two of them were. And what kind of man could love her sister?

They seemed incongruous. He was fit, robust, confident. Considering his nearly new pickup truck, expensive shades, and good jeans, he radiated affluence, and maybe that was the draw. Roseanne would view him as a target. A mark.

So did that mean he was stupid?

And if they were a couple, did he live there? She grimaced. How could anyone in their right mind?

Then her heart stopped. If they were a couple, would Roseanne leave it to him? Maybe *he* was playing *her*.

Sue steeled herself. She would hire attorneys, she would go to court, she would fight until her fingernails were bloody to possess this land that had been stolen from her in the first place.

Glancing over his shoulder, Rafael caught her ruminating, and he grinned, almost as if he understood her thoughts. "You need not worry, Susan."

"But I am worried." She gestured at the disgusting interior.

"It will all work out for the best," he said.

A hacking cough interrupted them. "You two gonna stand out there and flirt, or you gonna come in and say hi?"

Sue took a step back. That voice—that gravelly, smoky, cut-you-down-to-size voice from a lifetime ago—still had the power to unnerve her.

In the doorway, Rafael moved aside to let her pass. As she squeezed by, Sue felt the heat radiating from his chest, and she wanted to press against him, belly to belly, to let his warmth envelop her. She thought she'd buried her hormones with her husband, but apparently not. What an inconvenient time for them to awaken.

She inched into the room, her nostrils stinging at the reek of cigarette smoke and unwashed bedding.

Roseanne sat propped against a mound of pillows. Her long brown hair, streaked now with gray, swirled over her shoulders. Oxygen tubing snaked across the sheets to a canister propped in the corner. Her skin was greasy and sallow, the area under her eyes purplish as if bruised. She looked up, cracking a gray-toothed grin.

"Where ya been, bitch?"

Chapter Five

Sue forced a cheerful smile. "Hello, Roseanne."

Roseanne took a long draft of oxygen, her eyes closed. When they opened, her mouth turned downward in a scowl.

One yellowed plastic chair stood next to the bed in the cluttered room. Sue sat with Gypsy in her lap.

"What's that, a rat?"

"She's a Yorkshire Terrier mixed with something else. Maybe Chihuahua."

"Don't get all technical. Come here, girl."

Sue tightened her grip on the dog. "She doesn't like people."

"Me neither."

Roseanne made kissing noises at Gypsy, who wriggled and squirmed to reach her. Sue let go, and the dog leaped across the gap onto the bed. There she stood, one leg bent like a tiny hunter, sniffing Roseanne's outstretched hand. When Gypsy finished her inspection, she curled up, rested her head on her paws, and closed her eyes.

Traitor, Sue thought.

"I didn't think you'd come," said Roseanne.

"That was never in question."

"Yeah, you were always the good daughter, weren't you. But I still got the house, ha ha."

Rafael said, "Give me your keys. I'll bring in your luggage."

"You don't have to."

"It's dark, and you could trip and be injured."

Roseanne smirked. "Oh, how tender."

Sue stared at her sister, feeling hate radiating from her core. Was that the right word, even after so long? Whatever the term, something toxic festered when she looked at Roseanne. Reconciliation wasn't possible. All Sue wanted was to confirm that her sister intended to sign over the land. Then she'd arrange for an attorney, do the paperwork, and leave probably within two days.

Disturbingly, she envisioned the mental image of the circling vulture, but that was wrong. Roseanne's decision would right a wrong. It would right all the wrongs.

The two girls had been bitter enemies from the day Sue was born, even before that, as soon as four-year-old Roseanne understood what the bulge in their mother's tummy foreshadowed.

"So, where the hell you been?"

Sue's chest reverberated with her pounding heart. Adrenaline slipped through her veins. She wanted to bolt, never see Roseanne again. She took a draft of air through her nostrils, filling her lungs, calming herself. "I've been married. I raised two kids. Now I'm widowed."

"How Norman Rockwell." Roseanne scratched her armpit. "What else?"

How much to say, Sue wondered, knowing her sister didn't care anyway. Playing along, making small talk, she said, "Mike was in the military. We lived all over the country. When he retired from the service, he did civilian work for them. When he retired, we settled down in Visalia."

"What a shithole."

Sue didn't rise to the bait. The rudeness, the caustic remarks, were unpleasant but no big deal. She even felt sorry for Roseanne, seeing the oxygen tubing in Roseanne's nose, her sallow skin, her swollen belly.

"You know, I'm pretty tired from driving all day," said Sue. "I'm going to get a hotel room, and then in the morning, we can talk about your email."

Roseanne held on to Gypsy's leash. "You can't leave now."

"Why can't I?"

"There's an art festival going on, and everything's booked. You have to stay here. With me. Yeah, you're stuck." She pressed the cannula against her nostrils, her chest going up and down. "Anyway, I got a surprise for ya. Go get Rafe."

Sue found him sitting at a ramshackle picnic table in the backyard. He was leaning on his elbows, feet on the bench. He looked languid yet aristocratic. When he got up and walked toward her, she watched, enjoying the view, even though he smiled in acknowledgment. As a younger woman, she had been more covert. Now, what the hell. She was older and life was short.

He stopped in front of her, only inches away, a little closer than proper for a new acquaintance. "Did you want me?"

She lifted her chin. "Roseanne wants to talk to us together."

"What about?"

"I have no idea." She led him back inside. Near Roseanne's door, she brushed a spider web from her arm. "This place is a health hazard. If a fire started in here, it'd be a disaster."

Rafael shrugged. "What can one do? It's her life."

She glared at him. "One could have staged an intervention."

From inside the bedroom, Roseanne's voice croaked. "Shut up, the two of you. He didn't do anything about it because it's none of his business."

Sue went back to her chair. "Why did you invite me here?"

"Eh, I wanted to see your passive-aggressive little mug before I died." Roseanne laughed and then coughed. "Anyway, you should thank me. I made you tough." She leaned closer, one eyelid lower than the other. "But you're still not very smart. You came all this way, thinking I was going to give you the land, right? So predictable."

Sue stood. If she left now, she could be in Phoenix in a couple of hours. Coffee at Starbucks... She'd make it work. Gypsy wouldn't like it.

Sue reached for the dog.

Roseanne grabbed the leash and held it. "I figured if I gave you the land, you'd have to clean the place up first. It'll take years. You'll have even more reason to hate me. Ha!"

"Let go of my dog," said Sue.

"Aw, unpinch that face, ya big baby. You'll get something outta your long drive." Roseanne waved a hand at the room. "I'm leaving it all to you and Lover Boy here."

"That is not funny." Rafael crossed his arms.

"Yeah, I know. I told you that you could have it all."

"You did?" Sue was incredulous. "He's not even family."

"You don't like it?" Roseanne scowled. "Tough shit. He's my friend."

"Roseanne," said Rafael. "It is your property, and you're free to do what you want with it, but I assumed..."

"You assumed it was yours cuz I told you it was yours. And it is. But I'm leaving it to both of you. Not cuz I'm nice." She stopped to catch her breath. "Wish I could live to see you two fight over it."

"We are all tired." Rafael looked at his watch. "I suggest we discuss this tomorrow."

"You in a big hurry?"

"I have unfinished business in town. We're opening another sales office, and there are last-minute issues to address. Florence and John are waiting for me."

"How is Flo anyway? You still got her working as sales manager?"

"Yes. Why would I not?"

"You know she's got all-timers, don't cha?"

Rafael frowned. "I haven't seen evidence of that. In my opinion, she is the best agent in Arizona. Even now."

"She's gonna outlive me, the bitch. Tell her to come see me before I die."

Rafael said, "You're not going to die."

"And you're an idiot, but I love you. So that's why I'm giving you the property. With her." She waved a hand at Sue and coughed. "Cut it up, walk away, or kill each other over it. I don't give a shit. Now I'm tired. Leave me alone."

Rafael walked to the bedroom door, stopped, and looked back at Roseanne. "I'll be back tomorrow morning."

"Whatever." Roseanne closed her eyes.

Sue hurried after him, the sound of Roseanne's hacking cough trailing behind.

Leaning against the side of his truck, Rafael stared at the piles of garbage, a study in harsh shadows from the porch light. He ran a hand through his hair. "What a mess."

"So predictable." Sue joined him against the truck. His cologne wafted toward her, something like balsam and smoke.

"Why would she do this?"

"This is who she is. She pits people against each other. She has a way—" Sue forgot her point because he had turned to her and was listening so intently, her brain froze.

"She has a way?" His voice was low. Encouraging.

Sue's mouth formed a straight line. So he was gorgeous? He was the enemy. She couldn't allow herself to be distracted. "Listen, Rafe. May I call you Rafe?"

"No."

"Anyway, this is what you should have learned about my sister." Sue gestured at the junkyard mounded with garbage. "What she's doing to us? It fits her worldview. She believes the worst in everybody. Setting people up to fight? She thrives on that. It feeds her. Always has."

"What a dark heart," he said.

"Is this a surprise? I thought you knew her."

He shrugged. "She has always been good to me."

"What confuses me," said Sue, "is that she won't be around for the big show. The big blowup she's hoping we have."

"She is a mystery."

"That's putting it mildly." Sue leaned against the cooling metal of the truck, inhaling his cologne, wondering what he'd be like squaring off against her in court or wherever this conflict was heading. The site was a horrible mess, but it was half hers. All hers, if she were successful. Regardless of the circumstances, Sue felt a sense of calm wash over her. She was home, at last. It would be all right. She would have to figure out a way to dissuade the handsome man standing next to her, his arms crossed, jawline tense.

"We'll have to decide how to move forward," said Sue.

"Yes." He stared straight ahead.

"I don't know why you'd be interested in the property," she said, "but for me, it's home. I'd be coming full circle, having been on the run all my life."

He cocked an eyebrow. "Are you wanted by the authorities?"

"What? No! I'm the wife of a military man." She cleared her throat. "Was."

"My condolences."

He sounded so very proper, she wondered if her words would have any impact. But she had to try.

"We traveled from post to post, uprooting our two children every couple of years. And then Mom gave Roseanne the property, and I was so hurt I've never been back." She cut a glance at him, but he hadn't moved. "Today, coming down the lane, I felt the healing begin. I don't care about the trash. I intend to clean it up and make it beautiful again, in honor of my family. I want to live here. It'll help me feel close to my parents and my heritage, and maybe I can salvage my childhood."

Rafael turned. He gazed at her with a look that felt like compassion. At least, she hoped it was compassion. Though, she'd take pity too. Whatever worked.

"You think she wants us to fight?"

Sue shrugged. "She's counting on it. She's happy, thinking it will happen."

"Maybe it won't."

"Really?" Sue felt a flicker of hope. "That would be incredible."

"Yes, there is no need to fight. We simply sell it and split the proceeds."

Sue bristled. The nerve of this man. "Or you could give up your half since this is my family's land. Maybe you're the kind of person who would do the right thing."

Rafael gazed at her, his deep-set, dark eyes framed by those wonderful brows. He seemed to be looking at her with empathy.

She held her breath.

"Susan, do you know what this property is worth?"

Okay, maybe not. "But it's so run-down, and the trash..." She swallowed. "Probably a lot."

"It is worth much more than 'a lot.'"

"How would you know?"

He straightened. "I need to go to my office, but I'll return tomorrow morning. Would you like me to walk you to the door?"

"I'll be fine."

"Okay then. Adios."

"Fine. Goodnight." Sue headed for the oleanders, darkly mumbling to herself. What an audacious bastard. If he thought he was going to get her land, he was nuts.

Chapter Six

Rafael watched her go. What a fine figure and such wrath. Her every footstep sparked with anger. He did not start the truck until she disappeared into the oleander jungle. In truth, he had no need to rush to the office. He simply desired to get away, to think. To gather himself. Rafael wasn't accustomed to such mental disarray.

Seeing death in Roseanne's eyes tonight took him back to dark places. Mortality was a subject he tried to avoid. But to give half her land to her sister, after their long estrangement—such treachery he had not expected. Not that he was naïve. Roseanne was a sociopath, true, but he had seen worse.

And that made him feel foolish. He knew better. Stupid of him to have trusted her.

Driving into town, he thought about Roseanne tending bar at that dive in Cottonwood, back in the days when she was pretty and he still drank like a man going under. When she started missing work, he asked about her. Discovered she was sick and getting worse. Pretty soon, she couldn't be alone a hundred percent of the time, and he hired caregivers, but Roseanne burned through them. She didn't want help. She didn't want strangers around her stuff. Stuff! The place was a landfill.

He would get his crew to work on that, at the appropriate time, obviously.

Rafael had dropped by the house twice a day to see to Roseanne's needs, and she cursed at him but ate the food he brought, and some nights he slept in the old recliner in the living room. Years ago, his ex-wife had correctly accused him of being selfish. How surprised she would be to see him fuss over this dying woman.

He slammed on the brakes before running over a pedestrian, raising his hands in apology as the woman glared. Sedona was busy as usual. The crowds filled the streets and sidewalks on this warm summer evening. He would need to pay attention.

When the crosswalk cleared, he eased forward, picking up speed, his thoughts returning to Susan and his shock when he recognized her. Sister to Roseanne? She was a warrior, would have to have been, just to survive.

He drove slowly, adapting to the stop-and-go of a tourist season that, lately, seemed never to end. The crowds were annoying, but they were eager to spend money at this renowned vacation spot. And, of course, such enthusiasm was good for his own business.

Usually, the sight cheered him. Tonight, the crowds simply annoyed him.

Not because Roseanne had set him up.

Because Susan had him rattled.

The woman was beautiful, imperious despite her small stature, sure of herself. Her strength enticed him. Most women played up to him, trying to win his attention. Susan treated him as an impediment. The thought amused him. He loved a challenge.

They'd both felt the spark, but she kept her fists up.

Not a problem. He knew how to work around a reluctant prospect. His thoughts drifted as he considered his many options, but of all the weapons in his arsenal, the most logical in her case would be a seduction.

Of sorts.

The thought pleased him.

In the middle of town, he turned into his office complex, shut off the ignition, and exhaled. In the deserted parking lot, a big Harley occupied two accessible parking spaces.

Rafael tapped the elevator keypad, rode to the third floor, and unlocked the door to Palacios Development. Soft lighting illuminated the reception area, and signature projects adorned the walls. In one photo, he stood with the governor for a city hall ribbon cutting. In another, he joined a clutch of Hollywood celebrities at the opening of a performing arts center. Rafael had built everything from symphony halls to tiny sustainable homes. He should have felt more secure, but that wasn't his way.

He walked through the reception area, where family pictures covered Gabriela's desk, past the alcove from where Flo ran his empire. His employees were proud of Palacios Development. Most remembered the old days when the firm was housed in a trailer.

John's deep voice rumbled from down the hall. "That you, Boss?"

"It is." Rafael rapped his knuckles on the doorjamb, entering the office Matt and John shared. Blueprints lay everywhere, tightly rolled. Whiteboards scrawled with black ink covered the walls. Boxes stood in piles, half opened, as if the two men had just moved in. But Rafael let his employees have their processes, as long as they delivered. And John was like a brother.

Rafael dropped into the chair at Matt's desk. "Why are you still here?"

"Why are you?" In his midfifties, strong as a bull, John leaned back in his big office chair, its joints creaking.

"Roseanne." Rafael turned the chair so he could glare at the wall of glass. Beyond it, red rock formations darkened to purple with evening shadows. The view usually lifted his mood, but not today. He reached for a pen and clicked the cartridge up, down, up, down.

Up.

John flipped his tablet closed. "What?"

"She has a sister."

"The dead one?"

"Not anymore. I met her. At the house." Rafael explained what Roseanne had done.

John whistled. "How's that supposed to work?"

"I have no idea. And this woman, she is—" He searched for the word. How would one describe her, such power, such anger?

"Do you want to borrow my vest?"

"I don't expect her to shoot me, amigo. But it could get ugly."

"Throw money at her. What you always do."

"That's one possibility. First, I have to determine how she thinks."

They turned at the sound of keys in the lock. Moving to investigate, John returned with a stylish woman who was half his size and twice as old.

"Are you boys having a party without me?" Flo's eyes crinkled. She flashed a movie-star smile and loosened her designer scarf.

"We are debriefing." Rafael brought her a chair.

She settled into it, dropping her clunky leather bag on the desk.

John spoke from the doorway. "Anybody want a beer?"

"Not me," said Rafael. "I have to work."

"And I'm trying to keep my girlish figure."

"You people are no fun." John sat back down at his desk.

"I spoke with Roseanne this afternoon." Rafael spun his chair around to Flo. "She is annoyed at you. Says you have not visited in quite some time."

"I was there yesterday." Flo tapped her chin with a neatly polished fingernail. "Or wait. Was it the day before? Gosh, maybe she's right. I can't keep track. Sometimes I think I'm slipping."

Rafael exchanged a glance with John. They'd noticed Flo's recent forgetfulness. She was the best closer he ever had, but property work was highly technical and demanding. "If you are having memory problems, perhaps you should see a doctor."

"Don't get all hysterical." She tapped her temple. "The calculator might be slowing down, but it still works fine. And if I ever get brainless, you have permission to fire me."

Rafael nodded. He would hold her to it. As much as he appreciated the old woman, he was a businessman first. Palacios Development was one of the most successful firms in the area, having earned a reputation for quality development and talented staff. He made good money, his employees were happy, and subcontractors were eager to jump on board when he broke ground on new projects. Everything seemed to be humming along, but Rafael did not feel safe. He never did.

Running for your life from anti-government militias would do that to you.

Rafael had matured into a shrewd and astute businessman, but he would take that childhood insecurity to his grave. He did not fall in love easily, he guarded his money carefully, and he would never retire. He needed to keep moving, like a shark.

Flo spoke, "So, did she follow through with her crackpot plan?"

"You knew?"

"Well, I had an idea." Flo studied her manicure.

"Damn," said John.

Rafael glared at her. "Why didn't you say something? I could have tried to change her mind. Now the sister is going to make my life difficult."

"None of my business, Mister Palacios. Even with half, you'll still make out like a bandit."

"The business needs it." He would convince Susan to sell the property and split the proceeds. In any contest, Rafael knew he would win. He wasn't arrogant. Simply realistic. She would be well-compensated, but her passion for preservation would have to find another target.

"We'll be fine," said Flo. "You worry too much. Like I always say—"

"'Starvation and ruin are just part of the cycle,'" John finished for her.

"Exactly. You are a good student." Flo beamed at the big man, who grumbled and ducked his head.

"I'll leave you boys to your gossiping," she said. "I'm off to dine with a friend."

"Got a date?" The corner of John's mouth turned up.

"Wouldn't you like to know?" She scooted to the edge of the chair and pushed up with a delicate grunt. "Don't wait up."

"I'll walk you to your car," said Rafael.

"That isn't necessary."

"My mother raised me to be a gentleman."

Flo patted his cheek. "That you are."

The men worked a while longer, hashing over the specifics of a housing tract under construction. Later, after John roared off on his bike, Rafael remained at the office, buried in paper but making no headway. It was impossible to concentrate.

His thoughts returned to the incensed look in Susan's eyes. He enjoyed sparring with her, but his intent was deadly serious. And she would lose.

He snapped shut his leather bag and stood, flipping off lights on his way out.

He pulled into his garage and pressed the remote for the control panel just inside his house. By the time he entered his kitchen, lights were on low, music emanated from the sound system, and orange flames danced in the fireplace.

Dios, he was tired. He'd planned to work a couple more hours, but it was almost midnight. He pressed the control panel to shut everything down and climbed the stairs to his bedroom. He would get a good night's sleep, never a problem for him, and in the morning, fully restored, he would arrive at a solution. He would figure out how to send Susan on her way, clearing the path for his last big score.

Chapter Seven

After leaving Rafael in the driveway, Sue returned to the bedroom. Roseanne was propped up on her pillows, Gypsy snuggled against her leg. The television flickered in the dim light.

Sue stood in the doorway. "I thought I'd make dinner. What can you eat?"

Roseanne gestured at a case of Ensure.

"Is that all?"

"About it." Roseanne changed the channel to a wrestling match. "I don't even leave the bed anymore."

"What about the restroom?"

"Got a bag." Roseanne turned back to the TV. "There's a hospice person comes in and empties it in the morning. Lucky him."

Sue sat quietly, studying her sister. Roseanne had always been bigger in every way. Heavier, taller, stronger. Now she'd shrunk by a third. Her arms, no longer dangerous, looked like pale twigs against the blankets.

Roseanne muted the TV. "Katie told me about Mike."

"You two are in contact?"

"She answered my email," said Roseanne. "Don't go crazy. I asked her, she told me, I said thanks, and that was it."

"I'm just shocked she hid it from me. Like it was a big secret between the two of you."

"She knew you'd be mad." Roseanne adjusted the oxygen. "She said he had cancer."

"Yes. It was very quick." Sue didn't want to bring Mike's memory into this sordid bedroom.

"And you were in Visalia, in the old folks' home."

"We had just moved. I haven't even really had a chance to settle in, but I've made some friends." Sue looked around the room. "When did you turn into a—um, I mean, start accumulating things?"

Roseanne closed her eyes. "You think it's trash, but it's my bank account."

"Maybe the scrap metal is worth something, but there's so much here."

"A lot of it can be fixed. People used to bring me their broken crap, and I'd make it work, and they'd pay me for it. I can fix almost anything." Roseanne sighed. "Could."

Sue hadn't known that. "I'm sorry."

"Oh, screw off."

"I'm going to go poke around in the kitchen."

"Fine. Go."

Sue stopped at the door. "Why did you do your will that way?"

"You mean cutting the land in half?" Roseanne propped herself on one elbow. "I owed you."

"You owed me a big, new complicated problem?"

"Sure. Give you something to do in your retirement."

"I already have things to do. Anyway, why Rafael? This is family land."

"Rafael is family."

"Come on, Roseanne. All he wants is the money, which means I'll have to buy him out, which I can't afford. Or sell it, which will break all our hearts."

"You should thank me. It's worth a lot of money." Roseanne grinned. "You call Travis and Katie. I'll bet they don't give a shit about the property, just what it's worth."

"They wouldn't expect any money from it, at least not while I'm alive."

"But first"—Roseanne fixed a yellow-eyed grin on her sister—"you're gonna have to fight Rafael for it."

"So that's your plan? Die and start a war?"

"Yep." Roseanne scratched her armpit. "I'm a goddamn sociopath, right?" She removed the oxygen tube from her nostrils and stuck a cigarette in her mouth.

"Don't light that," cried Sue. "You could kill us both."

Roseanne shook the match out and flung it in the general direction of the waste basket. "Gotta die sometime."

Shaking her head, Sue left the room, wondering if she'd die in a flaming inferno that night.

In the kitchen, she felt along the wall from memory, found the switch, and flipped it. One bulb kicked on overhead. The room was cluttered but looked as if someone had used it recently.

After feeding Gypsy, Sue filled the kitchen sink with soapy water and washed out a pan for soup. The window over the sink was completely covered with bushes and trees. She remembered when her dad and uncle cut through the wall and put the window in, back when she was in elementary school. The morning sun could be fierce, but the view was spectacular in the evening. If you could see it.

After she ate, Sue explored the old house, flipping light switches as she went. Some bulbs worked. Others had long ago burned out, but she managed to see enough to feel her heart breaking. The walls were damaged in places by a leaky roof, the carpets shredded and stained, and all around lay piles of junk.

She found the decorative grate in the linen closet her mother had threaded with a shoelace, where the girls learned to tie a bow. A cabinet door opened to an old ironing board that folded out when needed and hid away when not. A bay window seat had served as the retreat for her Barbie dolls.

Sue wanted to throttle Roseanne. Their family's home had been a showplace at one time, its gracious rooms and breathtaking views accommodating family parties and more formal events. Now, the house served as a glorified dumpster.

As appalling as the mess was, she could make short work of it. After all her years of moving households at the drop of a hat, she was the right person for the job.

Her phone chimed, a text from Carol in Visalia, asking if she made it okay, saying it had rained, and did Sue want her sprinklers turned off. Sue texted back, thanking her for watching the house and promising to call tomorrow. It was such a small thing, having someone she could count on back at Golden Era. Before Roseanne's email, she had hoped for a future there with many such friends. Now, her future was uncertain.

Again.

With her pepper spray in one hand and her phone set to the flashlight, she picked her way back to the car to gather the bare minimum of supplies for Gypsy and her to make it through the night. Returning to the house, she blocked the back door with a heavy chair. She found a soft leather recliner in the den that looked fairly clean. A patterned Mexican blanket was folded on top of it. It would serve as her bed for the night.

Tired as she was, a low thrum of excitement ran through her. There was no place like Sedona, and she intended to move back. She would turn the property into a refuge for artists and for women who had become lost. She hoped the will would clarify that Roseanne was joking, but if not, she would figure out a way to thwart this man who was the co-owner.

The land was hers. She would not lose it a second time.

Chapter Eight

The next morning, Sue awoke, stretching her limbs in the recliner. She'd slept well in spite of the noise from the oxygen concentrator chugging away down the hall.

Apparently, Roseanne hadn't incinerated them in the night.

Sue went to see if the master bath was usable since the other two were buried under detritus. At the end of the hallway, she stood outside her mother's bedroom, one hand on the icy doorknob as she prepared herself. The door resisted as she pushed, crackling around the edges as if it hadn't been opened for many years. When it swung open, she stood frozen, mouth set in a hard line.

The room looked exactly as she remembered it, except plastic sheeting covered the bed and upholstered chairs in the bay window. The adobe brick fireplace stood cold and dark, the ashes were long gone, but the smoke marks remained. The drapes sagged, tearing away from the hooks. The room was cold, with an undernote of dust, mothballs, and the slightest tinge of something dead. Around the baseboards, mousetraps held desiccated bodies.

Heart in her throat, tears stinging, Sue resolved to make this room beautiful again. Her parents deserved better. The Mesa house deserved better.

In the master bathroom, Sue tried the faucets. One handle fell off, landing on the tile with a great clamor. But when she used it like a wrench, she started the water flow. At first, it was rust-colored, rinsing dust and cobwebs down the drain. When it ran clear and warm, she stripped off her clothes and washed up, leaving her hair to dry in the desert air. She pulled on yoga pants and a tee shirt, feeling a bit more civilized.

Padding down the hall, she pushed open the door to her old bedroom. Blinking in consternation, she took a careful breath and forced herself to bear witness. A motorcycle stood in the center of the room, leaking oil on the carpet. Two of the window panes in the French doors leading outside were broken and covered with taped cardboard. Shards of glass lay shattered on the floor. Red paint had been splashed on two walls and a dresser. Her jaw clenched in anger. Sue breathed through it. Were she to allow herself to feel, she feared she'd ignite the oxygen herself. Burn the place to the ground.

Quietly, she pulled the door closed.

The remaining doors opened to varying degrees of mess. One room was inexplicably filled with skeins of yarn, knitting needles, and looms, piled and bagged and stacked over every surface. A lawnmower blocked the rear hallway, whose door opened to the backyard.

Maybe Rafael was right. They should probably raze the place and walk away with the cash.

She shuffled down the hall, peeking in on Roseanne, who was so quiet Sue wondered if she was still alive, but the blanket moved lightly with her breath. Outside the bedroom window, the sun crested the eastern hills, gilding everything in the yard... The dented water heater, the ripped sofa, the bike frames.

The kitchen lay in darkness, the morning sun blocked by the oleanders. Sue turned on the light. The room sprawled, having been built proportionate to the feeding of a ranch crew, but now its counters were littered with broken appliances. Sue tried the coffee maker. The light glowed green, but the heating element remained cold. She poked and tinkered.

Gypsy walked into the kitchen and sat on the rug in front of the sink.

"Look who's back. Now you want to be friends?"

The dog yawned loudly.

Sue tried a few more tricks, gave the appliance one last thump, and gave up. She unplugged it and filled the dog's bowl with dry dog food. "Deal with it. That's all we have."

To Sue's surprise, Gypsy dove into the bowl as if she had not previously required lightly cooked chicken or beef cut into bite-sized chunks.

After hunting through the cabinets, Sue found a jar of instant coffee. She poured a cup of water into the saucepan and put it on the stove.

For the thousandth time, Sue shook her head at her mother's decision to give Roseanne the house, but Mom was weak and felt sorry for her wayward daughter. Roseanne had crawled home often, addicted, hungry, and impoverished. She'd stay long enough to get healthy, line her pockets, and leave.

Mom's decision was inexplicable, mind-boggling, and horribly unfair. Sue would never get over it. And now, it was worse. If Roseanne really planned to leave the property to her and a complete stranger, that decision would exacerbate the pain. As soon as her sister awoke, Sue would ask to discuss the will. Perhaps she could get her to scribble a new one or at least amend it.

If she managed to win the right to live here, she could wipe out the bad memories and cultivate the good. She could fill up her days with rich new memories and preserve her heritage for generations to come. At this point, having lost Mike and feeling a little distant from her children, it would go a long way toward restoring peace of mind.

But that was a big "if." Knowing Roseanne, what she said and did were two different things. Sue needed to get her hands on the will, read it precisely, and work with an attorney to resolve ownership. Maybe this Rafael person would be happy with a reasonable cash payoff, and Sue would be free to take the title on the place. Once that happened, she could clean it, repair it, and live here for the rest of her life.

Someone knocked on the back door, causing her to jump. Rafael was back. Why would he come so early? She would have preferred to be alone with Roseanne to try making headway and see if they might find any common ground.

She shoved the chair away from the door and opened it a crack. "Can I help you?"

"Good morning." He held a cardboard tray with two cups, his biceps flexing under a black tee shirt. "I brought coffee."

She opened the door. "Thank goodness. That coffee maker is useless."

"It's been broken for years."

"So why is it still here?"

"Because she was going to fix it."

"Right."

"Your sister could fix anything."

"Ha."

She led him into the kitchen. Feeling him looking at her rear end, she swung her hips to torture him a little.

He set the tray on the table and handed her a cup, their fingers touching. A shiver of delight ran up her spine, and she huffed out a breath, exasperated at herself.

"What's in here?" She reached for the paper bag, heavy and warm.

"Lemon Danish. I'll get plates."

Watching him reach into the cupboard with such familiarity, she wondered again about his relationship with her sister. The idea of the two of them together boggled her mind.

He set two small plates in front of her.

Sue hesitated. "Are those clean?"

"Clean enough." He sat down across from her. She loaded the Danish onto the plates. They smelled heavenly, oozing lemon filling from the buttery pastry.

"We need forks." He leaned back, extended one arm, and pulled open a drawer. Fishing out two, he scrutinized them, polished them on his shirt, and handed one to her.

Sue raised an eyebrow.

He shrugged. "It's clean."

Hesitating, she took it. "Thanks. I think."

"I'm not a complete barbarian." He cut into his pastry. "So tell me, Susan, have you decided on an asking price for your half of the property? Whatever it is, I can get it for you."

"You don't waste any time, do you?"

Chewing slowly, he eyed her. "Business never sleeps."

"Okay, here's my price. You walk away, and you get to keep your conscience."

"My conscience, of which you are not in charge, is clear." He dabbed at his mustache with a napkin.

"Have you ever looked up the origin of this homestead? The original kitchen and living room were built at the turn of the last century. Historically and architecturally, it's one of a kind."

"Yes, I know. Why do you bring that up?"

"Because I want you to get a sense of its value to my family."

"It's immaterial." He studied her over his coffee cup. "The new owners will bulldoze it."

"How can you be so cavalier?"

"That is reality." He reached into his wallet and handed her a business card.

Sue glanced at the card and sighed. Of course. The man was a land developer. He had his own office. He'd probably been conning Roseanne for years.

She dropped it on the table. "Congratulations. Looks like your hard work paid off."

"You misunderstand, but that's not my problem."

"I understand perfectly. I see now why you've pretended to be her friend."

He drained his coffee, crumpled the cup, and fired it into the trashcan. "Believe what you want. I'm going to say good morning." He walked down the hall, all broad shoulders and strong legs. Whatever else was wrong with Roseanne, her taste in men hadn't changed. They were always good-looking, and they were always assholes.

Now that she knew why he was here, the battle lines were drawn. He would not get this house just to demolish it to benefit some rich bastard who'd build a mansion on it. Not if she could help it. Rafael Palacios and his real estate development company would not desecrate this property.

She took another bite of lemon Danish. The pastry was buttery and fresh, and the sweet-sour tang of the fruit made her mouth tingle. If she was going to stay here any length of time—and her goal was the rest of her life—she'd have to find out where he bought them. Assuming they'd speak to each other once the fight over the property began. As soon as he left, she'd talk with Roseanne to see if she could change her mind. She would play all her cards—guilt, family, heritage, local history. She would beg if necessary. Whatever it took.

"Susan!"

His shout stopped her cold.

She flung the pastry and ran down the hall. In the bedroom, Rafael was kneeling next to Roseanne's bed.

"She isn't breathing," he said. "Her skin isn't warm."

Frozen in place, Sue stared at her sister's body.

She couldn't believe Roseanne was dead. She couldn't believe it was over.

He turned to Sue, his face gray. "Please get your phone. Call nine-one-one." His voice was gravelly.

"What?" She tore her eyes away from the body on the bed.

"Call."

Nodding, dazed, she murmured the words into the phone. The old address came automatically, as if it had moved ahead of twenty other addresses over the past thirty years.

"They're on their way," she said.

Rafael, holding the hand of her dead sister, nodded.

Gypsy jumped up on the bed and lay down, her head on her paws.

Sue leaned against the doorjamb. In a few minutes, the ambulance would come and take Roseanne away, and one more bit of Sue's childhood would disappear. She was the only family Sue had left. And not every single day of her childhood had been bad.

Well, most of them.

Rafael pulled the blankets up and sat beside the bed, his legs crossed, chin propped on a fist.

"Is there anyone else we should call?" Sue asked.

He blinked, nodded slowly, and reached for his phone.

She sat quietly on a nearby stack of newspapers.

He spoke briefly, made another call, and repeated the message.

They waited.

The ambulance rolled up, crunching over the rocks and trash, its siren quiet. Rafael went outside to lead the attendants around the back of the house. When Sue apologized for their difficulty navigating the mess, one of the men said he'd seen worse.

While the team disappeared into the bedroom, Sue and Rafael waited in the kitchen, not talking. Then they followed the gurney out the back door and stood nearby as Roseanne's body was loaded into the mortuary van. The driver closed the doors, nodded to them, and drove away. The van disappeared down the road into the shrub and piñon pines.

Quiet descended. She stared at the empty driveway. Her throat ached.

"Vaya con Dios." Rafael stood within reach, looking rugged and manly in his tee shirt, Levi's, and work boots.

Their eyes met and held.

For just a moment, she thought he would offer her a hug.

A red Cadillac drove up. The door opened, and an elderly woman eased out.

Rafael greeted her with a long embrace. The woman was so short she disappeared into his arms.

"Rafe, honey, I came as fast as I could."

"There was nothing anyone could do."

The woman broke away from Rafael and held out a hand to Sue. "I never believed you were dead. I'm Flo."

"Thank you, I guess. Would you like to come inside for tea?"

"There's tea?"

"I found some. The mice didn't care for it."

"I would love a cup." Flo looked at Rafael, who shrugged.

They took their positions at the kitchen table while Sue put on a pan of water. "The microwave doesn't work, so we have to do it the old-fashioned way."

"That's fine for me," said Flo. "So, the two of you both got the place?"

"How did you know?"

"Roseanne told me her plans. I tried to talk her out of it. She told me I was too old to have an opinion and to shut the hell up." The three of them fell silent. Then Flo smiled. "She was a hellcat, wasn't she?"

Rafael crossed his legs, a pose that struck Sue as aristocratic. "I met Roseanne at a bar near my office. She worked there. I stopped in every night. Sometimes earlier." He looked at Flo, who nodded encouragement. "It was a bad time. Every night, she would refuse to listen when I tried to pour out my sad stories. 'Everybody's in pain,' she'd say. 'You're nothing special.' Still, I drank and complained, and at the end of the night, she would pour me into a cab. I stopped because I began to see myself through Roseanne's eyes, so you might say she straightened me out."

"That's a surprise since she was always the one needing straightening." Sue set out the tea bags, cups, and spoons.

Flo laughed. "That's true. Do you remember the time..."

The two of them headed down memory lane while Sue listened and learned. Her sister seemed to have mellowed a tiny bit as she aged. Too bad Sue hadn't known. There might have been a slim chance at reconciliation.

But not so long as Roseanne owned the homestead. And now, having divided it between Sue and a total stranger, that would never happen.

Flo's voice intruded. "I understand you girls were estranged. And yet, she wanted you to come back and see her before she died."

Sue put down her mug. "She probably wanted to see my face when she played her final trick on me. And then she could die happy."

"Nobody dies happy," Rafael said.

Flo smacked him on the arm. "Before we get all morose around here, I suggest you two examine the actual will," she said. "For all we know, she left everything to the Sedona animal shelter."

"I have to go check on a site." Rafael finished his tea and carried the mug to the sink. The two women waited as he walked out the back door and closed it firmly.

"Now that he's gone," Flo said, "what are your plans?"

"Start cleaning."

"I mean, long-term."

"Can't you guess? Try to wrestle the property from him."

Flo sighed. "I don't like the thought of the two of you fighting. He's a good man."

"But it's my land."

"And I get that, too. Listen, I'll try to help you if I can do so without pissing off the boss."

"I appreciate that."

"Meanwhile." Flo tipped her head toward the kitchen sink. "You should have somebody cut those oleanders back. Get some light in here."

"I will."

"And just by the bye, how are you doing?"

"I'm fine. Really."

"She was your family."

"I haven't had feelings for Roseanne since I was ten." Sue swallowed a lump in her throat. "It's just weird, seeing the house after all these years. Thinking of my parents. Missing them. It brings it all back. And Mike." Tears welled in Sue's eyes. "Oh, for heaven's sake." She pulled up her tee shirt and dabbed her eyes.

"How long has it been?"

"Three years. Sometimes it seems like yesterday, though."

"Mortality can get to you." Flo nodded. "Just the whole stinkin' fact of it. But what can you do? That's life on the ranch."

It felt good to express the negativity out loud. Sue hadn't allowed herself, fearing she would have a hard time shaking the gloom. But now, sitting with Flo in the family kitchen, the pain felt like just another aspect of life. "Most of the time, I can distract myself. Other times, I wallow until it passes."

"Good strategy." Flo set down her empty mug. "I should go. I've got a couple of hot prospects, and mama needs new shoes."

Sue folded her arms. "He's going to dig in, isn't he?"

"Yep. I love the guy, but to Rafe, it's all about the money."

"Wonderful."

"Cheer up. Maybe Roseanne was joking and left it all to you."

"Or him."

Flo picked up her purse. "Walk me out. I don't want to break a hip."

Chapter Nine

Pulling into her driveway, Flo bent down and picked up the morning newspaper. She'd driven over it in her haste to get to Roseanne's place. Tire tracks attested to the fact.

She straightened, a bit lightheaded, and took a breath while admiring the view of the town from her perch atop the hill. For all its growth and traffic, Sedona was still a lovely place to live. The homes in her neighborhood were all old, like her. Flo and Henry had been among the first buyers, and as the other homes sprouted, she'd enjoyed making friends with the new neighbors. She made it a point to get to know them, to the extent she could, but with everybody busy, it was harder these days.

Shrugging off her jacket, she slid open the back door and eased onto a chair. With the day already warm, the sun-heated cushion was a relief to her old bones. After the flurry and drama of Roseanne's death, she needed to catch her breath. Her patio was the perfect oasis of calm.

From her unfenced backyard, creosote and sage rolled out as far as the eye could see, giving off a delicate fragrance, a light perfume Flo had loved all her life. Unfortunately, her sense of smell was fading along with everything else. It wasn't fair, but she didn't obsess.

A lizard watched from his perch atop a chunk of sandstone.

"You'll get old too, friend. If you're lucky." Eighty-five years on God's green earth, and she'd appreciated every minute. Seen her share of sunrises, been in love, earned a fine reputation in real estate, and lived well, whether poor or rich.

Maybe it was perverse, but she was looking forward to Roseanne's funeral. She would enjoy hanging out with her fellow employees and teasing their boss. Rafael was adorable, but sometimes his machismo had to be tamped down, and she was the only one with the guts to do it. Except John. John wasn't afraid of anybody.

Her stomach rumbled, having had nothing but tea on an empty stomach, and she thought about whether to fix a late breakfast or early lunch. Luckily, she didn't put on weight. Never had. Still had the metabolism of a hummingbird.

And if she got fat, so what? She'd simply change her fashion outlook and continue to eat.

The lizard cocked its head and did pushups. The wind picked up, a hot, fragrant desert breeze. She braced her hands on creaky knees and rose, struggling with fatigue. She hadn't slept well last night, an increasingly annoying reality.

Inside, she wandered from room to room, opening curtains and windows to take advantage of the fresh air. Her footsteps echoed on the tile floor, and she put on a sweater. Lately, she couldn't seem to get warm.

Flo started a packet of instant oatmeal heating in the microwave and opened the newspaper. The clock ticked over the sink. A siren wailed through the city streets, inspiring a coyote pack in the distant hills to yip and howl in response.

Her mood dipped as she remembered how Ava used to perk up at the sound of her wild cousins. Once in a while, she'd tip her muzzle upward and sing in solidarity right there in the house. Flo howled with her once or twice, laughing at the look of surprise on the dog's face. She considered howling now, just for old times' sake. Maybe Ava would hear.

The old sheltie had died on Easter Sunday. Nan, the vet, had come by with the blue juice, saying it was the right thing to do. "By the time you can see them hurting," she said, "they've probably been suffering for three years."

Flo's last memory of her sweet pup was of digging her fingers into Ava's fur, still warm after the heart stopped.

She wondered how long she'd be able to stay at this house, with its split levels and shiny floors to keep clean. There was no getting around it, everything was more difficult lately, and if something were to happen to her, no one would know. She sometimes considered moving to assisted living, but it would feel like jail. And although her body might be growing a little weaker month to month, her brain was as sharp as ever. She couldn't imagine moving into a facility where half her neighbors might not know who the president was.

Or *what* one was.

"Good grief, you're morbid this morning." Flo wasn't the type to ruminate. Considered it a waste of energy.

When the microwave dinged, she doctored up the oatmeal with peaches and brown sugar and carried the hot bowl to the table. Flo enjoyed the quiet. Living alone might not be an option in years to come, but she'd stick it out as long as possible. Flo couldn't imagine giving up her kitchen or her solitude. If she wanted to play the baby grand in the middle of the night, so be it. She valued privacy the way she valued fresh air or a night sky dark enough to turn the stars into diamonds.

Through the screen door, a breeze carried more sounds of the howling pack, a little closer now. Tomorrow, she would go back to work, selling those nice new condos on the edge of town, making money for Rafael and herself, and matching enthusiastic buyers with the house of their dreams.

Flo gazed around her beloved home, allowing herself thirty seconds of aching self-pity.

Then she straightened her shoulders and tucked into her breakfast. The morning was getting away from her, but it was still Thursday, and she always dusted and vacuumed on Thursday.

Chapter Ten

Once the red Cadillac was gone, Sue returned to the silence of the house. Such a sad, cold place. Nothing like the vibrant, warm home she remembered.

I'm here now, she thought. *I can make it beautiful again.*

From the den at the back to the living room at the front, the rooms looked like storage units. Roseanne had kept anything and everything.

But now the house was Sue's, at least for a while. And regardless of the fight ahead with Rafael, she would not live in a garbage dump. She would throw herself at the cleanup and hope for the best. She would do what she could before Roseanne's decision was official, its impact known. And thereafter, if possible.

Because Sue would fight for what was hers.

So much work to do. Before Rafael saw the place again, she wanted to declare it her territory.

Rafael. Damn.

She shook herself.

No time to waste.

She put Gypsy in the car and headed for town. After so many moves over the years, living in base housing, Sue was an expert at fast, cheap cleaning. She pulled in at the local dollar store and loaded up paper towels, cleansers, rubber gloves, and trash bags. A broom and dustpan. A mop and pail. She made a face at a display holding mousetraps but then threw a half dozen in her basket.

Driving home, she swung by a fast-food restaurant for lunch.

It took all afternoon to clean the kitchen. Sue dumped the useless microwave, coffee maker, and a dozen other small appliances outside and emptied trash into a five-gallon bucket. She scoured the sink and counters, emptied and wiped out the cabinets, and cleaned the stove. Last, she swept and mopped the floor, using disinfectant liberally. Little by little, the kitchen began to breathe.

She was filling up Gypsy's bowl when a trap went off. Her stomach lurched. The dog barked. Sue went to look and found a tiny mouse dead of a broken neck. Pulling on rubber gloves, she took the trap outside and flung the carcass into the brush. The coyotes would be happy.

By late afternoon, the kitchen and dining room were clean and Sue was filthy. She took another shower, slipped into a breezy sundress, grabbed a bottle of wine and a glass, and wandered out to the bunkhouse with Gypsy leashed alongside. The old building was half adobe, half wood, and it still looked solid. Its covered wooden porch offered a killer view of the canyon. She sat gingerly in one of the two shredded patio chairs. It held.

In the golden light of early evening, dark purple clouds retreated to the horizon. Thunder rolled in the distance, but the sky was clear overhead, and a light breeze rustled the pine trees. A cactus wren warbled its gravelly song from a nearby perch. The sound was unique to the desert, rarely heard anywhere else. It reminded her of her childhood, and she loved it.

She set the bottle of wine on a rickety table between the two chairs and filled her glass. The cold chardonnay warmed her belly. A raven cawed, swaying at the top of a distant tree. With the nastiness of the junkyard behind her and out of sight, Sue could pretend the homestead looked as she remembered it from years ago.

Back then, her mother kept a garden near the front of the house. The ranch workers had rigged up an automatic watering system for the roses and fruit trees. The outbuildings rang with industry, and the corrals held whinnying horses or milling cattle, depending on the time of year. If she used her imagination, she could hear her father calling out to the hands, giving them instructions for the day's work. She could smell breakfast cooking and the aroma of a fireplace on the breeze.

The memories were almost painful, but they were submerged by a tiny ripple of joy in her veins. She was home. She was safe.

A car door slammed. Gypsy barked. Alarmed, Sue headed back down the path toward the driveway.

Rafael stood by his truck, hand raised in greeting. She waved him forward, surprised to find herself glad for his company. His walk was commanding, shoulders back, all confidence. He wore an olive-colored tee shirt, dusty khaki shorts, and the infuriatingly opaque, reflective sunglasses.

"Can I help you?" she asked.

Rafael's lips twitched, acknowledging their first greeting, his mouth lush under a dark mustache. Honestly, the man looked like he'd just come from digging ditches, but on him, it looked regal. "I apologize for not calling ahead," he said. "Especially as I see now that you are enjoying your solitude."

"I'm taking a break from cleaning."

"You look very nice."

"Thank you." She liked that he had noticed.

He leaned down to greet Gypsy, petting her gently. The dog closed her eyes in pleasure.

Rafael eyed the wine bottle on the small table between two folding chairs. "Will you be needing help with that?"

Sue bit back a smile. The man was audacious. "There's only one glass."

She wondered if His Highness planned to glug straight from the bottle.

He tossed his keys on the table and refilled her glass, rolling the bottle to avoid spilling a drop. "You first."

"Oh, so we're sharing?"

"We're sharing much more than that, it would seem." He sat in the other chair and stretched out his legs.

"Not necessarily." She took a sip. Then another, this time a gulp. What the hell. She might not get it back.

He held out his hand for the glass, took a sip, and sighed. "Such beauty."

"I've loved it all my life," she said.

Rafael gazed off across the landscape. "This is my second favorite place in Sedona."

"What's your first?"

"My home."

A Blacktail doe stepped out of the brush at the edge of the creek. She stood, head raised, sniffing the air. Twin fawns, their spots almost gone, appeared beside her. The doe lowered her head and drank, ears twitching.

While Rafael studied the deer, Sue studied his profile—his deep-set eyes, straight nose, and strong jawline. His fingers curled around the edge of the chair arms, as if hanging on.

"As far as the funeral goes—" she began.

A branch snapped, and the doe bounded into thick chaparral, the fawns chasing after her. In two seconds, they were gone.

"Gabriela is working on it," said Rafael. "It will be at my house. I have a big yard, nice view, and a caterer I have used often."

She fixed him with a glare. "Are you always this pushy?"

He shrugged. "I am efficient. I know the community, the service providers, her friends."

"She had friends?"

"Some. She was difficult to know, as you are aware."

"Difficult. That's tactful." Sue reached for the glass. "I have questions about my sister."

"What do you wish to know?"

Sue raised the glass and took a sip. She swallowed and gazed across the canyon.

Rafael waited.

She set the glass down. "Did she ever talk about the family?"

"No."

"Not one word?"

He removed his glasses. "I'm sorry. No. Not about you."

"I wasn't asking about me." But she was, and he knew it, because she saw pity before he averted his eyes. Humiliation heated her face.

A sightseeing helicopter thrummed through the air, growing louder as it flew over them. Sue imagined the occupants expecting to see a happy couple enjoying their beautiful home on the Mesa.

Oh, wait. It was a landfill.

The helicopter veered off.

She turned to Rafael. "Who was Roseanne to you?"

"A friend. Someone I cared about."

"How much did you care about her?"

"Ha." Smirking, Rafael scratched at a sideburn.

"'Ha' what? Don't evade."

"I am not evading. I am amused at your question."

"Why?"

He put his glasses back on. "When was the last time you saw her?"

"My wedding day. Thirty-two years ago last month." She realized she was twisting the gold band and stopped. "What difference does that make, anyway?"

"None." Rafael reached down to scratch Gypsy behind the ears. The dog closed her eyes and sighed.

Sue gave up. She would pursue the question another day. "Do you have someone who can officiate at the funeral?"

"Reverend Marguerite. You'll like her. She and Roseanne were motorcycle friends when they were younger." He reached for the wine bottle, topped off the glass, and handed it back.

Sue sipped her wine. The service would be a formality to mark the end of her sister's existence on earth. Sue would attend because it was the correct thing to do and because her mother would have wanted it, but she would hate every minute.

"Also, I set up an appointment with the attorney who wrote her will," said Rafael. "He will meet with us tomorrow morning at eleven."

Sue blinked at him. "You're really running with this, aren't you?"

"I don't like to waste time," he said. "I assume your calendar is clear?"

"Aside from cleaning the house, yes."

"There is no need to overtax yourself. Since we're going to sell it anyway."

"I'm not selling anything," she said. "This is my land. You're not family. You don't get to have it. It's mine, and if I have to, I'll fight you for it."

"Is that your first offer? It lacks finesse."

Her angry retort died at the look of amusement in his eyes. "This isn't a negotiation."

"Everything is a negotiation."

"You're infuriating. Can't we just enjoy our wine in peace for one minute?"

"Susan." He leaned toward her and gazed into her eyes.

She felt her skin burning. The man was gorgeous. His eyes, his strong nose and chin, that neat mustache... He leaned closer, reaching for her, his hand so near her face that she could feel its warmth. She struggled not to close her eyes and nestle her jaw into his palm.

Rafael plucked out a strand of her hair.

"Ouch." She pulled back. "What the hell was that?"

"An insect." He tossed it on the ground, stepped on it, and rose to his feet. "I'll pick you up tomorrow morning." Giving Gypsy one final pat on the head, he strode off into the sunset with the air of a landowner, done checking on the servants.

What an infuriating human being.

But that walk.

She finished the wine. The man was messing with her head. Yes, he was gorgeous and confident and powerful. So what? She had only one mission. Once the attorney told them what was in the will, the battle could begin.

Sue watched until he disappeared around the corner of the bunkhouse, leaving her alone.

But alone in this place didn't seem like a bad thing.

For all the sadness of losing Mike, and the tragedy of Roseanne, and the desecration of the property, Sue felt a powerful sense of peace here on the Mesa. It wasn't just the sprawling nostalgia of the house, or the view from every window to the red rock formations in the distance, or the clear sky or purple sage hillsides. It was proximity to her kin. To her parents and grands, who were buried only a few miles away in an ancient Catholic cemetery. She felt a kind of safety here that she hadn't in years. Knowing her ancestors would want her here, knowing she would treasure and preserve the land and their legacy for as long as she lived.

And it was only fair that she should inherit the house. It was her turn, finally. She would fight Rafael for the land, even if she had to sell her soul to buy his half.

How difficult would he make it?

Maybe he'd do the right thing and bow out. Life was never that easy, but for tonight, she allowed herself to dream of an easy resolution, pretending he was nothing more than an acquaintance, a person with no claim on the property.

A person she wasn't attracted to.

* * * * *

RAFAEL DESCENDED THE STAIRS TO HIS BASEMENT.

Troubled by his visit to the bunkhouse, he set out the tools from his work in progress. He hadn't meant to cause Susan further anxiety. She was a good person, a homemaker at heart, the foundation of her family. If given the chance, she would turn the Mesa house into a cozy refuge.

Not like this place.

Upstairs, his home was a showplace. It would never be described as cozy. He didn't care for knickknacks and tchotchkes, preferring smooth, clean lines and no clutter. If someone wanted to buy it, fine. He was a businessman, and if the price was right, he would sell and go, because a house had never meant that much to him. But with Susan, it was different. The Mesa meant everything to her.

He couldn't afford to think of it.

Humming a tune, Rafael sanded one of the spindle legs of a custom writing desk he'd been crafting for the past month. This shop was his refuge, a sprawling cave with a back wall tucked into a hill and front windows offering an endless view.

After his parents had been murdered, he lived with relatives, with strangers, in the back of a church, in a ditch. He had never really had a home, but he'd had houses. For the most part, they were structures providing shelter, nothing more. But when he reached a certain age, a certain level of income, he always had a carpentry shop.

He set one of the legs down and picked up the next. This piece was a treasure, with finely milled legs, decorative curlicues he'd shaped by hand, and a drop front suitable as a writing surface. Inside were five small compartments: two drawers, a shelf, and two vertical slots.

He barely noticed his hands moving smoothly over the surface of the wood, so familiar were the movements. His skin bore old marks from nicks and cuts from his work and several that were worse from his youth in Central America. Susan would be battle-scarred, like him, because she was similar in age. It was inevitable, even if the scars were invisible. She had suffered but survived. As had he.

Rafael replaced a worn sheet of sandpaper with a new one, shaking his head in wry amusement. He was becoming a sentimental fool. And there was a price for sentimentality, as he knew. Susan would find that out, unfortunately. It was too bad that in order to achieve his goals, he would have to thwart hers.

But this was the way of the world. At the heart of it was the question of survival. It was in her own interests to let him sell it. She would be wealthy and could live anywhere, and her family would benefit as well. He would be doing her a favor by forcing her to focus on an alternate goal.

Her question about Roseanne had hurt him. He didn't like the feeling, but he had sympathy. She wanted to be strong, but sometimes, a person couldn't.

He was attracted to her. That was undeniable. More reason to be on guard.

Rafael often dated and had even fallen somewhat for this or that local woman, a few of whom he still considered friends. Most had come to Sedona seeking spiritual enlightenment, instead finding Rafael on the other side of a margarita glass. These women were a joy, a comfort. He enjoyed each and every one of them.

But they were temporary visitors passing through his life.

Susan would come to hate him because he stood in the way of her goals. The Mesa represented her family, her roots, and perhaps even her peace of mind.

It wasn't his problem. He couldn't let it be.

He set down the square of sandpaper and brushed off his hands. He could compartmentalize. He had learned to do so at an early age.

Going back up the stairs, Rafael whistled a happy little tune, realizing with a shock that the melody was from his childhood. He stopped and ran a hand over his eyes, his face. He couldn't have been more than five years old the last time he heard his father whistle the tune.

Shutting the door to the basement, he went outside to breathe in the scent of pine needles and mountain air.

Chapter Eleven

Sue slipped in the second of her diamond earrings, fluffed her hair, and stepped back to look. The black slacks, knit top, and black pumps—appropriate for a funeral—would show she was serious. Although she was also very nervous. And it had less to do with the attorney and more to do with the man who would arrive in ten minutes to pick her up and debate their future.

Rafael made her aware of herself as a woman. The knowledge annoyed her greatly. He was just a very handsome man looking out for his own interests. She'd certainly dealt with such people before and knew how to work around them.

Unfortunately, when in his presence, her brain melted. She wouldn't let that happen today. There was too much at stake.

What if Roseanne's will turned out to be different from what they expected? What if she left everything to Sue—the logical, ethical thing to do—and had only pretended to split it with Rafael as a way to entertain herself in her last hours? Or what if the arrangement was even worse than co-inheriting with a stranger who was a land developer? How many ways could this thing go wrong?

Sue chewed on it, working herself into a ball of nerves by the time he drove up. Tossing the lipstick in her purse, she checked again to see that the dog had food and water, then hurried around to the front of the house.

To her surprise, he was getting out of a low-slung, black Corvette.

Watching him, her breath caught. He looked like Mafia, only better. Black silk shirt rolled at the elbows. The silver bracelet. Those arms. And always the sunglasses.

He held open the door as she slid in, then closed it gently. The Corvette rumbled to life. Rafael angled toward her as he backed out, and she could almost feel the heat coming off him. No, it was her imagination. But that cologne. What did they call it, *Woman Slayer?*

"This is a big day," he said, his eyes on the rear camera. "Who knows what your sister has planned for us?"

"I'm hoping her last act on earth was to do something civilized."

He chuckled, turning onto the highway toward the traffic and bustle of Sedona. Beautiful red rock formations against a deep blue sky created a stunning backdrop to the town. She remembered those ridges and peaks from so long ago, even as far back as riding the bus to school. Or stepping out the church door with her parents after Sunday Mass. Shopping at the local grocery store.

They were always there, always the red rocks, standing as silent sentinels to her childhood. She had missed them so badly, but following Mike around the country, nostalgia was a luxury she couldn't afford.

Now, she would be able to enjoy and appreciate them every day. Relaxing, Sue took a deep, easy breath, the air scented with his cologne. Whatever happened in the next couple of hours, she was home.

Rafael parked in a shabby business complex on the outskirts of town. Inside the office, the dark furniture was old and dusty. On the floor, a rotating fan rustled the cheap drapes.

"Come on back," a high-pitched voice called out from down the hall.

Sue followed Rafael into a dark, cramped office. Files and law books were stacked on every horizontal surface. A heavyset man, sweating at the temples, shook their hands and invited them to sit. After introductions and condolences, he opened a folder. "I have to admit, this is unusual."

"What does it say?" asked Sue.

"Do you want it quick and dirty, or should I read you the whole thing?"

"Please read it all," she said. "From the beginning."

"Well, the headline is that Roseanne wanted it split equally. Fifty-fifty, to the two of you, split right down the middle. You got that?"

"We understand." Rafael's fingers drummed the desk.

The attorney's big head rotated from one to the other. "And you're okay with it?"

"Not at all," said Sue.

"Yes," said Rafael.

The attorney dipped his chin and continued wading through pages of minutiae. All the lawnmowers on the property were to go to an acquaintance of Roseanne's who owned a repair shop. A stack of lumber went to one old buddy, roofing materials to another. Her mother's jewelry was to be donated to a particular little shop in Sedona.

"What little shop?" asked Sue. "And why would she give it to her instead of her only surviving relative?"

"The proprietor was a good friend to Roseanne," said Rafael. "You'll meet her at the funeral."

"Can't wait." Sue's tone was flat.

When the attorney finished reading, he handed the folder to Sue. "I wish you the best, but if you need an intermediary, my card's inside. And I know a good realtor if you want his name."

"We're not selling," said Sue.

Back in the car, Sue thumped the folder. "This is unbelievable. She really did it."

"I suggest we discuss it at lunch," said Rafael. "There is a Mexican place—"

"I'm not in the least bit hungry," she snapped.

Rafael backed up the car. "It's lunchtime. We may as well eat. Why is this so difficult for you?"

Because it's you, she thought. "Okay, fine."

He took her to Tlaquepaque, where they strolled through the outdoor shopping plaza to an upscale restaurant. A stroll that, under other circumstances, would have been lovely. Instead, Rafael walked quickly, with Sue marching silently beside him.

The hostess seated them at a shaded table on the patio, bringing chips, salsa, and menus. Without looking, he ordered lunch and drinks for both of them.

"You act like we're celebrating," she said.

"I feel like, in a way, we should be." He crunched on a chip. "Because this is the beginning."

"Of the end," she said.

He chuckled.

Their drinks were delivered. She took a sip, the salt and tequila brightening her day in some small measure. She licked the salt from her lip and noticed he was watching. She set down the glass. "What exactly are your intentions?"

He smiled that wolfish grin that showed his teeth and gave her a shiver right down her spine.

"With the house," she said.

His smile widened. "I already have people lined up to buy it, in its entirety, as is, right now."

"With garbage dump and everything?"

He shrugged. "Perhaps not that."

"So we sell it and walk away."

"Both of us wealthy."

"In your case, wealthier." She narrowed her eyes at him.

He shrugged. "I'm not embarrassed by it. But yes, then we split the proceeds and walk away."

"And you expect the house to be destroyed."

"They'd want to rebuild. Something of their own taste. Very likely, they would put it near the edge of the Mesa to improve their view. The bunkhouse would be gone, replaced with perhaps a pool and casita. You have to admit, it would be a beautiful property."

"And you could build it."

"Of course."

"Thereby making money on both ends."

"I would have earned it. And so would the people who work for me."

Their food came. He had ordered carnitas to split, flour tortillas for her, corn for him. They spent a few minutes serving themselves from the main plate.

Sue rolled the meat, beans, cheese, and salsa into her tortilla and took a bite. She lied when she'd told him she wasn't hungry, and now the buttery, salty, spicy blend nearly overwhelmed her senses. She washed it down with the tangy margarita and sat back to think.

The man sitting across from her had it all figured out. Of course, the money sounded appealing. If it were only about that, she'd say yes in a heartbeat and walk away wealthy, as he had said.

He looked at her, smiling.

"What?"

"Your sister told us you died of a drug overdose in your twenties."

"Huh. What a disappointment to have me show up after all these years."

"Not at all." His eyes lasered in on her.

She held his gaze. "You're pretty sure you can convince me to sell, aren't you?"

"My buyers are motivated. I have international reach. The property will go like this." He snapped his fingers.

"Sounds like you've got it all planned," she said.

"I've been thinking about it for months, ever since Roseanne said she would leave it to me."

Sue bristled. He almost seemed to want her to feel guilty. But he was the interloper. "I have a different vision. Would you like to hear it?"

Rafael inclined his head. "Please."

She leaned forward. "Imagine the ground cleared of every last tire, every cement block, every electrical appliance and derelict vehicle. I would hire a landscape designer to bring back native plantings, fountains, and hardscape. There would be arbors and sitting areas, especially the patio on the far corner over which I would rebuild the ramada."

"It would take a lot of money," he said.

"Please. I'm not finished," she said. "I would refurbish the outbuildings as individual studios and rent them to local artists who would work on the Mesa, producing in various forms of media. The old bunkhouse could be repurposed as a guest house. It would be an artists' retreat, celebrating the beauty of Sedona. As for the house, I would rehab it and preserve my family's heritage, perhaps even allowing tours if the local historical society was interested. This would represent artistic fulfillment and ancestral preservation for me, and my life's purpose in these later years would be fulfilled."

She stopped, realizing she'd ranted to this stranger, this adversary, so carried away was she with the beauty of her dream. She looked away, off into the restaurant, bracing for him to crush her vision.

Reaching across the table, he took her hand.

Shocked, confused, she let him.

"That is an exquisite picture you have painted," he said, "and I wish I could give it to you."

"Why can't you?"

"Five million dollars, Susan."

She pulled her hand back. "I'll buy your half."

His eyes flickered. "You have two point five million to give me?"

"Maybe you wouldn't need that much." Sue fiddled with her napkin. "Maybe you could discount your half so I could afford to pay you."

"Or I could sell it for even more. Six, seven million. Think of it, Susan. So much money for both of us."

"Why so greedy? You already said you're wealthy."

"I am wealthy on paper, but my business is like the tide. It comes in, it goes out. My line of work depends on a constant influx of new projects."

"Right. For you, it's just business." She shoved her plate away.

"What, do you think that's wrong? It's what I do. It is my life's work."

"Business, I understand, but compared to destroying what's left of my family history, it's crassly materialistic."

"If you want to be cynical, that's all any of it is."

"So we're at an impasse."

"Not at all. We are simply at the opening of negotiations."

"What if your potential buyers were to see what it really looked like?" She sat back, munching on a chip. "For example, what if drone footage emerged online, depicting the volume of garbage currently on site? Would that scare them away?"

"You would not—"

"But I might."

"You are evil, Susan."

She smiled.

Rafael signaled for the check. "As far as I am concerned, John could clear the place in two days. You would need to get your drone up quickly."

"I could have one up this afternoon if you push me."

The corner of his mouth turned up. "Why don't we agree to a time to clean up the property, the slow way, as you insist? Say, two to three weeks?"

"It would take months to clear that front acreage and then another several months to clear out the house."

"With my heavy equipment and crew, I can have it cleaned up in ten days."

"I want two months."

"One month for you to entertain your fantasy. That is all the time I can agree to."

Sue sighed. A month wasn't very long, but she was motivated. They could work on the property while she found the funding to buy him out. Or convinced him to love the land as much as she did.

"So." He put both hands on the table and leaned toward her. "Do we have a deal or not?"

"We have a truce."

"Truce, then." He raised his glass. "*Salud.*"

"*Salud.*"

As she savored the last of her beverage, Rafael's phone rang, the ringtone a 1940s swing tune.

He glanced at the display. "It's Flo. Excuse me."

"Sure." While he was gone, Sue considered their arrangement. It was good he'd volunteered to have his crews clear the site. She hadn't actually planned for that, and it would be a great solution. In one month, she had to have Plan A, B, and C in place to secure the homestead for herself. Taking out a pen, she did calculations on a cocktail napkin, not noticing his return.

"Flo fell at her home," he said. He looked pale. "She is at the ER. We have to go."

Sue looked up in alarm. The old woman was frail. "How bad is she?"

"I don't know."

At the hospital, they found Flo in a hospital bed, her leg elevated and iced. She was happily flirting with a male nurse. "I sprained my ankle," she said. "Tripped on a rug."

"How bad is it?" Rafael asked.

"Bad enough they want to ship me to a convalescent hospital. I won't have it."

"They won't let you go home?" asked Sue.

"Not by myself." Flo looked up at the ceiling. "I hate being helpless."

"This should be seen as a wake-up call," Rafael said. "Maybe you should move to a group-type facility where you are not alone."

Both women glared at him. He put both hands up as if to fend them off.

"If you're suggesting I go live in one of those old-age places, please don't. I don't care if I fall a hundred times; I won't be warehoused."

Sue felt the same way, but there were practical matters to consider.

Rafael said, "Then I will find help for you. An attendant. Someone who can stay at your house with you for a few weeks."

"I'll call Vicky," Flo said. "She always knows the good-lookin' ones."

Sue looked at Rafael. "Would you give us a minute, please?"

He tilted his head, questioning.

"Girl talk," Sue said.

Rafael ducked out the door.

Sue leaned a hip against the bed. "Listen," she said, her voice barely above a whisper. "I know the Mesa house is a dump right now but give me two days and I can have it cleaned up enough for you to move in with me."

"That's too much to ask."

"I'm a fast worker. I can have it ready in no time."

"Rafael wouldn't like it."

"Big deal. Anyway, you could stay until you feel able to return home."

Flo reached for Sue's hand and gave it a squeeze. "That's kind of you, but I'll be happier in my own house. Vicky'll find somebody for me."

"If you change your mind, though..."

"Thank you. Now, get out of here and get to work. People are going to want to see it back to normal." With that, Flo laid back, exhausted.

Sue walked out to the car with Rafael. "She's going to ask Vicky to find help."

"She'll need a home health-care aide," he said. "And a visiting nurse."

"You seem to know the drill," said Sue. "Because of my sister?"

He nodded. "Though Flo is a procrastinator, and lately..." He twirled his finger at his temple. "I'm not so sure, you know?"

"Does she have family in the area?"

"She is a widow and has no children." He put the car in reverse. "We are her only family. My employees are very fond of her."

They drove the rest of the way in silence. Sue wished Flo wanted to come home with her. It would have been a nice roadblock for Rafael. Now she'd have to come up with another tactic.

He dropped her off in front of the house. "Don't forget, we begin work tomorrow."

Sue watched him drive away. She had a month.

No time to waste.

Chapter Twelve

When Rafael walked in the front door of his office, Matt, the burly engineer, jerked away from Gabriela like he'd been Tasered.

"Afternoon, Boss."

Gabriela straightened her skirt. "You're here early." She rounded her desk on four-inch heels.

Matt's eyes followed her.

Rafael suppressed a smile. The two of them were so hot for each other yet so conflicted, it was entertaining. He set his briefcase on Gabriela's desk.

She handed him a stack of mail. "Flo called."

"From the hospital? I was just there five minutes ago."

"She forgot to tell you, she has a couple of prospects for the new tract in Cottonwood. She wanted you to follow up."

"Even injured, she never slows down," he said.

"I need to get going," said Matt. "They're finishing up grading at Verde Wells today." He shot a glance at Gabriela, who eyed him hungrily.

Rafael went into his office and closed the door. Good for them. Young love and all that. Delusional but well-meaning.

Tapping his phone, he called Flo, checked on her status, and got information about the prospective buyers. He moved three pieces of paper from one side of his desk to the other and took two phone calls. Gabriela was at her desk out front, but other than that, the office was deserted.

Outside the tall windows, the sun had disappeared behind puffy white clouds. Possibly they'd have rain later. Not good for construction.

Frowning, he unfurled a set of blueprints, but his mind was elsewhere. He couldn't stop thinking about Susan. So full of fire and so determined. At barely five feet, she carried herself like a warrior. He found that amusing. When she narrowed those icy blue eyes at him, he wanted to pull her close, taste those lips. That mouth.

Also, he wanted to run for his life.

Rafael tried to concentrate on work, but the blueprints were as boring as blank paper. He couldn't get interested.

"I'll be back later." He hurried past Gabriela and out the door.

After five miles of bumping down a poorly maintained forest service road and another mile of ruts and washboard, he turned into John's driveway. Two dogs ran to the truck, barking ferociously until they saw who it was.

John stood on the front porch, arms folded, leaning against a wooden pillar. He wore a white tee shirt, Levi's, and heavy black boots. He greeted Rafael with a lift of his chin. "What brings you out here?"

"I was in the area."

"Nobody's ever in the area. Want a beer?" John went to the kitchen, returning with two opened bottles.

Rafael took one. Here in the starkly primitive atmosphere of John's cabin, he didn't have to dance around with pleasantries.

John could be blunt to the point of rudeness. He rarely smiled, and he didn't like people much. If they irritated him, he tended to climb on his Harley and leave the offenders in his literal dust. Yet he knew more about the trades than any subcontractor Rafael had ever hired, leading to a steady stream of projects over the years. During that time, he and Rafael had become good friends.

They kicked back in the chairs on John's porch. Two dusty hounds flopped at John's feet. His hand dropped idly to one's head, rubbing its ears. In the distance, heavy clouds gathered.

"This morning," said Rafael, "I accompanied Roseanne's sister to the attorney's office to examine the will. It was as we expected. Roseanne left it to both of us equally."

"Hard to guess why."

Rafael shook his head. "It is a mystery. Roseanne liked to play games, but this is a disaster. Both her sister and I desire the land equally."

"So now you guys are gonna have to fight over it." John rolled his bald head around on a bodybuilder's thick neck, the bones crackling.

"Yes, it's a problem. One I intend to resolve in my favor, of course."

"Throw some money at her. That usually works."

Rafael stared across the landscape. Rain had begun falling to the south, gray lines as straight as lead pencils reaching from sky to earth. "She doesn't want money."

"Not possible."

"She has love for the land because of her family."

"Sucks." John took a slug of beer. "So, up the offer."

"I intend to when the time is right. However, we have agreed on a cease-fire for one month in order to prepare the property for sale."

"She's agreed to sell?"

"Not exactly." Lightning flashed in the distance, followed closely by the roll of thunder.

John held up his empty beer bottle. "You good?"

Rafael nodded. John returned with another. "What's she look like?"

"She is attractive."

"Age?"

"Like me."

"That old. Wow."

Rafael shook his head. "She is a Molotov cocktail."

John's mouth twitched in a movement that almost resembled a smile. Rafael had confided about his childhood.

"You should make a move." John leaned back and stretched. Each knuckle was tattooed with a Celtic rune. "Before you get too old to snag a nice piece of ass."

"I have no trouble snagging anything," said Rafael.

"You need help with the cleanup? Want me to come by tomorrow?"

"For a few hours."

"Maybe I'll offer her a ride on my hog."

"She's not interested in your hog." The words came out in a growl.

John chuckled.

Rain began to splatter in the dust, then quickly increased. The men backed away from the edge of the porch. Rafael scowled at the desert. This gift of Roseanne's was already disrupting his life. She was undoubtedly looking down from the heavens—or up from somewhere else—and laughing at him.

Laugh away, he thought. He would triumph in the end.

He always did.

* * * * *

TWO POINT FIVE MILLION DOLLARS. There was no way she could cobble together that much.

Sue leaned back in her chair, eyeing the calculator on the kitchen table. Her head hurt. Long day, alcohol, and fear were a bad combination. And now, financial disaster.

She and Mike had been frugal, but a series of investment disasters had ruined their finances. She should have kept a closer eye, but she trusted Mike. And really, it was nobody's fault. The market turned at a bad time. They'd never recovered from it.

Sue let Gypsy out and sat on the picnic bench, waiting for the dog to do her business. Discouraged and tired, her thoughts drifted.

Lunch had been perplexing.

Rafael infuriated and intrigued her. She could waste the whole afternoon thinking of the way his hands gestured to make a point, the way his fingers held the fork and knife, the way his mouth enjoyed their shared plate of carnitas. He was polite, even solicitous. When he sat quietly listening to her, she felt as if he were hearing each individual word, assessing and contemplating.

She felt heard. It was flattering, to say the least.

He had to be aware of his effect on women. And the way he looked at her, as if studying a bit of prey he intended to consume. A delightful shiver ran up her spine.

But she couldn't let her guard down. After all, the man wanted her land. He would use everything possible to bring her around to his way of thinking, whether through words, trickery, or seduction. As a successful land developer, he was surely adept at achieving his objectives. She would have to be ready.

She watched Gypsy snuffling around at a pile of rusted cans. How long had it been since she'd been this attracted to a man? With Mike, they'd developed a rhythm over decades, a routine solidified by a thousand repetitions. He was a good husband and friend, and she'd poured every bit of her heart into caring for him, especially in the time it took for the cancer to kill him.

Remembering, her eyes stung. She'd give anything to have him back. The last time they made love had been just before his diagnosis. After that, all their energy was focused on getting him well, then easing his journey when that didn't work.

Crushed, horrified, she'd made it through the funeral on the arms of her children, Travis and Katie, grown and gone.

The first year was a fog, but in the second, she decided to live, and set about forging a new life for herself. Visalia had been Mike's choice, not hers, but she made inroads in the community. She took exercise classes and served on committees. Showed up, made a few friends. The aching loneliness had diminished somewhat.

When he died, she was grateful to the people who'd attended the funeral since they hadn't lived in Golden Era all that long. But within two months, things changed. Women who'd been friendly at neighborhood functions turned cool. Invitations to dinners and activities dropped off. Former friends were slow to return messages. Carol and her husband were the only people who stuck by her.

It didn't take a genius to see what was happening. They saw her as a threat.

As if! Most of their husbands were more interested in golf and football than chasing a widow around the clubhouse, and the feeling was mutual. Sue couldn't imagine any man ever appealing to her again, not after Mike.

And yet, here was Rafael, and wouldn't you know, he'd be competing with her for something she desperately needed, for her family's legacy and her own mental health. Because without her land, the future looked bleak indeed.

Calling Gypsy, Sue returned to the house. It wasn't her way to ruminate. She might not be able to control the future, but she could manage the present. And the first order of business was to call Carol and ask if she'd mind keeping an eye on the house a bit longer.

"Not at all," her friend said. "I went inside a couple times to water the plants, but these houses pretty much run themselves."

"It's all fun and games until a sprinkler head breaks off."

"Got that right. By the way, Chuck was asking about you."

"Chuck from the barbecue?"

Sue had danced with the man. He was pleasant and, if she remembered right, not bad-looking. But until recently, men hadn't crossed her radar.

"He's caught up with me, out walking, and he keeps asking. Seems like a decent person. What do you want me to tell him?"

"You can say I'm visiting family." Sue was flattered at the man's interest, but she didn't intend to return to California except to tie up loose ends. "Tell him I'm moving."

Carol was silent for a moment. "Is that true? Are you?"

"Oh, Carol. I don't honestly know." Sue explained her situation. "So I'm going to be fighting for my property with this developer, of all things."

"Don't back down, girlfriend. You deserve it more than him."

"That's what I say."

"Give him hell, then."

Laughing, the women hung up. Sue leaned against the kitchen sink, staring at the dusty oleanders pushing against the window. Her mood darkened. Carol was a good friend, and here Sue was, planning to pull up roots again. Just as she had all her married life.

Would it ever end? Would she ever find a friend or two she could stick with, live nearby, and see often? Have coffee or lunch with? Go to a movie?

If she won this house, if she remained in Sedona, it would be possible. All she had to do was claim the property for herself.

Restless, Sue grabbed a legal tablet and a pen and wandered around the house, taking inventory. At this point, the kitchen was clean and functional. The primary bath worked. What she really needed to do next, both for sanitary and psychological health, was to clean out Roseanne's room.

Sue groaned. What a mess that would be. The dresser and mattresses were too big and heavy for her to move alone. Especially when she considered the narrow path through the den to the back door.

Rafael had said he would help. She would take him up on that. He mentioned bringing in heavy equipment.

Why would he have access to heavy equipment?

On impulse, she got out her phone and looked him up online.

And then the air went out of her.

Rafael Palacios was a real estate developer.

His website was spectacular. His designs were some of the most fabulous she'd ever seen. Hello, Howard Roark. No wonder he wanted the house. Her little sentimentality must be charming to him.

Sue couldn't breathe. She needed to get out of the house, to clear her thoughts. Even though it was hot outside, she knew exactly where she needed to be.

She changed into shorts, a tee shirt, and hiking boots. After slapping on sunblock, she loaded her backpack with water bottles and clapped a wide-brimmed hat on her head. Snapping the leash on Gypsy, she practically ran down the path to the bunkhouse, below which lay a series of trails into the canyon.

The walkway down could be treacherous, so she moved carefully, holding Gypsy in one arm, reaching for handholds on nearby boulders with the other. The path leveled out, weaving through manzanita taller than her head and juniper bushes loaded with berries that smelled like gin. She made a lot of noise to scare away snakes, but a critter rustled through the underbrush every few feet, most likely a lizard or horned toad.

When she entered the cottonwood grove along the creek, she set Gypsy down. The dog waded into the shallow water, sniffing and tasting it. Sue rested on a rock, letting the breeze cool her, listening to the rustling leaves overhead. Not far from here was a series of rocks the native peoples used as mortar and pestle. Her mother had planted crucifixion thorn around them to hide them from random hikers.

She shoved off the rock, tugging Gypsy along. They followed the path down by the creek, under the shimmering cottonwoods, along the base of the canyon to the secret stairway. At least, that was how she thought of it. A series of steps, hidden by boulders and brush and a dozen native plants, cultivated into seedlings by her mother and then nurtured into drought-resistant adults, creating a screen for the only passageway up to the cave.

Sue ducked under a juniper bough and between a creosote and a manzanita plant, keeping Gypsy close. She ascended the narrow passageway, stepping over sharp rocks and smooth boulders, careful not to twist an ankle or break a limb in this most hidden of places. Higher and higher, she climbed, the steep slope no challenge, excitement pulling her forward. Branches scratched at her arms, but she had worn a long-sleeved shirt and did not feel their sharpness. Her steps were sure, their placement familiar. The carpet of dried leaves over sandy rocks did not frighten her. She slipped through the brush with the agility of a deer until the gateway boulder loomed in her path.

Without hesitation, she squeezed between the boulder and the dense branches of juniper. Edging around the boulder and out into the sunlight, she laughed with relief and joy.

Here, hidden from the canyon floor by the layers of scrub and cottonwoods and from all but the most dedicated copter pilots, was her beloved cave. The red earth under her feet revealed no human footprint other than her own, proof that her family had managed to keep the site secret. A miracle, one she hoped would continue.

She took a drink from the water bottle and then filled her hand for Gypsy, who lapped it eagerly. A cottonwood swayed gently overhead, shading her from the hot sun.

No one in the family ever spoke of this place, fearing it would be overrun by hikers and buried in trash. Worse, its secrets would be exposed.

At the end of the climb, Sue should have felt winded, but her body seemed to vibrate with energy.

The familiar slab of red rock at the cave's entrance was as familiar as her family sofa, the place where Sue's childhood imaginings took shape. She had invented magical creatures summoned to the cave for a royal tea party, or later, a critical secret mission. Or even later, the return of the ancestral Sinagua, led by a handsome warrior prince who, smitten by the beautiful young maiden, would gather her up in his arms and whisk her away to his palace in the clouds.

The cave was magical, but not just because of imaginary princes. The cave was magical because Roseanne hated it. She hated the tedious climb, hated the rocks and dirt and lizards, and hated the idea that a bat might fly into her face. Thus, Sue had it all to herself, and it was a refuge.

She petted Gypsy, tied her leash to a sapling, and went into the cave. It wasn't deep, going back only about twenty feet, and thus light from outside was sufficient for Sue to investigate without a flashlight.

Although shallow, the air inside the cave dropped almost immediately, and the quiet settled over her like a cool, comforting blanket. Along the back wall, stick figures painted with charcoal and plant dyes marched in a line. Two human figures, whom Sue had always thought of as the warrior and his mate. A deer, a bird. Another person, this one wearing a long cloth or cloak. Another bird. A snake.

Sue touched the figures, her fingers light on the cool stone. *Here I am*, she thought.

A breeze rustled around the edges of the cave, tossing dead leaves inside.

Sue pressed her palms against the cave wall, eyes closed.

I'm back.

She breathed.

Peace settled over her. Her arms felt light and strong, and her spine and muscles relaxed. The cave supported her back. She felt welcome.

She felt safe.

By the time Gypsy yipped, an hour had passed. Sue stood, stretched, and marveled at the fact that she wasn't tied in a knot. In fact, she didn't feel achy or stiff at all. She had only ever come here as a youth, before the aches and pains of middle age. If the cave conveyed some kind of youthful energy, it was a good thing the family kept it hidden all these years. Otherwise, the whole world would trample a path here.

She made her way back down the dirt walkway, surefooted and agile. Her head felt clearer, her body lithe and strong. Collecting Gypsy, Sue made her way back down the path, as surefooted and agile as on the trip up. Near the base of the secret stairway, she hunted around for a length of juniper, sweeping the red dust and obliterating her footprints from the last thirty feet of steps. Then she tossed the branch away, checked the opening to make sure her passing through was not obvious, and headed toward home. Although hikers often followed the path alongside the creek, their numbers were usually low, even during the tourist months. Now, in the humid air preceding the monsoon season, the canyon was deserted. A good thing, given its tendency to flash flood.

Once, as a child, Sue had been playing at the cave, lost in her made-up stories, when the rumble of thunder urged her to head for home. But at the bottom of the path, another rumble sounded, along with the smell of the rain-swept desert. It had sounded to her eight-year-old ears like a freight train heading down the canyon toward her.

Alarmed, she had darted back up the path, through the brush, past the boulder to high ground just as the flood roared by. It was gone in a few minutes, leaving dead trees and plants clinging to the cottonwoods down at the creek, which had been scoured with black and rocky water.

Sue should have been terrified by what she saw. Instead, she was entranced by the power of the canyon, the power of the red rock desert.

Then and now, that entrancement remained.

The fragrance of ozone followed her home.

Chapter Thirteen

The next morning, the sound of knocking woke her. Sue clawed her way out of the recliner, every joint and muscle aching.

After returning from the cave, she'd worked late into the night as if in a fever. Starting in the bedroom closest to the kitchen, she sorted through mountains of craft supplies stacked in boxes against the walls. Paints, brushes, fabrics, sewing notions, skeins of yarn, knitting needles, and looms of every size went into black leaf bags, which she carried out to the backyard or loaded into her SUV for donation. If she had spent fifty years doing nothing but crafts, Roseanne still wouldn't have been able to use it all.

When the room and closet were empty, she swept, dusted, and mopped until her body couldn't take any more. After a microwaveable dinner and half a bottle of wine, she'd curled up in the recliner, exhausted.

If she managed to wrestle the property from Rafael, how would she feel about moving so far from Katie and the grandchildren? Was she really ready to make such a move? All during her marriage, she and the kids had followed Mike from airbase to airbase. It was a difficult way of life.

Her kids came through it differently. Where Katie seemed permanently insecure and needy, Travis went blithely on his way through college and into a good career, reluctant to settle down with one woman. Whereas Katie had married and given her grandchildren.

Grandchildren she rarely saw, due to geographic distance, which would only increase if she moved to Sedona. It was a difficult part of the equation. Her remaining family was scattered to the winds, but with this land, she could create an enduring home for them. The Mesa was their legacy. If she could hang on, she could give her children a permanent connection to their ancestors. She could atone for their childhood.

Thinking and planning, Sue fell asleep in the recliner.

Now someone was pounding on her back door. She could see his shape outlined against the dusty curtains.

She lurched to her feet and pulled on her robe. Glimpsing herself in the old mirror over the fireplace, she grimaced. Her hair looked like a silver tumbleweed, and leftover mascara formed half-moons under her eyes.

Rafael knocked again.

She smoothed her hair, tightened her robe, and opened the door.

He held a cardboard tray from the coffee shop.

"Good morning." After a slow assessment of her general appearance, his eyes locked on hers. He was trying not to laugh.

She straightened her shoulders. "I thought we said seven."

"It *is* seven. May I come in?" He brushed past her without waiting for an answer.

"Please do," she muttered at his back, then ducked into the bathroom where she washed her face, brushed her hair, and threw on a pair of jeans and a cotton shirt.

At least she looked less hideous.

In contrast, Rafael looked like a model for a calendar featuring old-guy construction workers. He wore a light blue tee, offsetting tanned and muscular forearms. Faded jeans fit his strong legs, which ended in scuffed work boots.

Not that she noticed.

She sat with him at the table, uncapped her coffee, and blew on it before tasting it. She felt his eyes on her and glanced up.

He lounged in the other chair, leaning back, an ankle resting on the other knee. His arm rested on the table, fingers drumming a restless beat. "Your SUV is filled with trash bags."

"I cleaned out the craft room. Those bags are going to the charity drop-off."

"A good idea. Do you need help with that?"

"No but thank you for asking."

"De nada."

The man had the most compelling accent. So elegant. She could listen to that rich voice all day long. And that mouth. She loved a man with a mustache. Mike had never worn one. Said he didn't want to look like a hood.

Funny word. Who said that anymore?

"Susan."

She blinked. "Hmm?"

"I asked if you are ready."

"For...?"

"To begin work."

"Oh, right." *Snap out of it*, she told herself. *He's your adversary, and you have work to do.* "Let's start on Roseanne's room. It's the worst in the house."

"Worse than a leaking motorcycle?"

"So you know about that. Why is it here? And why is it in the house, for Pete's sake?"

"Who is Pete?"

She smiled, shaking her head.

"The bike was Roseanne's." His hand rested on the table. He wore a ring on his right ring finger, silver like the bracelet, though that piece was absent today. Some cultures wore wedding rings on the right hand.

Stop it.

"So. The motorcycle?"

A strand of dark hair fell across his eyes. "Rosie loved motorcycles. She was fanatical. When she was younger and stronger, she owned a Harley-Davidson, an 883, as I recall." He sighed.

"Did you ride together?"

"Occasionally. I still have my bike, and sometimes a small group of us—" He fell silent.

Sue waited, watching emotion play across his face, wishing she knew what he was feeling.

He glanced down at the floor. "I knew she was sick, but I had hoped she would take measures."

"I think nothing would have helped short of a transplant."

"At the very least."

"Why didn't she try?"

"She was a renegade to the end."

"It sounds like you admired her."

"I did. She wasn't afraid of anything."

"Maybe she should have been."

"No one could tell her how to live. She loved her cigarettes, and when her doctors told her she'd have to quit, her response was graphic." He chuckled. "Your sister was one in a million."

Sue rose and walked to the sink. "Were you together?"

Rafael brushed his mustache with a thumb and forefinger. Tugged on his lower lip. "Roseanne and me? As a couple, you mean?"

She leaned against the counter. "It's a simple question." Too bad if she shocked or offended him. She was getting brash in her old age.

Rafael grinned, his teeth bright.

"Is something funny?"

"Suzy, are you joking with me?"

"Why would I be?"

"Your sister preferred women."

"She did not. I would have known."

"I assure you, she did."

Sue turned her back to him. Roseanne, gay? How had she missed that?

Of course, thinking back, it wasn't hard to believe. Roseanne went after anything she wanted, man or boy. Why not women too? It probably wasn't even about sex. Power, more likely. Power and abuse.

Rafael pushed the chair away from the table and pulled a set of leather work gloves from his back pocket. "If you're ready—"

"Yes, fine." She slipped past him and hurried out of the kitchen.

Roseanne's bedroom, thanks to Sue's success at wrenching open a window, at least had fresh air coming in. The room was a dump, and it contained ghosts. The sooner they cleared it, the better.

She stripped the sheets. The mattress sagged and bore stains from years of use. Shamed, she threw the sheets in the corner.

Seeming not to notice, Rafael simply seized the mattress and set it upright on its side. She held the back end upright as he slid it out the bedroom door into the hallway. Together they duck-walked the mattress and box spring out to the patio, threading their way through the junk, knocking things over as they passed. That done, they returned for the rest of the decrepit furniture from Roseanne's bedroom, which they also placed outside the back door.

When the bedroom was nearly empty, Sue rolled the closet door open. The space was filled with clothing, shoes, and cardboard boxes. None of it looked salvageable.

Standing beside her, Rafael said, "My office works with a disposal company. There will be a dumpster here by tomorrow morning. If you put that into bags and leave them on the patio, my men can get rid of them. And you might need these." He handed his gloves to her. They were well-worn leather, the fingers bent to the shape of his hands.

"Thanks, but I have my own."

"You should watch out for snakes and scorpions when you're outside. The warm weather brings them out."

"I grew up here, remember? I've been bit and stung by everything in the desert." She picked up a broken picture frame and tossed it on the pile. "So you can stop with the fear campaign."

"You and Roseanne. You're like Amazons."

"Yes, we are. Were." She unrolled a leaf bag. "I need to get back to work."

"And I as well. I'll return tomorrow with my crew."

"Good." She walked outside with him into the heat of midmorning. A road runner darted away as they approached. "Thanks for the help."

"See you then."

She watched him walk away. Such a fine backside, and those shoulders. The man got her hormones up and moving again, something she thought was well in the past. She felt young and hungry and allowed herself to enjoy the view.

And then he turned around and busted her. She gave a little wave and a smile. So what if he saw? Men liked to be ogled too. She went back inside, her thoughts bubbly and scattered. This would never do. He was her adversary.

After Rafael left, Sue discovered a washing machine on the rear patio underneath a tarp. The machine appeared to have been used recently. The electric cord snaked into a nearby window, and a nearby garden hose indicated the water source. A flat blue drainage hose stretched out to a weedy area with tall, very green grass. Sue went back inside, plugged the cord into a nearby outlet, and loaded the machine with her dirty clothes and towels.

Hours later, while the ancient washer chugged away on the back porch, Sue took a break, sitting on the patio table in the pine tree shade. Wind chimes jangled from the branches, a pair she'd found while unearthing the craft room. Sitting on the wooden bench, listening to the old agitator swishing back and forth, brought her a sense of peace. It was primitive but would do the job. She had such a setup at the first house she and Mike lived in, in Yuma. Like this one, her washer had emptied into her yard, and as a result, her flower garden was a thing of beauty. Fond memories of the hard old days.

But she'd been young then. In contrast, this was how Roseanne ended up.

When the bedroom was so empty it echoed, she dusted and cleaned the windows and used her new broom to sweep the floor. She filled a five-gallon bucket with water and disinfecting cleaner and mopped until the tile shone. Working her way out the door, she straightened up and rubbed her lower back. If Roseanne were watching right now, no doubt she'd be laughing uproariously, having thrown the gauntlet. *You can try to get the house, but I'm going to make you work for it.*

Sue showered and dressed, loaded Gypsy into the SUV, and drove into town. After dropping her donations at the local charity, she headed over to the hospital to see Flo. The double doors whooshed open, releasing the smell of pine-scented disinfectant and beef stew from lunch. Flo was in a private room, sitting up in bed and reading a novel.

"Hey there," she said, tapping on the doorjamb.

"Come on in, stranger." Flo set the book aside. "Pull up a chair."

"I brought you a new *People*."

Flo wore no makeup and looked refreshed. "I'll read it at home."

"So you're getting out? When?"

"Couple days."

"I have an extra bedroom now. Not to bug you or anything."

"Thank you, honey, but I can't wait to be in my own bed again. Eating my own food." A look of distaste crossed her face. "My refrigerator must be a biological horror by now."

"Gabriela went by and cleaned it out."

"She's a good girl." Flo gazed out the window. "This has jarred my thinking, I'll be honest."

"How are you going to manage?"

"I've got Vicky on the case. She'll find somebody. Maybe a handsome young person who'll help out long-term in exchange for cheap rent."

"That's a great idea. Vet them carefully, though."

"Of course." Flo struggled to sit up. "When my Pa got old and weak, anytime anybody suggested he move to a facility, he'd wave his fist in the air and holler, 'You'll carry me out of here feet first.' It made me mad because he was so weak and needy it about killed my mother. I resented the hell out of him. But now I understand. You want to be in your own place."

"Will you at least get one of those bracelets in case you fall?"

"I don't like the idea of Big Brother watching me all the time," Flo said. "How's the property split coming along? You killed Rafael yet?"

Sue smiled at the deflection. "No, but I'd like to."

"Then you could have the whole thing."

"I might be able to buy him out if I can get him to be reasonable. If I can get him to see the value of my family's legacy. How sentimental the property is."

"Wouldn't hang my hat on it. Mr. Palacios isn't a sentimental person."

"But if I can get close to affording his half..."

On the way to the hospital, Sue had spoken with the California realtor about selling the Visalia house. The realtor told her to expect top dollar in the current market, but it wasn't nearly enough.

"That, plus guilt, might work."

"I have to try." It was important to keep a positive attitude, to go into this as if it were a done deal. She had to commit fully, or not at all.

And if she failed, she could always return to Visalia to live out her days. Join a crafting club. Go to water aerobics, pickle ball, and book club. She would try again to make friends. Her life would be safe and placid.

What a depressing thought.

Her only hope was to find a pot of gold somewhere or, equally unlikely, to change Rafael's mind.

At least she had two clean bedrooms, a kitchen, and one halfway-decent bathroom. Soon, Rafael's crew would start on the exterior. The Mesa house would feel like a home again. Even if the future was uncertain, she would enjoy it as long as possible.

She gave Flo a hug. "I have to go. I'll call you."

"You do that. And stick to your guns. You have a right to live there."

Sue hoped Rafael would come to see it that way.

Chapter Fourteen

Sue tucked her purse under her arm and clipped down the walkway to the front door of Rafael's house. A uniformed worker answered and led her across the cold gray tiles, past the soaring great room and dining area to the rear wall, which was covered with two-story-high blue-tinted windows. It was exactly what she expected after seeing his Howard Roark website. Cold and austere.

Putting on her company face, she stepped outside.

Two-dozen people, dressed in everything from black formal to flip-flops, chatted under a vine-covered ramada. Flo held court from a bright red wheelchair. A good-looking blond man stood behind her, holding the handles as if ready to go. Rafael and John stood shoulder-to-shoulder at the crowd's edge, chests out, hands in pockets like twin statues.

Sue caught her breath at the sight, Rafael in his sport jacket and black dress shirt, John in a black tee and jeans. Rafael had a full head of hair, while John was completely bald. Both wore the same mustache, but John had a goatee. Both wore dark sunglasses.

As if sensing her presence, Rafael looked up. He said something to John and walked toward her. "I wasn't sure you would attend."

"How could I not? She was the last of my family."

"Of course." He tucked her arm in his.

She liked the comfort of it. Beyond his warmth, there was reassurance, a sense that they were friends despite the conflict between them.

Rafael began introductions. "This is Gabriela, my office manager."

Sue shook hands with a twenty-something Latina wearing a short skirt, high heels, and an elegant updo.

"You look so much like her." Gabriela's grip was strong. "I'm sorry for your loss."

"Thanks."

"And what a weird situation for you two, right?"

Sue cocked an eyebrow, but Rafael steered her toward a burly redhead. "This is Matt. He operates our heavy equipment."

"Hello. Wow." The young man blushed. "I'm sorry, but you look just like her. I mean, on a good day. I mean—"

"Matt," cautioned Rafael.

"Sorry for your loss." The kid was red from his shirt collar to the roots of his hair.

Sue smiled at him. "From the time we were kids, people mistook us for each other." At least until Roseanne shaved her head.

"And John."

The big man simply nodded, hands in his pockets.

Flo waved her over.

Sue leaned down to hug her, whispering, "Is he your guy?"

Flo murmured, "I found him at the hospital."

Sue peered into the old woman's face. She wanted more info, but the young man was right there.

Flo beamed up at her attendant. His muscular biceps bulged from a blue polo shirt, sunglasses hiding his eyes. "Eric, dear, would you mind getting me a glass of water?"

The guy stared at Sue before walking toward the refreshment tables.

"He came in to do therapy, and we got to know each other," said Flo. "Turns out his apartment lease was up, so it was perfect."

"He's living with you?" Sue splayed her hand on her breastbone. "What do you know about him?"

"Look at him. What else do you need to know?"

Eric headed toward them.

"Let's talk later," said Sue.

A motorcycle rumbled up, interrupting them.

"The Reverend Marguerite," said Rafael.

He extended his arm, and Sue took it, loving the feeling of closeness. It was an act, of course. The man was gracious in everything he did. Very old-school. She wondered if he'd come from wealth.

Although she walked along with him as if it were any other day, inside, her stomach fluttered.

The reverend cut the motor and climbed off the bike.

Removing her helmet, she shook out curly gray hair. "Hello, my dears. I'm late as usual." The woman spoke with a British accent. She flashed a bright smile, skin deeply creased. Her blue eyes fell on Sue. "My goodness. You are Rosie all over again. I am so very sorry for your loss. May I give you a hug?"

When the reverend's arms encircled Sue, she felt such love, it almost made her sad about her sister. She closed her eyes, letting the woman's kindness wash over her.

Rafael took the minister's sacramental bundle. "Our guests are waiting."

Marguerite unsnapped one of the saddlebags, extracted a funeral vestment, and slipped it over her head, the multicolored silk fabric spilling like a waterfall down to her western boots. On her way to the podium, she greeted those in attendance as old friends.

The reverend took her position at the front of the seating area. A card table held Roseanne's picture, along with a beer glass from Rattler's Bar, a vaping device, a deck of cards, and an eagle feather. Behind it, the mountain dropped off to a sweeping view of the valley. People took their seats. Sue sat next to Rafael, his hip and shoulder touching hers, raising completely inappropriate thoughts in her mind. She shifted a half-inch away.

Whether it was intentional or the way of men everywhere, he shifted closer, taking up the free space.

Sue concentrated on Reverend Marguerite, who stood with her hands clasped for a quiet moment. A jay called from a nearby pine tree, and a breeze tossed the reverend's long hair in her face. She brushed it back.

"Dear ones," the reverend began, "Roseanne Louise Mercer was a handful. When you stepped into her territory, you took your life in your hands. And I'm not speaking metaphorically. Roseanne had a weird sense of humor."

Sue frowned. She wouldn't call it humor, exactly.

"Roseanne was a difficult woman. She hurt her family. She hurt her friends. She lied. She tricked people. She stole one of my motorcycles and sold it to a chop shop.

"Now, I ask you, good people, why would God, in Her infinite wisdom, put someone like Roseanne in your midst?"

Good question, Sue thought.

The reverend caught her eye. "I might suggest it was for our enlightenment. Or, as someone once said, 'If you can't be a good example, then you'll just have to serve as a horrible warning.'"

A skinny woman with thinning, gelled hair laughed out loud.

"Now, given that Roseanne was so difficult and had few friends," said Marguerite, "why are you all here? Anyone? Come on, speak up. We can learn from each other. I'd like to understand what motivated you to attend."

Matt stood. "Our boss told us to."

He sat down to laughter.

"It's the decent thing to do," said Flo.

"Karma?" volunteered a hipster young man with lots of metal on his face and ears.

"All of those are good," said the reverend.

"I am here to pay a psychic debt," said a pale woman in a gauzy white sundress. "Because Roseanne facilitated my spiritual enlightenment."

"How the hell'd she do that?" muttered John. His voice carried in the silence.

The woman, ethereal, simply gazed at him. "Once upon a time, Roseanne took me to the cave. She said it was an undiscovered vortex. It was like a religious experience for me."

Sue groaned inwardly. Great. Now it was out.

"There's a cave?" asked Gabriela.

"Yes, but it's a secret," said the woman.

"Believe that at your own peril," said Rafael, his voice carrying through the crowd, silencing them. He sat forward, fixing them with cold eyes. "Roseanne liked to fool people into wandering around the canyon, searching for a nonexistent cave. She once sent an elderly couple who nearly died of snakebite."

"But I was there," said the pale woman. "We did a spiritual ceremony."

"Probably involving mushrooms," said Flo.

Sue leaned toward Rafael, her lips almost brushing his ear. "Thank you," she whispered.

He leaned back. "You are welcome."

"I wanna say somethin'." A toothless man in a biker vest jerked a thumb at the woman next to him. "Me and the old lady used to ride our hogs to Rosie's bar all the time. She was real nice to us. Gave us free drinks."

"She could be generous," said the reverend.

"She was a dick," the biker's woman said, blinking with disbelief at her partner. "She only did that to see if we could wrap ourselves around a tree afterward. Ever think of that?"

The man scratched his head. "Not 'til now."

"Hey everybody, I'm Vicky." A petite woman with long, curly reddish-silver hair waved from a wheelchair. "Hey, Sue. I knew your sister since she'd always come to my consignment shop to sell things. I always thought she was kind of a jerk." Vicky spoke with a slight drawl, left over from someplace southern. "But then, couple months ago, when my shop was about to go under, she brought in a bunch of stuff to sell. Good stuff too. Jewelry and antiques. And she didn't want anything for them. She flat-out gave them to me. It was weird, but I couldn't say no, cuz I was desperate. Wasn't for that, I would have had to close up for good. So it was kind of a miracle, and I'm still grateful."

"Glad she helped you out." Sue wondered which of her mother's precious heirlooms Roseanne had donated.

"That makes two of us." Vicky grinned.

Clenching her jaw, Sue looked away.

"I would like to say something," Flo said. "Roseanne was a piece of work, I agree. But I always wondered if she had a choice, or was she compelled somehow? What if her brain was off? And there but for the grace of God go any of us."

"Thank you for your compassion," the reverend said. "Sue, would you like to speak?"

Sue considered telling them that the happiest day of her life was when Roseanne ran away for good. That Sue felt betrayed when their mother gave everything to the bad sister, the cruel one. That she couldn't bear the thought of what Roseanne might have done to manipulate, con, or torture their mother into such an act. And that she felt guilty about not being around to protect her.

What could she say to these people? The jay squawked while she considered.

Before she lost her nerve, she stood and approached the table. Her sister's picture showed a younger Roseanne, unsmiling, dark hair hanging. It would have been taken around the time she moved in with their mother. The frame was cheap wood, brittle and dry, as if dug out of a pile at the house.

Some of the mourners smiled with encouragement. They probably wanted to know if she was crazy too.

She looked to Rafael, who gave her a slight nod.

Sue squared her shoulders. "Roseanne and I were estranged for most of our adult lives. I often wondered if she had changed and if I should have reached out. But that's the question that will never be answered. I will have to live with my decisions."

"Honey," said Flo, "don't beat yourself up."

"Yeah, she scared the hell out of people," said the biker guy.

Gabriela held up a hand. "And how come she never contacted you? That phone works both ways."

"Well, anyway, thank you all for showing up to remember my sister." She bit her lip. "My parents would have appreciated it."

In silence, she returned to her seat.

"Let's reflect for a moment, shall we?" said the reverend.

Sue closed her eyes. Funerals made you think about more than the immediate loss. They made you remember you were mortal, and so was everyone you loved. They reminded you that time here was short. This was why she hated funerals.

Her chin quivered. She missed Mike. She missed Travis and Katie. She missed their old life, when the children were small. She missed their little books and stuffed animals. Car seats and homework and making breakfast for them before school. She missed falling asleep next to her husband; the reassurance, the safety of him.

How was it possible all that was gone, as gone as if she had only dreamed it? It was more than just Roseanne. It was the whole rough business of being human, something that seemed more profound now that she was older. She looked up at the sky, blinking back tears.

Rafael's arm encircled her shoulders. She leaned against him, her head on his shoulder. It was so comforting she was almost embarrassed. As if they knew each other well. As if they were friends.

She was old enough to know that life could be hard, and you took kindness as it came.

After a few minutes, Marguerite returned to her post. People shifted, waiting. Sue eased away from Rafael, needing to maintain her distance yet grateful for his warmth. Almost afraid to meet his gaze, she did anyway and was rewarded with a gentle smile.

The reverend clasped her hands. "I say this next thing with love. Rosie could be a menace, but I suggest you forgive her. Not in the sense of letting her off the hook, because she was wrong, and she knew it, and that's her deal, and she'll have to answer for it, if, in fact, there is any kind of answering, which I believe there is, cosmically or otherwise.

"What I mean is forgive in the sense of letting it go. Whether you believe in hell or karma or whatever, there is one real truth you can rely on: she is gone, but you are here. Don't take that for granted. Be mindful. Be grateful. And be good to each other. Because in the end, that is all you have. And that is the greatest of riches. Let us pray."

As the reverend invoked cosmic benevolence, the scent of pine needles, warmed by the summer sun, wafted around them. Sue felt her shoulders relax.

When Marguerite finished her prayer, she tapped the urn. "Okay, Rosie, let's eat."

At the buffet line, Sue loaded her plate with snow crab, mini-quiche, and three different kinds of salad, then found a seat.

Vicky, sitting across from her, shook out a napkin. "I heard about Roseanne leaving me all your mom's jewelry. I'd offer to give it back, but I'm not that nice."

"So you two had something in common," said Sue. Nearby, someone gasped. Sue felt bad that it had slipped out, but too bad if they didn't like it. She was done pleasing the world, and anyway, Roseanne had no right.

Vicky cocked her head, studying Sue. Then she chuckled. "Smart mouth you got there. Which is good. I hate boring people. We can be friends."

"You might want to see her shop," Flo said to Sue. "It's really a gem itself."

Vicky gave a halfhearted smile. "Look, I feel sort of bad about this. I could split some of the profits if you want?"

"Keep it. Roseanne must have had her reasons."

"Maybe she gave it away so you couldn't have it," said Gabriela.

"That would be consistent," said Sue.

"She felt sorry for me being in a wheelchair," said Vicky. "Been like this since I went naked skydiving on my fiftieth birthday."

"Seriously?"

Vicky just laughed.

Marguerite turned to Sue. "I understand Roseanne left you the property. Do you intend to clean it up and move in?"

"That's the plan," said Sue.

Gabriela laughed. "Yeah, the boss will love that."

"I don't understand," said Marguerite. "Why would Rafael have anything to say about it?"

"I guess you haven't heard," said Flo.

Rafael picked that moment to come by with a bottle of wine. "Heard what?" He glanced around. "What did I walk into?"

"Roseanne left it to both of them." Vicky held out her glass. "Rafe wants to sell it, and she wants to keep it."

"Nothing is secret around here," said Sue.

Gabriela nodded. "Sedona's a small town, really."

"The fact is, it's worth a lot," said Flo. "They stand to benefit greatly if they sell it."

Rafael nodded. "That is exactly right."

"Except we're not going to," said Sue.

Flo held up her hand. "On the other hand, it's rich in family history and, according to legend, a deeply spiritual location."

"We're in the property business, not the spiritual business," said Rafael.

"That's quite a dilemma," said Marguerite. "How will you work it out?"

Sue straightened her napkin and looked up, chin set. "He's going to sell me his half."

"Are you rich?" asked Vicky.

"At a discount," said Sue.

Rafael laughed out loud and walked away.

"I get the feeling he disagrees," said the reverend.

"We've agreed to bury the hatchet for a month while we clean up the property," said Sue. "At the end of the month, we'll come to a mutually agreeable solution."

"Any ideas?"

"Not a one." Sue rubbed her temples. "I honestly don't know what I'm going to do."

"I hope it works out for you," said Gabriela. "And for my boss. Otherwise, he'll be a beast to work with."

Sue tossed back the rest of her wine, set down her glass, and looked around at them. "The way I see it, it's him or me," she said. "And this time, it's going to be me."

"Atta girl," said Vicky.

"Yay," whispered Gabriela.

"I'll pray for you both," said Marguerite.

Sue finished her lunch and stood to leave. She hugged and thanked people on the way out. Although she hadn't had a horrible time, the weight of the afternoon dragged on her. She needed solitude and time to process her thoughts. To shrug off the nice clothes and complicated feelings.

"Are you leaving?" Rafael caught up with her. "Please wait."

She stood by John in uncomfortable silence while Rafael strode to the mementos table and retrieved the bronze cube holding Roseanne's ashes.

Sue backed away. "I don't want it."

"You should have it," said Rafael. "Who better than the last member of her family still alive?"

"But you were her family too. That's what you said."

He shook his head.

Reluctantly, she accepted the urn. He was right. It was hers now. Her burden and her responsibility, although for a moment, she fantasized about flinging it over the wall down the side of the mountain.

Rafael smiled, as if reading her thoughts.

She warmed at his glance. It was kind of him to handle the service for the benefit of the community, but she wondered, after hearing the speakers' sentiments, why exactly they had bothered. And now everybody knew about her mission over the coming month.

She tucked the bronze box under her arm and walked to her car.

* * * * *

RAFAEL WATCHED HER GO, her slender body wrapped by the gold sundress, her hair lit by the afternoon sun.

John's voice rumbled beside him. "Can't believe how much she looks like her sister. Hell of a lot prettier, though."

"She is stunning."

"If I had to work with that, it'd be hard to keep my hands to myself."

Laughter carried from the patio.

"There is too much riding on this," said Rafael. "I will treat her like a work colleague, nothing more."

"Right." Skepticism colored John's response.

"You think I am joking, but I have no interest in mixing business with pleasure. Besides, Susan is too strong-willed. She would not be good for me."

"Oh, she'd be plenty good for you. Way she walks."

"Exactly what Roseanne had in mind, I'm sure."

John's lip turned up in the hint of a smile. "She was Roseanne to the last."

Chapter Fifteen

Sue set the urn on the kitchen counter and eased out of her heels. The funeral had made her melancholy, despite her intentions not to feel anything. Although it was the middle of the afternoon, the kitchen lay in shadows, amplifying her gloom.

While the home was rich in history and sentimentality, it was a humble place, one cobbled together by the earnest efforts of her ancestors. No wonder Rafael wanted to raze it. By comparison, he lived in a palace, something fit for the cover of *Architectural Digest*.

Not what she was used to. Sue and Mike had always lived in base housing, moving every few years and making the best of each assignment. Visalia was the first brand-new house she'd owned. During the first weeks of living there, she couldn't believe how every surface sparkled, how white the baseboards were, and how smoothly the kitchen drawers slid shut on their own. There were no dings on the walls, and the sinks and toilets gleamed. The front and backyards stood waiting like blank canvases for Sue and Mike to fill in with color and texture according to their desires. Even if it was cookie-cutter, it was theirs. No more renting, no more moving. And then Mike got sick and died before they'd had a chance to enjoy it.

Her lower-class roots stuck out now more than ever. Oh, sure, she'd acquired polish. Back in the day, she'd grown comfortable visiting with the base commander's wife and her circle, no problem. But this situation was different. With his wealth, his home, and his elegant manners, Rafael was like old Spanish royalty. Probably never knew a hungry day in his life. And now he expected her to hand him the Mesa on a silver platter.

He had no idea how rich the history was.

The original family had lived in a tent while her grandfather built the house on a rock foundation, with a kiva fireplace and log walls. They eked out a living, ranching and farming while battling weather, illness, varmints, and outlaws. Now it was the twenty-first century, Sue was back, and she'd be damned if she'd let somebody run her off.

And this dark kitchen was about to get a makeover.

"Come on, girl. We can't sit around moping." Sue rattled her keys, and Gypsy scrambled to her feet.

At the hardware store, she bought pruning shears, twine, gloves, and safety goggles. The oleanders were going down.

Back at the house, she hacked and chopped with a vengeance. When she finished, six bundles of branches lay tied and stacked on the ground. The windows were filthy, so she hosed them off, not wanting to get close to the cut branches oozing poisonous white sap. One day, she'd arrange to have them removed completely, but for now, it would do.

With the bushes cut low, the kitchen glowed in the afternoon sun. The room felt cleaner and larger. Sue's spirits lifted. She had made a stand, however small. The work had begun. The Mesa house was steps closer to becoming her own.

As she rolled up a rug to haul outside, her phone rang. Sue plopped down on a box in the living room. "Hey, honey!"

"So, have you sold it yet?" Her daughter's voice was flat.

"Um. Well, I'm trying not to." Sue bit her lip. Until now, she hadn't shared her plans with Katie or Travis, fearing they'd resist.

"Seriously, Mom? I mean, I looked at it online, and it should be worth a fortune. We'd be rich."

"Actually, I'm more interested in the memories. So I'm going to fix it up and live here."

There was a long pause. Then Katie spoke, tone accusatory. "You said you'd move closer to us."

"I want that, too, but the house—"

"Sophia and Ethan are so big already. I'm afraid you're going to miss their growing up."

Me too, Sue thought, but Katie's family was a challenge. Every time she babysat, she had to shop for groceries, do laundry, and clean. It was as if Katie and Jason were two college roommates, but with kids. And they fought constantly.

"So, what do you think?"

"Honey, I don't know."

"Come on, Mom. You're retired. Don't you want to spend your golden years watching your grands grow up?"

"But I'm in Arizona, and I'm fighting with this developer—"

"Wait. You've got a guy who wants to buy it? How can you not be interested?"

"The money's not the point."

Katie sighed.

Sue's mom-radar pinged. "Honey, what's going on? Talk to me."

"I don't know. I just hate my life. Every day, it's all on me. I have to make breakfast and lunches and get the kids to school and myself to work, and I have to do all the cleaning and shopping and cooking, and I am just so damn sick of it."

Sue didn't want to interfere, but she wanted to help. While she fought her inclinations, the silence stretched between them. Finally, she broke. "Can the kids do more? Or what about Jason?"

"He's a man, okay?"

"Men aren't necessarily—"

"Come on, Mom. Look how Dad was."

"Watch yourself." Sue bristled, but Katie wasn't wrong.

Mike had been old-fashioned military. Expected the house shipshape and the kids and wife to be respectful and obedient. For the most part, Sue went along with it because she loved him and because he was decent and good.

"My dryer just went off, and somebody's at the door," Katie said.

"Honey, call me—"

"I have to go. Bye."

"I love you," Sue said, but Katie had hung up.

"Great." Sue exhaled in frustration. Now the house was causing problems with her family. Glancing across the room, she spotted the bronze cube holding Roseanne's ashes. Wherever she was, she was probably having a good laugh at Sue's expense.

"I'm tempted to dump you in the canyon, Roseanne." Sue clambered to her feet with a groan, her muscles already aching from the oleanders. "You and the rattlesnakes can keep each other company."

Chapter Sixteen

She'd barely taken her first sip of coffee when the ground began to rumble. After living in California, her first impulse was to dive under the kitchen table, but the sound was coming from the driveway, accompanied by warning beeps from someone backing up.

Outside, Rafael was gesturing with one hand, guiding a truck carrying an industrial-sized dumpster. When he closed his fist, the truck's brake lights flared and died. A man jumped out of the cab, pulling on gloves. He headed for the rear of the flatbed and grasped the gear handles, tilting the truck bed and rolling the dumpster off into the dirt with a heavy thump.

Rafael accepted a clipboard and pen from the driver, signed for delivery, and shook the guy's hand. The man climbed back in the truck and drove away.

"Good morning." Sue shaded her eyes against the rising sun. "You're early."

"We are eager to get started." His eyes hid behind his sunglasses, but his smile was blinding. "First day of work."

She couldn't help but smile back. His enthusiasm was catching. Regardless of motive, both were anxious to clear the property of Roseanne's filth.

Another vehicle arrived, a dump truck towing a piece of construction equipment.

Sue tensed. "You brought a bulldozer to clean up my property?"

"It is properly called a front-end loader. But, yes," said Rafael. "For a big job, you need big tools."

"But there might be something valuable in there, underneath all the scrap."

"We will keep a sharp eye out. I will tell the men now." He walked over to the truck, where John and Matt worked together to release the tie-downs from the dozer's treads.

An auto wrecker arrived, and the men stopped what they were doing to clear a path to a tire-flattened station wagon. Hefting old tires and pipe lengths, plywood pieces, and broken furniture, they soon opened up access to the vehicle. The operator dragged the rusted hulk onto the tilted-steel flatbed, secured the load, and drove away.

Rafael returned to Sue's perch near the porch. "I arranged to have them also take those other three." He gestured at the rusting carcasses in the front yard.

She frowned, glad to have the help but piqued by his take-charge air, as if he already owned the property.

Well, perhaps he did, but she didn't have to like it.

While John went back to the front-end loader, Matt came over to say hello. "This property's gonna be a showpiece," he said.

"And today, you guys get to play."

Matt grinned. "That's what it's all about."

A sharp whistle pierced the air. John stood glowering at them, his muscular arms hanging ape-like from massive shoulders.

"Is he mad about something?" asked Sue.

"Naw, that's his happy face." Matt trotted away.

With a great rumble and growl, the front-end loader roared to life. John shifted gears and backed it off the trailer, its treads clanking and jangling. Rafael and Matt positioned themselves near the bucket, monitoring the flow of materials gobbled into the big scoop. When it was full, Rafael gave a thumbs-up, and John backed around, rolled forward, and released the load with a great clamor into the dump truck, which rocked on its chassis at the impact.

Over and over again, they repeated the routine. John worked the controls, expertly scooping up an air conditioner, a water heater, a pile of bricks. He collected cement rubble, old appliances, and auto parts, dumped them into the truck, and returned. Shifting gears, he shoved the bucket forward to collect a load of old fencing. He went back and forth, moving on to a stack of weathered lumber.

After watching for a while, Sue concluded there was nothing left of the old days. Whatever might have held sentimental value was gone forever, buried under garbage as far as the eye could see.

She went inside, fed Gypsy, and left a text for her son to check-in. It was the third message in as many days, but

Travis, like most young men, wasn't very good at getting back to his mother. He worked long hours for a lobbying firm in Washington, DC, where he kept an apartment. He never spoke of dating or a personal life. She knew better than to pressure him—what good would it do?—but hoped for the day he'd announce he'd found the woman of his dreams and would be settling down.

A loud crunch jarred her out of her thoughts. John was starting on a new pile, this one of concrete remnants. She shook her head in disbelief. Amazing that Roseanne would have allowed the property to be used in such a way, corrupting the precious homestead for a few bucks taken in payment for allowing garbage to be dumped on the land.

What a complete mess. What a crime against her family, who had started out life here with such high hopes. How hard they'd worked, only for it to come to this. Sadness and anger twisted her gut.

She couldn't watch anymore. Turning away from the kitchen window, she decided to attack the family room/den, the large room where the ranch hands used to share meals with the family, where Sue and her parents would read or watch television, where her mother would do her mending in the evening in the light of a long-ago floor lamp.

Heaving a sigh, she began collecting books, clothing, and small appliances into piles. Once the room was clear, she could use it as a staging area to empty the rest of the house. The rear patio would be the last stop for the junk before it left the property.

She went back and forth, carrying loads in and out, occasionally pausing to exclaim over a few sentimental memorabilia and decide whether she really wanted to keep it. Some of it was precious—her Little Golden Book about puppies—but some of it, like her father's torn and stained tennis shoes, required the heartbreaking act of placing them in a trash can. Over and over again, she was forced to make such decisions, and within a couple of hours, she was an emotional wreck.

Pausing to catch her breath and gather herself, she looked out the kitchen window to see how the men were progressing. Rafael had climbed on the hood of an old car and was directing John with hand signals.

She filled a glass of water and drank. The men were easy to look at. Rafael especially. He jumped down from the car, lithe as a jungle cat, walking around the place like a fighter heading for the ring. The guy looked hot, and not just from working demolition in the Arizona sun.

Back in Visalia, after she emerged from the fog of grief, Sue dated a little, but she always went home alone. Men flirted, but they seemed so transactional, looking for a no-strings sex partner or a nurse with a purse.

She wasn't interested. Mike was the best. No one else could compare.

She leaned against the sink and watched Rafael give orders, his motions certain and authoritative. She wondered how it would be if they weren't standing on opposite sides of the land. If she moved to Sedona and were free to date him, even if it were just for pure, meaningless sex—

She set down her glass and squinted at the rubble.

A figure was emerging from the scraped earth. It looked familiar, with that benevolent face and faded blue veil. With a little yelp, she galloped out the back door.

"Stop!" she yelled. Rushing to the front-end loader, she fell to her knees in front of the bucket just as the bladed edge scraped close. Swearing, John stomped on the brake. The machine juddered to a stop. He grasped the top of the steering wheel with both hands and lowered his head. Rafael and Matt jogged over to see what was going on.

With her bare hands, Sue dug through the debris, flinging bits of cement, wood, and cardboard aside as she unearthed her prize, a chipped and faded statue of the Virgin of Guadalupe. "You almost ran her over."

"Crazy girl. I almost ran *you* over." John patted his shirt pocket for his smokes.

Rafael took Sue's hand, pulling her up, her knees covered with dirt.

"I can't believe we found her. I loved this statue." Sue stood the figurine upright and brushed the dirt from Mary's face. "Every spring, Mom and I would make a flower crown for her. We called her Queen of the May."

"I will put it in the backyard." Rafael hoisted the statue onto his shoulder. "Come with me."

The front-end loader rumbled back to life. Cigarette smoke and diesel wafted past her nostrils in the hot sun. Following Rafael around the side of the house, Sue realized she was trembling. She hadn't thought of the danger. Her impulse was only to save the statue, so meaningful to her childhood.

With a gentle thud, Rafael set it under a pine tree. "You could have been hurt."

"Another ten seconds and she would have been destroyed."

"Your hand is bleeding."

She'd cut her thumb, and her knees were scraped and crusty with dirt and gravel. What else had been destroyed under Roseanne's watch? The loss was countless. Ageless.

Rafael stuck his sunglasses in his shirt pocket and secured the statue, moving it back and forth on its base until it was level.

"Thank you," said Sue. Her voice cracked. She turned away, embarrassed.

He grasped her shoulders gently. "Your statue is fine. Why don't you go inside and tend to those cuts?"

For a moment, their eyes met and locked. She studied his face, his strong jaw, his deep-set eyes. Sue wanted to collapse against his broad chest and let him hold her.

Seeming to read her thoughts, he gave her shoulders a squeeze. "Are you all right?"

Swallowing, wordless, she nodded. She could feel the heat radiating from his shirt front, the weight of his grip on her shoulders. She needed to move. If she stayed there one more second, her weakness would be revealed, and she needed all her strength to deal with this man, her adversary.

"Fine," she croaked, stepping back, slipping from his grasp. Wobbly and flustered, she turned her back on him and went into the house.

Stumbling past Roseanne's ashes, Sue was tempted to kick the urn. What sacrilege. Her sister had let that poor statue die out in the yard with no more concern than if it were an old tin can. And not just the statue. The land, the house, her family's memory.

Thank God John had stopped. And Rafael. The look in his eyes had held such compassion. And something else she didn't want to think about right then.

For the rest of the day, she avoided the front yard and him. Without once looking out the window, she labored on the inside, he on the outside. At noon, the equipment fell silent while the men broke for lunch, then again at three when work ceased for the day.

Rafael knocked at the back door. "We are almost finished with the heavy loads," he said. "The salvage yard will return tomorrow and collect the remaining materials."

"I underestimated the amount of work it would be," she said. "You were right to bring your big equipment."

Humor glinted in his eyes. "Any time."

She walked with him to the front of the house. "I can't wait to start landscaping. It'll be so good to see plants and flowers again."

"That is questionable. The ground in some places is saturated with oil. We may have to scrape and backfill most of the lot before it can be sold."

"What a horrible thought."

"One we need not address today." He reached over and removed a clump of fuzz from her hair.

She looked away.

"Susan."

"What?" She focused on a point in the distance.

"We did good work today, and your statue is safe. Don't think too much of the future. Today you can feel satisfied."

Sue took a deep breath, surprised to feel as if she'd been holding it in. Although today had been wrenching, he was right. In the weeks ahead, she would work toward her goal, and he toward his, both of them absolutely determined.

But perhaps they could work together amicably. He had shown himself to be a nice man and a gentleman. It might be possible to enjoy the next few weeks. Maybe they could even be friends.

After he and his crew left, the house fell silent. Restless, Sue wandered from room to room, trying to get interested in the next project, but she was tired. Depleted.

She leaned against the doorjamb of the empty bedroom. Now cleared of all the yarn and crafts Roseanne had inexplicably collected, it stood clean and open, ready for a new purpose.

The idea hit her like a lightning bolt.

Grabbing her keys and Gypsy's leash, Sue locked up the house and headed for town.

Chapter Seventeen

Parking in front of an art supply store, Sue cut the motor. On the drive here, she hadn't allowed herself to think, to question her motives. But now she was here.

If she went inside and bought canvases and paints, it would mean she was serious about resurrecting her hobby. Pursuing a dream when the future held no guarantees. She might get started, only to be kicked off the land and forced to leave, heartbroken and disillusioned. Besides, she had enough already.

But she could look.

Carrying Gypsy, Sue pushed open the door. Her nostrils filled with the rich, memorable aroma of oils, paints, and supplies. The aisles went forever, the shelves packed with brushes, canvases, and tools. Wandering up one row and down the other, she tried to gather her ideas, to remember her goals, but there was so much. It was daunting. Where would she start? What did a person use these days? The bright arrays were overwhelming. Clutching Gypsy, she spun in a slow circle. Color, form, light—she felt as if she knew nothing. She didn't recognize anything. It had been too long. Discouraged, she turned toward the door.

"Do you need rescuing?" At the end of the aisle stood a young Black woman, her dark hair a nimbus of curls around a heart-shaped face.

"I don't know." Sue bit her lip. "I used to paint. I thought I might want to try again. It used to be so much fun. And I'm here. You know, Sedona."

"Right. You almost have to."

"But I don't know." Sue looked wistfully at all the shelves filled with potential. "I was pretty good a long time ago."

"I hear you. You'd be surprised how many women..." The girl shook her head. "Anyway, I'm Marissa. Can I make some suggestions?"

"If it's not too expensive."

"What medium?"

"Not sure anymore." A small gallery stood at the rear of the store. Sue paused in front of an oddly primitive painting of a javelina. "That's interesting."

"A local man. Just recovering from a stroke. We're trying to encourage him."

Marissa placed brushes, cleaner, and a palette into the cart. They wandered through the store, discussing canvases and easels and the local art scene. "This store's gorgeous. Is it yours?"

"My mother's. She bought it; I run it. I live in the apartment over the store."

"Easy commute."

"There's another person who works here, Franny, but she couldn't come in today." She stepped behind the counter. "I can give you a list of places to paint."

"I have a pretty nice view from my house." When Sue explained, Marissa gaped.

"Get out! I would kill to paint there."

"Why haven't you?"

Marissa laughed. "I don't actually want to die."

"I'm working on that. My late sister owned it. It's in terrible shape, but I'm going to make it beautiful again."

"Everyone in town will be happy to hear that."

"You should come by sometime to paint. Here's my number." Sue scribbled on a piece of scrap.

"Welcome to Sedona," said Marissa.

Driving home, Sue could hardly keep herself from speeding. She was so eager to try painting again. And she felt as if she'd gained a new friend.

Sue arranged her art supplies in Roseanne's old room and got to work. Humming a little tune, she applied paint to brush and tentatively dabbed it on the canvas. In her mind, she saw red rock mountains against a backdrop of storm clouds.

As the time passed, though, the picture was going in another direction. As it took shape, Sue stepped back and frowned.

Her storm-surrounded mountains looked like camels lying in an oil spill. She tried a little more of this, a little less of that. But it was no good.

After repeated failures, Sue gave up and texted Marissa. *I need a landscape class. Anything coming up soon?*

Marissa answered right away. *Can I see what you did?*
Sue took a picture. *911, right?*
Marissa: *How about 8 am tomorrow at your place?*
Sue: *It's still a dump.*
Marissa: *I have pepper spray.*

* * * * *

AT DAYBREAK THE NEXT MORNING, Sue had been up for an hour, drinking coffee and doing calculations on a tablet, trying to figure out how she could afford to buy Rafael's half. Headlights flashed across the kitchen windows just as the sky began to lighten. Sue gathered up her supplies and hurried outside.

"That was rough," said Marissa, climbing out of her sedan.

"I know. It's way overdue for a load of gravel."

"Or ten."

The other door opened, and a birdlike woman with a gray ponytail climbed out.

"This is Franny," said Marissa. "I mentioned her yesterday. She works with me at the store."

"Good to meet you." Franny's blue eyes crinkled briefly as she and Sue shook hands. Franny's hands were tiny, strong, and warm.

Sue picked up her gear. "Watch your step."

The women hiked past the bunkhouse and set their easels at the slope's edge. With the sunrise casting dramatic shadows, the view provided a rich subject for their canvas. Sue extended the legs on her easel and set it up next to Marissa. She had brought out a small table on which she laid out her palette, paints, and brushes.

Sue had painted before but never stuck to it long enough to become proficient. Today her dreams would become real under the guidance of her new teacher.

They fell silent as each concentrated on her work. From time to time, Marissa offered pointers.

Before too long, Franny's phone rang. She stepped away to speak privately.

"That's probably her husband," said Marissa. "He gets worried when she's gone."

"She barely got here."

"He's a very anxious person. Keeps her on a short leash."

Franny returned and picked up her brush. "I handled it," she said. "I called his buddy to go over and have coffee with him."

They painted in companionable silence for the better part of an hour until Sue gave up, deciding her work was hideous.

"You're trying too hard," said Franny.

"Let your emotions flow," Marissa said. "Come on, let loose. Don't worry about what it looks like."

Sue grimaced. "Maybe I should find another hobby."

"Is that what this is?"

"I don't know."

At the sound of a rumble, the women looked toward the house. Two vehicles arrived. The delivery truck from the mattress store. And Rafael.

He gestured at the delivery truck. "What is this?"

"We're going to head out," said Marissa, gathering her supplies.

She and Franny drove off.

On the way home yesterday, Sue stopped at a sleep store to buy a new bed. "Did you think I would sleep in the recliner forever?"

"I didn't think it would take forever." He frowned at her.

"Well, I couldn't bear one more night. Don't worry about it, Rafe."

"I asked you not to call me that."

"Sorry." Sue brushed past him to greet the workers and show them the path to the craft room. She returned to find Rafael in the kitchen, helping himself to coffee.

"Do you want one?" he asked.

"Please."

They sat wordlessly at the kitchen table, the clang of wrenches against metal carrying down the hall. When they finished, she signed the delivery order and closed the door. She couldn't wait to make up the new trundle.

Rafael stood and rinsed out his cup. "You seem to be moving in with determination."

"Only bowing to necessity."

"And what is next? A kitchen remodel to keep you happy during negotiations?" He pulled out a chair, scrubbed at his face, and sighed. "What is your plan for the day?"

"I have a list." Slipping on her reading glasses, she referred to her yellow tablet. Over the past few days, she'd made a rough inventory of the entire property, identifying every aspect needing to be cleaned, repaired, or removed.

"Let me see." Palm out, he wiggled his fingers.

Sue handed it over, slightly embarrassed. The list was exhaustive.

He ran his finger down the page. "You intend to save the ramada?"

"I do."

"And the bunkhouse?"

She nodded. "And most of the outbuildings."

"To what purpose?" He shook his head and continued reading. "This is extensive. You're very organized."

She shrugged. "It's something I like to do."

"I can see that," he said. "You went to a lot of work. And your penmanship is excellent."

She grabbed the list back.

"But Susan."

"Yes?"

"That list is long, and it will grow as you think of more things. Have you considered the time, labor, and expense?"

"I'm aware."

"Are you equally aware that, instead of all that effort, you could simply sell it and pocket a large amount of money?"

"I don't want to talk about that."

"But do you ever allow yourself to consider it?"

Her eyes narrowed. "No, I do not."

"I know what it means to you," he said. "You have lived in many homes where you made a sanctuary for your husband and children, no?"

He was right. Her homes had been sanctuaries for her family. She hadn't thought of it that way before.

"Yes."

"And even though each posting was relatively brief, you were able to find happiness anywhere."

"This isn't like that, Rafael."

"I know. Your roots are here. Years and years of memories. Not all good. Many painful."

She stood up. "I thought we could start with the living room. Make a path to the front door so we can get it open and start using it."

Rafael stared at her. Sighing, he rose. "We should separate things into trash or salvage and pile them on the patio," he said. "For instance, this table. Do you want it?"

"No, it's not important." She gestured toward the back door. "I already started a donation pile."

Rafael picked up the table. "Show me where."

They developed a routine. She identified items to get rid of and things to save, and he carried the heavier items outside.

Mementos were everywhere. She couldn't help sharing them with him. For the dozenth time, she called out, "Rafael, look!"

Resigned, he set down a washtub filled with shoes.

"I can't believe it." She held up a red-and-white box. "This is the record player I got when I was in kindergarten!"

He eyed it skeptically. "Do you wish to keep it?"

"I might. And look at these doilies. Mom embroidered them. See how intricate they are? Those I am absolutely keeping," she said. "I'm kind of undecided on these two chairs, though. What do you think?"

He glanced out the window in the direction of the dumpster.

"Don't even think of it," she said. "My father made those. By hand."

"I might work outside for a while."

"Wait, look at this." Sue held up a baby blanket. "I crocheted it for my hope chest."

Rafael bolted out the back door.

All morning, she ran across sentimental items, stacking them in a corner of the den and hauling everything else to the back patio. In turn, Rafael transported the discards to the dumpster and the donations to the back of his pickup truck.

By noon, the dumpster and the truck bed were both filled. Rafael stood on the front porch, glugging water from a jug.

"Are you sure I can't make you a sandwich?" Sue asked. She was sweaty and covered with dust, but the den was nearly empty, and she was delighted.

He shook his head. "I have to go. Later, John will come by to take away the furniture."

"That'll free up a lot of space."

"Also, we need to get the front door open."

Sue nodded, thinking of making room for her Visalia furniture.

Rafael capped the jug. "I cannot help you tomorrow. I have an appointment in Scottsdale, but I'll be back the day after. But Susan."

"Yes?"

"The furniture is supposed to go out of the house, not come in. So, no more beds, agree?"

"Have a productive day in Scottsdale," she said.

After Rafael left, the house fell silent. It was almost too quiet. Thank goodness for Gypsy.

Sue went down the hall to her parents' room.

She hesitated, her hand on the door.

Then, steeling herself, she started on the closet. Taking down her mother's clothing, Sue's heart threatened to shatter again and again. Every blouse, every housedress conjured a memory. Worse were the photo albums, box after box. She and Roseanne posing on their new Stingray bicycles. Sue's first pony. A pet duck. Class pictures from kindergarten all the way through her college graduation. Sue and Mike on their wedding day, and then the children, from gurgling babies through surly teenager-hood. Photos of their postings, from Japan to Germany, to nearly every state in the union.

Her mother had saved them all, a chronicle of her good daughter's life.

Hours later, Sue was wrecked. She took Gypsy for a walk to the edge of the property, trying to clear her head. The work seemed insurmountable, not just the piles of work on the outside but the mountains of memories inside the home. Sue had a headache, and her eyes were red from tears. The worst part was that she had to do it alone. She was the last one for whom those photos meant anything.

Though she could call Katie.

No, Katie was still mad.

Travis hadn't messaged her back. Probably in some jungle somewhere. She shivered, remembering the times Mike went off on some kind of mission. Something he couldn't talk about.

Sue had friends from around the country, from her many postings, women she missed and phoned and stayed in touch with on social media and email, but this was different. This was that deep need for family that only a parent or sibling could satisfy.

What was she going to do with all those photos? Who would look at them after she was gone? Travis and Katie wouldn't care. Yet she couldn't just throw them in the trash. Digitizing them would reduce their size, but it would take weeks of work, and for what? Would Sue really ever look at them again, beyond the first few dozen? Would anyone?

It was all so overwhelming.

Maybe Rafael was right. She should take the money and let the past remain in the past. Savor her memories of the good times and leave all this behind her.

But regardless of the future, she needed to resolve the past, so she returned to the task. As the sun moved across the sky and the shadows lengthened, she moved a lamp from her bedroom to her parents' room and kept working. With wine and music, Sue dove back in, sifting through hundreds more photos. Hours passed as she sipped, laughed, and cried.

At midnight, she closed the door, sick with loss. How many lifetimes they'd all lived. Roseanne, with her cruelty and manipulation, their father dying young, their mother as a capable young mother and housewife who then deteriorated when Roseanne came to town, Sue and Mike crisscrossing the country, never letting the kids anywhere near the Mesa. Sue's mother dying, and Sue not hearing about it until three weeks later.

There had been no funeral.

And now her children were in their late thirties, adults in full, Travis somewhere working for the government, Katie battling to save her marriage.

Sue snuggled into her new bed, wondering if a person ever just got tired of dealing with it all.

Chapter Eighteen

Sue pushed open the door of the little shop and stepped up to the counter. The store was deserted.

This morning, she'd awakened filled with determination to reclaim her legacy. Somehow, she would raise the money to buy Rafael out. Starting with the ring.

The beaded curtain parted, and Vicky rolled her chair to the counter. "Hey, it's you. Didn't think you'd come. Nice little dog."

"She isn't, really."

"Something I can help you with?"

Sue slipped off her wedding ring. The three large diamonds flashed at her. "How much can I get for this?"

Vicky frowned at the ring and then at Sue. "You sure you want to sell it?"

"How much?"

"Let me get my loupe." Behind the counter, a raised platform ran from one side of the store to the other. It was wide enough for the wheelchair to turn around at any point and high enough that Vicky sat at eye level with her customers.

While Vicky examined the ring, Sue examined the store. It reminded her of the gift boutique in Big Sur, next to Nepenthe. That shop offered high-end hippie clothing, expensive wind chimes and sculptures, and odd, precious jewelry.

But it would serve as a mere backdrop for this place. Stained glass windows portrayed a peacock, a hummingbird, and a tropical parrot. Custom shelves held elegant watches, bracelets, and necklaces on velvet backdrops. Loose gemstones lay sprinkled throughout the locked cases, reflecting the light and drawing the eye.

Vicky removed the ring from the cleaning solution, rinsed it, and dried it. She turned it over and over, looking at it under the magnifier, not speaking. She was very thorough.

Sue waited, hoping for a high number. If she were going to buy Rafael's half of the Mesa, she would need to cobble together every asset she owned and then try to get a loan for the remainder. It would be a long journey to that number. The ring was only the first step.

Vicky glanced at Sue, green eyes narrowed. Then she turned and glared at the window. A couple walking past stopped to argue.

"Well? How much?" asked Sue.

Vicky placed the ring back on the velvet. "You don't want to sell it."

"But I do."

"But you shouldn't. It's too precious. You'll hate yourself afterward."

"What is this, the Dear Abby Advice and Pawn Shop?"

"I'm doing you a favor. That's a one-of-a-kind piece, and it's old, isn't it?"

"Yes, which is why it should be worth a lot."

The two women stared at the ring, as if waiting for it to speak.

Vicky sighed. "If you're sure about this, here's what I think you can get for it. Within range, anyway." She scribbled a number, her fingers sparkling with a half dozen rings.

It wasn't as much as Sue had hoped, but it was a start. "Okay, it's yours."

"But I'm not taking your ring." Vicky pushed the velvet cloth toward Sue. "I couldn't live with myself. Anyway, it won't make a dent. You'd be better off sleeping with Rafael."

Sue exhaled in frustration. "What would that get me? He'd still want to sell."

"Yep. He can be a blockhead." Vicky rolled up the black velvet square. "He's fun to fight with, though, isn't he?"

Sue pretended to study the items in the jewel case.

"Thought so," said Vicky. "Every woman in town feels that way. You're not immune. That's a good sign."

"Is it?"

"Yep." Vicky smiled at her, and this time, it seemed genuine. "Means you're still alive."

"I already knew that." Sue stopped on her way out the door. "What's this about?" She pointed at a poster in the window.

"It's a charity event for local art students," Vicky said. "Can I sell you a ticket? Everybody goes. You could meet people." She reached under the counter and pulled out a cashbox. "Hundred bucks apiece."

"Holy crap." Sue blanched at the price, but she needed to do some serious networking. Get to know the people in town. Folks who might want to come to the Mesa to attend classes and workshops or reserve space for a small event. A catered luncheon or a special retreat. If she truly believed in her dream, she needed to invest, even if it was painful. She opened her purse and pulled out her wallet. "I'll take two."

"Got somebody in mind for that second ticket?" Vicky waggled her eyebrows.

"Not yet." Sue gathered up Gypsy and headed for the car. As she pulled open the door, Vicky's voice stopped her.

"Lot of rich people going to be there. Like filthy rich."

Sue turned around. "So?"

"So, maybe you might be able to get one to buy out his half. Rafael's. Like a charitable donation, you know? I mean, if you wanted to donate it."

"Donate it to who?"

"The city? I have no idea, but if it was my property I was trying to save, I'd figure it out."

Driving home, Sue considered Vicky's suggestion and felt ill. Sure, she'd thought about offering tours of the place to the local historical society, the community college, or whatever civic organizations wanted to see it. But to donate the entire homestead site? It was too much to imagine. And if she did that, would she simply give up her dreams and move back to Visalia?

But if the alternative was a forced sale, wouldn't this be the lesser evil?

Rafael would never go for the idea. He'd jack up the price to make it impractical.

But it would be easy money to pocket a couple million dollars and walk away.

Would he? If she could find a donor?

She was still deep in thought when she pulled into her driveway and realized the satellite installer guy was there early. And not only him.

Rafael.

She tapped on the installer's window, got him started on the work, and went looking for Rafael. She found him at the bunkhouse. "I thought you were in Scottsdale."

Rafael's brows were knitted, his forehead furrowed. "You are installing satellite service?"

"I think I deserve to be comfortable," she said.

Arms crossed, he gestured with his chin at the house. "In a few weeks, this property goes on the market, regardless of your nesting activities."

"So you keep telling me. Why are you here?"

He walked away from her, running his hand through his hair. He turned and scowled. "I intended to invite you to a picnic."

"A picnic?" Sue pointed at herself, then him. "You and me?"

"Tomorrow is Sunday. A day of rest. We should not work."

"An actual recreational activity?"

"A person can't work one hundred percent of the time, and Sedona is beautiful now. First a hike, then a picnic."

"It's hot, though."

"You, the native of Arizona, should have no trouble with the heat."

She glanced up at the sky, which was heavy with dark clouds and the smell of rain. "We'll have to go early. We won't want to be outside if it starts raining."

"Rain would be very nice." Thunder rumbled in the distance. "But I agree. We will leave early."

She wanted to say yes. The crowds were dissipating with the onset of the August monsoons, and a picnic and hike could be very beautiful as long as they kept a weather eye out. "What should I bring?"

"I will be in charge of everything. Six a.m. tomorrow. Adios." He walked away, shoulders back, head high.

What the heck was Rafael planning? They were enemies, but they were drawn to each other. She didn't know if he intended to seduce her or push her over a cliff.

When the satellite installer finished, he gave her the paperwork, showed her where to hook everything up, handed her the remote, and left.

Sue turned on the new satellite service and found a music station. Then she flopped into the recliner.

Rafael said he was only interested in settling their property interest, but they were both trying to play each other. And now a picnic.

Was it recreation or manipulation?

Sue would have to keep her guard up.

Chapter Nineteen

After a great night's sleep on her new mattress, Sue felt energized and ready to hike. Telling the dog to be good, she locked the back door. Rafael was leaning against his truck, waiting for her. He wore khaki shorts and an olive-colored tee. He looked as capable of striding through the wilderness as managing a land development company.

His strong brown arms reached for her backpack. "I am happy to see you remembered a hat."

"I know what to expect. Where are we going?"

"Little Horse."

"Wonderful. I haven't been there in years." Sue remembered the trail as an easy hike through dry arroyos and up through the red rocks to beautiful views of the Cathedral and Bell Rocks.

He drove through town and headed south. She inhaled the fragrance of his aftershave, something light and promising. Sitting in the truck with Rafael threatened to upset her equilibrium, but she had a plan. She would enjoy the outdoors while getting to know him better, like any good negotiator. While they drove, she imagined him agreeing to relinquish the property because it was the right thing to do. In her daydream, he said yes, and they continued on as friends.

Platonic friends.

She looked out the window, smiling at the indulgence. Today she hoped to revisit the beauty of long-forgotten places and perhaps find another location to set up her easel.

At the trailhead, Rafael clapped on a wide-brimmed canvas hat, shouldered her pack, and set off. The morning air was fresh and cool. Sue took a deep lungful and exhaled, relaxing into her stride, grateful to be fit and healthy. Rafael set an energetic pace, the entire time unspooling a travelogue of the hike's high points.

When they stopped to rest, she said, "You sure know a lot about the area."

"I have it memorized for my clients."

"You take them on hikes?"

"I do what they need." He shrugged, repositioning her pack. "Ready?"

Sue fell in beside him. "It's good to be back. I love the sense of spirituality here, with the rocks and the clouds and the view."

He didn't answer.

"You don't feel it?"

"Spirituality from the rocks? No."

"It's real, you know," she said. "And thanks for shutting that woman down at the funeral. The one who talked about the cave."

"I have no interest in crowds overrunning the area."

"Have you ever been there?"

"No."

"Aren't you curious?"

"Roseanne told me she feared it."

Sue laughed. "The one time she went there, a bat flew at her. She freaked out and fell on her butt. And then, on the way home, she walked through poison ivy. But it is lovely. You should see it." They climbed over a series of rocks. "I think it would be a good idea for you to see what you're about to destroy."

He looked at her askance. "We're not fighting today."

Every day is a fight, she thought. *I have to keep up my guard.*

A couple of hours later, hot, sweaty, and hungry, they drove to a picnic area by Cathedral Creek, shook out a blanket in the shade from the cottonwoods, and splashed around in the water, cooling off before lunch. Rafael opened the basket for a cold bottle of white wine, plates, napkins, and a wedge of brie.

He poured their wine, hers first. He carved a bit of brie, placed it on a square of bread, and gave it to her.

Impressed with his manners, she enjoyed the bite.

Then he did the same with pâté spread on crackers.

"I can feed myself," she said.

"Am I doing it wrong?"

He wrapped prosciutto around a bite of melon and extended it to her on a fork.

"Thank you, but look, Rafael, you have to stop this." She chewed the morsel, savoring the bright flavors.

"Stop what?"

She wiped her fingers on a cloth napkin. "You're acting like this is a date."

"Me feeding you is a problem? Why is this? I enjoy your company."

"And I enjoy yours, Rafe."

He grimaced at the slang.

"We're adversaries," she said. "There's nothing about this day that equals romance."

"I am not romantic. I am friendly."

"Too friendly."

"With what I have seen of the world, there is no such thing. More love is needed."

Her head jerked up. "You did not just say that."

"I mean it in a general sense. You know, like the Beatles. All you need is love." He bobbed his head as if hearing the song. It made her laugh.

He grinned back. "Susan. Relax."

"I am relaxed. It's just, you know, you're annoying."

"You struggle to resist my animal magnetism."

"Stop." But she was laughing, and so was he. He refilled her wine, and they enjoyed their lunch alone in the growing heat and humidity that portended afternoon monsoons. Although it was hot and sticky, there was a breeze, the sky was beautiful, and no tourists bothered them. The only sounds were those of the birds and the creek.

"Thanks for the break," she said. "You were right. We needed it."

"A respite. Time for us to know each other better." He sipped his wine and eyed her over the glass.

She snorted. "Who *are* you?"

"I am Rafael Antonio Palacios de Verdugo Cantón."

"What I meant was *what* are you. It's like you're always on."

"It's not my fault." He shrugged. "Women bring it out in me."

"All women? How do you manage a trip to the grocery store?"

"I allow extra time."

"Ha."

"I am a single man, and I behave a certain way, which women seem to like."

"So it's probably just a habit."

"Exactamente. It means nothing." He reached over to brush a strand of her hair from her forehead.

"See?" She leaned away. "That's what you do."

"You have beautiful hair."

"Listen, Rafael, you have to stop."

"Don't you like it?"

"Of course I like it. But that's beside the point. You like me, I like you. Where does that get us? We have a big problem, and we need to remain focused. Stop trying to distract me."

"You find me distracting?"

"I find you incorrigible."

"Yes, probably." He finished his wine. "I like to flirt, but I'm casual with everybody. That's the way it will stay. I like my life the way it is."

"Me too," she said. "I had a great marriage, and I miss my husband every day, but life with him was one way, and now that he's gone, it's going to be another way. I'm independent now. I need to be my own woman."

"I feel the same."

"You need to be your own woman?"

"I am being honest here."

"So am I. And honestly, we need to be strictly platonic."

"Precisely. We are friendly competitors." He reached out his hand to shake, but he held on to Sue's for so long she had to tell him to let go.

"Sorry." He grinned.

"You are not."

They put everything back in the basket and went to wade in the creek, splashing cold water over themselves and then, with much laughter, each other.

Sue followed him up the bank, and they laid on the blanket, her on her back, him propped on one elbow.

"My parents used to bring us here." She gazed up at the trees waving gently across the cloud-studded sky.

"With Roseanne?"

"Yes." She cast a sideways glance at him. "My mother would bring baloney sandwiches and lemonade. Potato chips and cookies. We'd eat until we were stuffed. Then they'd take turns napping while Roseanne and I played in the creek. All afternoon. Sometimes it rained on us."

"Roseanne was good then?"

"Well, it's relative. She wasn't quite so mean," said Sue. "But then she got older and changed. Our picnics stopped. My dad died. It was pretty awful."

"I am sorry for your hardships." His eyes were filled with sympathy.

"Everybody has something."

Billowing white clouds drifted across the sun, providing welcome shade. They lay on the picnic blanket together, shoulders almost touching. They were silent for so long, she thought he might be asleep.

Then his voice broke the silence. "I have a daughter," he said.

"I didn't know."

"Her name is Natalia. My wife took her to Argentina when the girl was two."

"Your wife left you?"

"No note, no nothing. I was frantic, but then I received a divorce notice and a warning about further contact."

Sue was stunned. Hurt for him. "She must be in her thirties now?"

"Thirty-two."

Travis's age. "Have you tried to find her?"

Rafael covered his face with his hat. Thunder rumbled in the distance.

Sue left him alone. She wanted to know, but it wasn't any of her business. Lying next to him, she stared at the leafy green patterns against the sky. Rafael began to snore lightly. Her own eyes grew heavy.

When thunder boomed, she awoke to find him propped up on one elbow, watching her.

A raindrop hit his arm. Another splashed her in the face. They grabbed their things and ran to the truck just as the clouds opened. Laughing, they jumped inside and slammed the doors. She shook out her hair. "We look like wet dogs."

"I might. You don't."

The wipers slapped back and forth as Rafael drove through town. He turned on the radio to a soft jazz station. Neither spoke, and the atmosphere inside the truck was cozy, peaceful. It reminded Sue of earlier days, coming home after picnicking with her family, worn out and happy. At this moment, Rafael felt like family, especially having shared with her about his daughter.

She turned to the window. He wasn't family, and he wanted to kick her off her land. There was no way she could afford to buy his half, so why was she even bothering to clean the place? Why even dream?

She had to fight back a big, self-pitying sigh. *Don't go there*, she told herself. *It'll pass.* "Rafael, would you ever consider donating the house to a historical entity?"

"No."

"But think of it. What a great way to preserve the heritage. Future generations—"

"No."

The atmosphere in the truck turned cold. "Fine."

He switched on the blinker and headed for the Mesa.

Ten silent minutes later, they pulled up in her driveway and got out. He handed her the backpack. "I'll be back tomorrow," he said.

Slinging her pack over one shoulder, she turned her back on him and went inside.

The man made her crazy. She wanted him, even for just a fling, even if it was totally a bad idea, but she did. Good thing she'd made that big speech about remaining platonic or she might have hauled him inside.

Her reaction to Rafael amused her. Even though he was her opponent, she could waste the whole evening thinking of the way his hands gestured to make a point, the way his fingers held the fork and knife, the way his mouth moved as he spoke. As he ate.

When he looked at her.

Platonic or not, she had enjoyed watching him. It had been a long time since she'd been so captivated by a man.

Still, Mike was hovering in the background. Sue wasn't sure she believed in the afterlife, but if he was up there somewhere, would he be watching her? Would he be hurt by her moving on with her life, perhaps dating other men? Perhaps more?

No freakin' way. Mike was territorial.

But Mike was in his next phase, and she was here, alive, and it had been far too long since the shroud of widowhood fell over her, darkening her horizon. Surely Mike would want her happy.

She sighed.

Even though Sue was lonely, she wasn't interested in men or dating. It was like her body had shut down.

Except around Rafael. And they would be working together for the foreseeable future.

Might she allow herself a little fun? Could she perhaps enjoy him in a superficial way? Her imagination ignited with possibilities. And hunger.

But then there was the matter of her body. It still worked, but time had taken the usual toll. She looked good in her clothes, but to take them off in front of a stranger? Men aged, too, but it wasn't the same.

Her breasts were still good. She'd never thought small boobs would turn out to be a blessing, but they were still up there. She was slender, but her skin wasn't as firm and her bottom was no longer sweetly rounded. If she let Rafael see her, she'd have to back out of the room. And be careful not to be on top, unless it was dark. Candle light would be okay. She could invite him to stay after dinner one of these nights. Once the house was cleaner. They wouldn't want to make love in a junkyard.

She grinned at the realization she was staging a seduction, at the frank acknowledgement of the hunger to feel his hands on her body. His mouth. To touch him everywhere.

She wasn't that kind of girl, but maybe at this point, she'd become that kind of woman.

In the dark kitchen, she peered out the window. The truck was still in the driveway. For a moment, her hopes flared. If he got out and came to the door, she would let him in.

He was sitting in the cab, looking at the house.

She waited.

A moment later, the motor rumbled to a start, and Rafael drove away.

Disappointment knifed through her.

She changed into dry clothes and tried to get interested in a project, but the house seemed too large and silent. The picnic had been fun. Rafael had a playful side, something she wasn't used to in a man. Mike, for all his strengths, was quieter, always dedicated to his work, focused on the mission.

Truth be told, her marriage had been challenging. Life with Mike was safe and predictable. She was proud to have been a good military wife, adeptly moving house every couple of years, keeping her husband's career in the forefront. She'd been both father and mother to their children for long stretches while he was deployed. Luckily, she and Mike were similar from the start: controlled. Squared-away. Thinking of him now, she missed him with every cell in her body.

Fat raindrops hammered on the roof.

In Roseanne's old room, she set a new canvas on the easel and prepared her supplies. She sketched out a rough design of the creek and the picnic arrangement from memory, tinted the canvas, and transferred the sketch. Touching a wide brush to the canvas, she began filling in broad strokes of sky and earth. In her mind, she saw red rock mountains against a backdrop of dark storm clouds.

An hour later, she started anew. Same result. Nothing was working. One effort after another, down the drain. She couldn't get the colors right, or the angles, or the dimensions. Frustrated, she capped her paints and called it a night.

* * * * *

RAFAEL STOOD UNDER A WARM SPRAY OF WATER, showering off the memory of their picnic. At the house, he'd needed to get away from her before his resolve weakened and he tumbled into the sanctuary of her embrace.

But that couldn't happen. Susan was adamant about remaining platonic. Which amused him because usually, women threw themselves at him. They couldn't wait to get him in bed. They hated when he left afterward.

Because he was the one who left, always.

He never brought them home.

Though he would like to, with Susan.

But no. He would abide by her rules.

He had wanted to chase her into her house, to pull her into his arms and kiss those lips. She had the greatest mouth, wide and laughing, wry when she didn't believe his bullshit. Searing blue eyes that saw through him. The combination would drive him crazy if he let it.

Rafael braced himself against the shower and dunked his head, drowning his thoughts. Shaking off the memory. He turned the water to cold and grimaced at the welcome sting of the icy needles.

Chapter Twenty

She kept herself busy until the next afternoon. When his work truck rumbled up, she took a quick look in the mirror and hurried to open the back door.

He climbed the steps, and she caught her breath. He exuded masculinity in his tee shirt, shorts, and work boots. She wanted to say something funny, to crack a joke and dissolve the tension between them. Instead, she simply stepped back to let him pass.

He moved by her, slowly, like a big cat, his eyes locked on hers. Under his mustache, one side of his mouth curved upward.

She looked away. "Let's start in the living room. It's driving me crazy."

"The living room is driving you crazy?" He was smiling that beautiful grin of his.

"Yes. I want to be able to use the front door."

"Then we will work toward that end. Help me decide what is salvageable or trash," he said. "Like this table. Do you want it?"

She shook her head. "But it's good for charity."

"So. We will put it in the donation pile." He carried it out back, returning for more items as she unearthed them. After a while, they divided their work; her inside, him on the front porch, clearing from the outside. They worked hard all afternoon, sweating and resting and working some more. The air was still and very humid. They took numerous breaks under an elm tree in the front yard to avoid heatstroke.

Sue kept reapplying sunblock. She offered him the tube, but he waved her off.

"I don't care for it."

"Don't you worry about skin cancer?"

"At this age, not really."

She twisted the cap back on. "How old are you?"

"How old are you?"

"Oh, now we're shy, are we?" she replied. "I'm sixty-five."

"Sixty-four."

They sat there, smiling at each other as if having discovered a great treasure.

She gestured at the front door. "It's clear on both sides now. Want to try opening it?"

He put his shoulder against the door, bouncing a little. Testing it. "Is it unlocked?"

"It is."

On his second attempt, the door scraped open. Dust and dirt rained down on him.

"Jesus!" He pulled up his tee shirt and mopped his face. Sue ran for clean towels, wetting them under the hose for him. He shook out his hair, and she brushed at him, removing the larger bits of debris.

"I think I just received an asbestos shower," he said.

"Good thing you're not worried about cancer."

"Give me the hose."

He peeled off his shirt, and she caught her breath. He was brown and strong, with a furry patch of silver on his chest. "Rinse my back."

He bent at the waist, and she held the hose over him, sluicing the cool water over his warm, smooth skin.

"My head."

She complied as he scrubbed his scalp with both hands, finishing with his biceps and forearms. He stood, raking furrows through his wet hair, water trailing down his back and dampening his waistband.

Sue busied herself with turning off the hose to avoid being caught salivating. Rafael grabbed a clean shirt from his truck. Thunder growled to the south, and a breeze picked up.

When he returned, she was using the shop vac to clean up the debris. She switched off the machine. Her face glowed.

"What are you so happy about?" he asked.

"Good show." She rolled up the vacuum cord.

"You weren't supposed to notice. Remember, we are platonic."

She held up both hands. "I'm sorry. You're right. Let's call it a day."

They got Gypsy and a couple of cold beers and headed out to the bunkhouse to watch the monsoon approach. In the distance, long gray threads connected the earth with the underside of purple clouds as the storm rolled across the land.

"We made serious headway today," she said.

"We did."

She slipped off her sandals, rested her bare feet on the middle railing of the porch, and sighed. "I enjoy this."

"It was a good idea to come out here and relax after our labors."

"But if you sell it, it'll be off-limits, which would be a shame, don't you agree?"

He looked upward as a trio of ravens squawked past. "I already have this experience from my house, as you saw at the memorial service."

"But it's a different view."

"There are many, many good homes with spectacular views all over Sedona. In fact, I could show you some."

"No, thank you."

"Susan, the list you showed me—it will be a lot of work. Not just removal, but repair, as you noted. The painting and cleaning, fine. That's within reason. But that's an old house. It has deterioration you can't see, which will be expensive and difficult to fix."

"I don't care."

"For example, the ductwork. A new compressor for the AC. Possibly new wiring. There are a thousand things that might need work. But other properties wouldn't. Some of them are very fine, requiring no renovation."

"Rafael, do you ever feel guilty about helping yourself to land that belongs to my family?"

He glared at her, but she held his eyes.

"Sometimes." He stood and reached for his keys. "But I don't let it interfere with my objective."

* * * * *

RAFAEL DROVE HOME, LISTENING TO MUSIC and not quite happy about spending the evening alone. The house was spacious and quiet and somewhat cold. He knew this but assumed he'd be selling it, so he didn't care. But tonight, he felt the absence of other humans.

The absence of Susan.

After dinner, he went online and tried tracking his daughter again. He'd tried so many times over the years, although not for a long while now. Natalia was grown. There was nothing he could do for her now; he had missed her childhood, and her feelings for him were established. Why intrude?

And this is what he had told himself for the last ten years.

But things had changed. The internet and social media now made searching possible. No one had secrets anymore.

Rafael stared at the screen, debating with himself. After a few moments of consideration, he began typing search terms, using his own name, his wife's name, her maiden name, his daughter's name with all the combinations.

And this time, after all those years, he found a lead. A law firm in Buenos Aires with a woman attorney on staff. In the photo, the woman was laughing along with her coworkers. She looked carefree and beautiful, and his breath caught in his throat. It was as if he were seeing his ex-wife on the screen.

It was as if he were looking at himself.

He closed the laptop and went outside to the patio to sit in the dark and contemplate the day's events. Being with Susan had awakened something in him—the need for authentic connection.

She was threatening his strategy.

He wished Roseanne had left her sister alone. If she had simply passed the property to him as originally promised, it would be on the market by now. Instead, all these complications.

The yard fell silent, and he sat and listened. After the funeral, it had seemed as if Roseanne's spirit were hovering over his property, as if she were nearby, all around him.

His voice broke the silence. "Was this your plan, Rosie?"

A mosquito whined by his ear. Rafael swatted it away.

In the distance, an owl hooted. Breezes sighed through the tops of the pine forest where his house sat.

But it was just wind.

Rafael chuckled. Hijole*, you're losing it. Talking to a ghost.*

"Because if you wanted me to fall for your sister, it's working. But you died before you could see your little plan play out."

The sound began far down in the valley, below his hillside perch, a low moan ascending the hillside, the sound of a great gust of wind in the trees, roaring through the pines, hitting his house and blowing dirt and pine needles into his face and his eyes, threatening to blind him.

He threw up his arms to protect his face.

As soon as it arrived, it passed. A pine cone fell to the ground from a nearby tree. It hit so hard, it splintered on the sidewalk.

Rafael got to his feet.

"I am obsessed with your sister," he said to the darkness, "and I have no idea what to do. Your mischief worked. Now leave me alone. Go now, Rosie. Rest in peace."

Chapter Twenty-One

In the morning, Rafael was back, not hungover in the least, which was a surprise since he'd found himself staring into the bottom of a tequila bottle before staggering off to bed the night before. Not like him at all.

When he awoke that morning after tossing and turning for hours, he flew down the hill, anxious to start the day. At her place.

With her.

Screaming around the curves, his tires complaining, Rafael had to tell himself to slow down. No sense in getting into a wreck.

Sue answered the door with a big smile, her hair piled on top of her head in a messy bun, ripped jeans, and a thin tee shirt. She went to get him coffee. He followed her, inhaling her fragrance. Citrus? Jasmine?

It was just the two of them, alone in this house, alone in this small room. She felt the same way he did. He could see it in the way she remained unmoving, waiting for the coffee pot to finish while he sidled up near her. The way she tilted her chin up, a question in her glance.

He smiled down at her. Those blue eyes, like flecks of diamond, cold at times, warm now.

What if?

The coffee pot stopped. She was about to reach for the mugs, but before she could, he reached around her, gathering her in, his arms bracketing her, holding her.

She gasped when his body pressed against her.

"Rafael," she whispered. "I don't know if—"

"It is." He nuzzled her ear, her neck. She smelled so good.

Her arms tightened around him, her hands flattened against his back.

* * * * *

SUE FORCED HERSELF TO STAND PERFECTLY STILL because if she moved even the slightest bit, she would be crawling all over him. She squeezed her eyes shut. "We have work to do. We have to—"

Jesus, he was kissing her neck, his mustache tickling her skin, his breath so warm.

Her knees wobbled.

"Work can wait."

That was worse. His voice rumbled in his chest, his closeness amping up the heat, the attraction. And his scent, like honey and smoke. She had to stop him. She tugged on his arms. They loosened. "We're just friends, remember?"

"Yes. Friends." He raised an eyebrow, asking a question without words.

She cupped his jaw, his beard scratchy under her hand.

Rafael lowered his mouth to hers, and God help her, she was gone, lost in the heat and the softness and the hunger. His kiss was searching, and she responded in kind, pulling his head down to hers, holding him close, ferocious with need. He drew her close, and she knew his need was as great as hers. Sighing, she gave in to the kiss, a little moan escaping, her front pressed against him, his arms strong against her back, her waist, lower.

HONK!!!

They broke apart, and Rafael muttered a flamboyant Spanish curse.

Of course, it was John, driving up in a Mad Max–style three-quarter-ton pickup with twin stacks and a dump bed.

Sue's back was pressed against the kitchen counter, Rafael's arms still bracing her. She grasped his biceps, reluctant to let him go, feeling the taut muscles under his shirt. Her hands savored his skin, his heat, the reality of him. Every part of her wanted him. She was starving for his touch, his mouth on hers.

He leaned in, kissed her again but more lightly this time, then rested his forehead against hers and sighed. "*Madre de Dios.*"

John gunned the motor a couple of times, rattling the whole house.

Sue wriggled free and combed Rafael's hair with her fingers, trying to restore normalcy.

"Do I look that bad?" he asked, a rakish grin on that luscious mouth. It was all she could do not to taste him again.

She glanced down at her front. Everything was still buttoned and zipped. "We need to go outside before he comes in."

"He won't." Rafael straightened his shirt. "Are we good?"

She gave him a lopsided smile. "Really good."

John was leaning against the side of his truck, hands hooked in his pockets. He glanced from one to the other, and his face changed to a smirk.

Sue returned his look. Let him think what he wanted.

John said, "Got the truck, Boss. What do you want me to fill it with?"

Rafael looked at Sue. "Backyard?"

His smile held her. She didn't want to move, but with John there, eyeing the two of them, she forced herself. "You know what to do. I'll be working on the inside."

With Rafael directing him, John backed the monster down the ancient driveway to the backyard shed. Sue returned to the house, determined to regain control, but her entire body buzzed with the memory of Rafael's embrace. It was crazy, it was stupid, they were on opposite sides of the property deed, it went against everything she had decided...but damn, the man could kiss. She wanted to flop down in the recliner and think about it. No, she wanted to pull up a chair and watch him work. Watch him move.

More than that. She wanted him.

Not just a kiss or his arms around her.

All of him.

Wrenching herself away, she threw herself at the interior, trying to keep from wondering if he'd slip inside the house to steal another kiss. Despite her resolve, her ears were tuned to their movements. Now they were in the front yard, now the back, now taking a break. She longed to hear the door open. If he came into the house and demanded her body, she would happily share it with him.

She worked like a tornado over the next hour, burning off the hunger. Outside, it seemed Rafael was doing the same. Chunks of metal, cement, and wood rained down into the truck bed with a clang-banging that could be heard inside the house.

Then the noise stopped, and Rafael tapped on the back door. "We're done for the day."

They couldn't touch each other because John stood nearby.

"Okay. See you tomorrow."

"Actually, I have business in Phoenix," he said. "I'll call you when I get back."

"Okay." Her voice was soft. She wanted to reach for him.

John made a derisive snort.

Rafael grinned. "We'll speak soon." He trotted down the steps and disappeared around the side of the house.

After they left, Sue collapsed in a chair to think about his kiss, about his strong arms trapping her against the kitchen counter, about the heat radiating from his body. Rafael had animal magnetism, but it was more than that. She hadn't kissed anyone but Mike in thirty years, and frankly, she never expected she would again. She hadn't wanted to. But now she felt like a teenager, head over heels, drowning in hormones. In lust.

This wasn't helpful. What good would it do to have an affair with the man who wanted to steal her land? Worst-case scenario, she'd develop feelings for him right before they had to face each other in court. That would be awkward.

No, she had to have her priorities straight. As much as she got weak in the knees, thinking about him, it couldn't happen again.

* * * * *

LEANING ON RAFAEL'S TRUCK WINDOW, JOHN POINTED at the satellite dish. "Looks like your girl's getting comfortable."

Rafael started the engine. "She is not my girl."

"Aren't you worried about her digging in? Eviction is long and bloody."

"Not at all. The outcome will be the same."

John shook his head. "I wouldn't trust her."

"You don't trust anyone."

"Life's better that way."

Rafael glanced at his buddy. As confirmed bachelors, they reinforced each other's worldview, but sometimes he wondered if they were taking it too far. John, in particular, had become bitter, had grown a shell. Rafael's wasn't as thick, but still, he'd been this way most of his adult life and was no more interested in change than John was.

"She's got you by the balls, man," John said.

"This is none of your concern." He couldn't believe he'd lost his resolve so completely. The memory came rushing back in a wave of warmth and desire. He wanted to rush into the house, pin her to her new mattress, and own her.

He'd been with beautiful women before, women who were generous with their bodies. He would enjoy their companionship for weeks or, in one or two cases, for a few months. But then he would extricate himself, remaining happily alone until the next woman came along, and the cycle would repeat itself.

Rafael had what he needed. He'd been happy. It was a good life.

Until now.

What was it about Susan? More than chemistry, he was comfortable being around her. Sitting out on the bunkhouse patio, enjoying a single glass of wine, her bare feet resting on the fence rail, her strong, tanned legs—but also, she was smart, and determined, and almost scary, with her icy blue eyes and the heart of an Amazon. Burnished with age, with maturity. She was formidable, with a mind of her own, a compelling body, and determination sparking from her fingertips.

He realized John was speaking to him. "What?"

"Said if it had to be anybody, she's pretty fine."

Rafael stared at the house.

"Yeah, you're pretty much screwed," John said. "I gotta go." Giving the truck's roof a slap, he walked away, waving idly over his shoulder.

Rafael rested his elbow on the sill and started the truck.

Chapter Twenty-Two

After a restless night filled with even more restless dreams, Sue set up her easel at the bunkhouse. Marissa had returned, hoping to take advantage of the morning light. While her friend planned to paint the riverbed canyon, Sue faced the house, hoping to recreate what it looked like in its heyday. Armed with a compelling rendition, she would use it to convince the historical society of the need for preservation. One of the managers, Ms. Novak, had grudgingly agreed to see her.

Marissa was speaking. "I think you should try mixing these two colors..."

Sue tried to portray the beautiful image in her mind onto the canvas, but she wasn't having much luck.

"Don't get discouraged," said Marissa. "You've improved just in the last hour."

"I've been waiting so many years to do this, and now I find I'm terrible at it."

"Your sense of composition is good, and you have a feel for hues and colors."

"But?"

Marissa gathered up her supplies. "At some point, you have to let go. Become more yourself."

"Not sure I know who that is. Painting-wise, anyway."

"But see, that's the fun of it," said Marissa. "It's a process of discovery. Let it happen."

Sue tried, but her mind kept returning to a certain dark-eyed man with the most amazing kisses. And then she'd remember what she had to do this morning, and the warm feelings would turn cold.

The historical society was housed in a Spanish-style office reminiscent of California. A receptionist asked her to wait. Sue studied the paintings on the office's walls, most depicting ancient Native ruins. Nothing so modern as the Mesa house. As the clock ticked, her spirits sank.

Twenty minutes later, she was greeted by a middle-aged woman in a short blue skirt, sleeveless silk blouse, and high-heeled sandals. Her honey-blond hair was piled atop her head in a messy updo. Her posture was erect, her smile sparkling, her handshake firm.

Sue followed Novak into her office, a showplace of native art and figurines. The light tan wood was artificially distressed, making it look vintage, and the carpet on the tile floor would certainly be expensive. Sue had done a bit of volunteering at the historical society in Visalia, a temporary building salvaged from an overcrowded school, and felt a rush of envy.

"I understand you have a property you believe is of historical significance that you think the society might be interested in?" Novak settled in an easy chair adjacent to the office sofa.

"That's right." Sue clasped her hands in her lap. "It was homesteaded in the late 1800s by my great-great-grandparents." Having practiced her speech, Sue's description of the homestead went well, and her passion carried her along. She thought she was doing a good job, but Novak's face was unreadable.

She listened politely, nodding at times, occasionally asking a follow-up question.

Ten minutes later, Sue wrapped up her pitch. "So, if the society is interested in buying out my co-owner, I'd donate my half. But I need funding to pay him to go away."

Novak chuckled. "Who are you working with?"

When Sue told her, Novak sat up straighter. "Rafael is a part of this?"

"He is. While I'm trying to save it for the community, Mr. Palacios would prefer to sell the parcel for private development."

"I'm sure he would." Novak shrugged. "Unfortunately, our budget is already committed for the year."

"But this property is unique. Parts of the home are still original, like the stone foundation and log walls in some rooms. It's an architectural treasure."

"We really don't have the funds."

Scrambling, Sue thought of the charity dance Vicky told her about. "I might be able to find an additional donor."

"I don't think we're interested."

"Or maybe even do an online fundraiser?"

Berkeley Novak leveled a cold gaze at Sue. "Let me be blunt, Ms. Weston. That house is a heap. Your sister ruined it. And before that, it was probably modernized. That would diminish its historical value."

"But visitors would still find it compelling," Sue pleaded, "and it would be a beautiful event location. Events that would generate revenue for the society."

"It's a bridge too far," said Novak. "The society would have to update certain aspects of it, most likely plumbing, for example, which would be expensive." She glanced at her watch. "If circumstances change, I'll give you a call."

"I only have a few more weeks. After that, Palacios will destroy it."

"I'll let you know." Novak stood, ending the discussion.

Thanks for nothing, Sue thought. "What else would you suggest I do to save the place?"

"I have no idea."

"I guess I could try social media," said Sue. "Rally the masses over Rafael's intent to desecrate the place."

Novak was staring at her. "That's an appalling idea."

"I was joking," Sue said, "but I'm feeling a little desperate. Wouldn't you be?"

Novak held open the door. "I wish you well."

I'll just bet you do, thought Sue. The heavy wooden door whispered shut behind her as she left the office. Her only hope now was the charity dance, and she needed a confidence boost. Determined, she headed for a cute boutique downtown. She would attract a donor if it killed her.

Chapter Twenty-Three

Standing in front of her mother's full-length mirror, Sue gave a twirl. The floral skirt flared out, flattering her shape, as did the white boatneck top and delicate, heeled sandals. Grabbing a tiny blue leather clutch, she told Gypsy to be good and headed for the old part of Sedona.

At Tlaquepaque, the summer night was filled with the splash of courtyard fountains and the sweet scent of honeysuckle. Balconies of delicate wrought-iron overlooked tiled alcoves and carved wooden doors. On this balmy evening, she felt quite girly in makeup and perfume, especially after all the scutwork she'd been doing.

Music and song drew her toward the Calle Independencia, the promenade decorated for the evening's event. A stage featured a band, and off to the side, a display of student artworks from high schools in the Verde Valley.

The street was filled with people laughing, drinking, and dancing.

She found Vicky easily, following the identifiably raucous laugh that sailed above the crowd. The redhead, at a table with a half dozen friends, waved her in. Her wheelchair was decorated with flower garlands.

A server approached with a tray of tequila shots.

"Might need two of these." Vicky handed one to Sue, who downed the smoky heat in one gulp. Vicky made introductions. Most of her friends were people from town.

Sue pulled her aside. "Are these guys potentials?"

"Heck, no." Vicky laughed. "They're as poor as us. But the night is young. Just wait."

Marissa appeared in the crowd, laughing as she danced with a muscular young man in a tight tee shirt and fedora. The two of them looked like an ad for a singles resort. The crowd closed behind them.

"Oh, to be thirty again." Vicky took a glug of margarita and wrinkled her nose. "I'm gonna be sixty in a few months and I hate it."

Sue sipped her drink. She didn't mind her age, especially on a night like this when the monsoon had given them a break and the air had cooled, and she felt pretty and had a nice little heater going. And then there was that kiss—

"Hey, look who's here," said Vicky.

"Hello, gorgeous." A pale man wearing gold-rimmed glasses, Bermuda shorts, and loafers leaned down to kiss Vicky on both cheeks.

"Charles, how great to see you," said Vicky. "This is Sue. She's restoring a historic property in Sedona and looking for donors. Sue, Charles owns a chain of car dealerships throughout Arizona, so he's loaded." Vicky poked an elbow in Charles's ribs.

"Is that right?" He smirked. "I wish you luck."

"Oh, come on," said Vicky. "Open that wallet, dude."

"I don't think it's for me. But if you're ever in the market for a car." Charles handed Sue his card, gave Vicky another hug, and hurried away.

"I feel like a beggar," said Sue.

"Don't get discouraged. Remember, you have to get twelve rejections for every sale."

"Who says that?"

"It's a known fact," said Vicky. Suddenly her eyes bugged out. "Holy shit."

"What?" Sue's head swiveled to see.

"Well, hello, strangers!" Vicky greeted the couple approaching their table. "This is Celeste Waterbury and her husband Geoffrey. They're snowbirds from Massachusetts."

Sue held out her hand. "Isn't this the wrong season?"

Geoffrey, a lean, tall man in a blue polo shirt, looked her up and down. "It's not by choice."

"We flew out for the event." Celeste was a willowy silver-blonde with a low voice and the posture of a ballerina.

"Glad you did," said Vicky. "And lucky for you two, I have great news. My friend here is restoring the Mesa house."

"About time. That place has been a dump for years." Geoffrey looked at Celeste. "Let's go."

"I'll be right there." When he walked away, Celeste gave Sue an unhappy smile. "We own a vacation home in the gated community next door. I'm glad you're trying, but frankly, I'm skeptical. It's a monstrous project."

"Not anymore," said Sue. "I've been working on it. Much of the land is cleared."

"Good for you. That took fortitude, I'm sure."

"Sue's looking for donors to invest in the property, so she can donate it to the local historical society," said Vicky. "If you and Geoff helped her out, it would go a long way to helping you sleep at night."

"And to preserve the history for future generations," Sue added.

Celeste nodded vacantly. "I want to be supportive, but Geoffrey." She glanced toward her husband, who stood, unsmiling, gesturing for her to join him.

"He looks happy," said Vicky.

"Right. Well, I must go," said Celeste. "The best of luck to you."

"We'll need it."

Sue watched her rejoin her husband. "Another fail," she said.

"Yeah, but actually, that was kind of like seeing a unicorn," said Vicky. "I'm surprised she's out."

"What's her story?" asked Sue.

"Something about her work as a therapist. Something bad happened. That's all I know."

Sue felt sorry for the woman and almost regretted hitting her up for money. Almost.

But as the evening wore on, she felt discouraged. None of the dozen prominent citizens she'd chatted up wanted to come on board. Everyone thought preserving legacies was a good idea, but no one wanted to fund it.

At least she had fun dancing, breaking away from her fundraising failures to whirl around the tiled piazza for a fast number here, a slow dance there. Many of her dance partners were younger, and at least that helped salvage her self-esteem. Her last partner of the night was Jerry, a nice guy who showed interest in the Mesa. When the dance ended, they agreed to have brunch the next morning and talk further.

Jerry kissed her on the cheek. "I'm looking forward to tomorrow."

"Me too." She beamed at him.

A resonant voice interrupted. "I hope you are not here trying to sell my half of the property." Rafael, appearing out of nowhere, reached for Sue's hand.

She couldn't help grinning as he pulled her onto the dance floor.

"I didn't expect you here," she said, nuzzling into his neck. "How was Phoenix?"

"Great. Incredible." He leaned her backward in a heart-stopping dip. "Like you, I have been looking for investors."

Sue laughed with the pure joy of dancing with an expert. "Vicky told you."

"Jerry is a good man," said Rafael. "And he has money. Did you know he donated a museum to the city of Phoenix?"

"A whole museum?"

"Precisely." He spun her away and reeled her back in. "So he would be a good target for you."

"Are you taunting me?"

The dance ended, and they returned to Sue's table to say goodbye to Vicky, but she was already gone.

"I'll walk you out." Rafael tucked Sue's arm through his, and they strolled toward the parking lot. A soft breeze wafted around them, perfumed with a row of jasmine.

"That was so much fun," she said, unlocking her car door. "You're a very good dancer."

"We make a good team." Bracketing her with his arms, he leaned her against her SUV.

She felt the cool surface against her back, felt his heat against her front as he moved in, his hands on her arms, gently caressing her.

His cologne—fiery spice and dark wood—drifted over her, and she closed her eyes. When his lips met hers, she felt a jolt of heat up her spine. His kiss was probing, curious, hungry. As she gave herself up to it, his arm went around her waist, pulling her against him.

When they broke apart, she ran her fingers along his jawline. He grasped her hand and kissed her wrist.

She pulled back. "It's late."

"I would be happy to follow you home. Since it's dark on the Mesa."

"Rafael, if you did, I'd have to invite you in." She let her protest hang, waiting.

Sighing, he held her hands to his chest and touched his forehead to hers.

His lashes were so long, she couldn't help but kiss them, every touch of her lips a tiny message of regret. "I should go," she said.

He didn't protest, helping her into the car and closing her door gently. "Drive safely."

"I will."

In the rearview, he stood, hands in his pockets, watching her depart.

At the front door of the Mesa house, she fumbled with her keys while Gypsy yapped on the inside. Coyotes yipped and howled in the creek basin below. Changing into sensible shoes, she took the dog out for a last bathroom break. In spite of the darkness, Sue felt safe here. The memories of her childhood, the good ones, lifted her up. It was as if the warmth of her family surrounded her now that Roseanne was no longer a threat.

She needed that warmth, given her new confusion over Rafael. The man lit a fire in her, that was for sure, but the fire could burn down her life, and she'd already had too much disruption in the past few years. Now, she craved stability. No more drama.

She couldn't afford to fall for the man.

Tomorrow, she would meet Jerry for brunch at a famous restaurant in town. A man who could drop an entire museum on a city would surely need a place to dump some cash. What was three million to a billionaire? She felt good about her chances.

And yet, each step toward finding the money meant one step closer to severing her relationship with Rafael.

Chapter Twenty-Four

Rafael pulled up in Sue's driveway, parked his Corvette, and tapped on the front door. He knew she was home because her vehicle stood in the driveway, but she wasn't expecting him. He'd planned to go to the office and get some work done today, but all he could think of was her.

Thunder rumbled across the canyon.

He knocked again.

On a hunch, he went around to the back.

And then he stopped.

Sue was kneeling at the base of the statue, gardening. She wore cutoffs and a blue cotton blouse. Her hair was tied in a bandanna.

A breeze swirled across the yard, and she tugged at her blouse, flapping it to cool off her midsection.

Feeling like a thief, he allowed himself a few moments to appreciate the loveliness of her backside. She was humming a little tune as she worked.

The dog noticed him and wagged her tail.

Sue turned around and stood, tearing the bandanna off and wiping her forehead. "You could have said something."

"I was about to."

A strong gust of wind whipped her hair across her face. "Doubt it."

"Very soon, I would have."

"What do you want, Rafael?"

Ignoring her tone, he gestured at the statue. "What are you doing?"

"My mother intended it to honor my grandparents. I wanted to preserve their memories."

"I realize that," he said. "But isn't it a wasted effort? Since they'll only be here for such a short time."

"Real nice, Rafe."

"Please don't call me that."

"Why not? Everyone else does." She gathered her tools. A few drops of rain splatted on the cement.

"You're not everyone else." He stood between her and the house. "Did you have a nice brunch with Jerry?"

"Are you spying on me now?"

"You hugged him. You were out in public. I was driving by."

"So?" She brushed past him. "It's none of your concern."

"Why are you angry with me?" Rafael caught up with her at the door. "Susan?"

"I woke up this morning, got dressed, and went to brunch with a total stranger, pitching my heart out to accomplish something that'll never happen but that you could fix with one word." She swiped her arm across her forehead. "So even though I like you, and—" Sue glanced at his mouth and took a breath. "But we're not allies. This is my family's land. You have no part in it except my sister wanted to make sport of us."

The corner of his mouth turned up. "She wanted to make sport?"

"Play with us. Throw us together and make us fight. It was her plan all along, and you're just playing into it. Why don't you end the misery?"

"What misery?" He stepped forward. "Susan, are you in misery?"

She wrapped her bandanna around her wrist. A streak of dirt smudged her cheekbone. "Why don't you admit you're a usurper and do the right thing?"

Rafael threw back his head and laughed. "You make me sound like Genghis Khan."

"If the shoe fits—"

"Hey." He brushed his thumb over the streak, erasing it.

Raindrops began to fall, fat drops that drenched them immediately.

Sue called to Gypsy and opened the door.

* * * * *

HIS EYES FOLLOWED HER AS SHE POURED two glasses of lemonade. Outside, the rain hammered down, no doubt drowning her new plants.

It was probably a mistake to invite him in. She was growing tired of his domineering behavior. Questioning her about Jerry, making her feel evasive.

Was he jealous?

She set the glasses on the table.

It was too bad he was her adversary. Despite his ego, Rafael was really so appealing. Handsome and smart. Confident. Good hair.

He lifted his nose in the air. "What is that smell?"

"What smell?" She returned the pitcher to the refrigerator.

He left the kitchen and stalked down the hall with Sue in pursuit. At her parents' bedroom, he pushed open the door. His nose led him to the primary bath, where the tilework had been re-caulked. "It's this. What are you doing?"

"I hired a guy."

"You hired a guy."

"Yes, and I cleaned up all the dead mice too. So shoot me."

He shook his head. "Don't you understand?" Heading back down the hall to the kitchen, he pointed at the rooms she'd emptied, cleaned, and refurnished, one with a twin bed. "And here you have a guest room!"

She hurried after him. "I might have guests."

"An art gallery!" He flung an arm in the door of the yarn room, now dominated by a big easel in the corner. A table held all her paints and supplies.

Lightning flashed through the window.

"It's not a gallery, exactly. More of a studio."

"And this." He walked right into her bedroom, stopped in the center, and took it all in. The new curtains, the lamps, the patterned area rug. The trundle bed, set up with both singles to equal a king, covered with a patterned throw.

"It's a bed, Rafael. Where did you think I was going to sleep?"

"A hotel. We could have had this place sold by now."

She smiled. "You're so obvious, Rafe."

His head jerked around.

"You think if I'm uncomfortable in the recliner, things will go faster, or if I'm in a hotel, you can bring in your tanks and flatten the place. But I'm not giving up my plans."

"Your plans will not work." He stepped toward her. "You're just wasting time and money. The new owners will want to start from scratch."

"Stop reminding me. How can you be so cruel?"

"And how can you be so delusional? This house won't be here in three months, and a new one will be. All of this is going under the blade."

"I'll never allow that."

"You have no choice."

"I have the choice to fight you every inch of the way."

"You are intransigent," he said.

"And you're a gold digger." She glared at him.

"A what?" One side of his mouth quirked up. "Did you just call me a gold digger?"

"Yes." She straightened her shoulders.

He took a step closer. "Like a beggar, sitting on the steps of the post office, waiting for handouts?"

"That wasn't my first thought."

"Perhaps something more flattering. Like a hacker? A swindler?" His grin became wolfish.

She lifted her chin. "You got close to Roseanne to finagle the land."

"How conniving of me." He was standing right in front of her now, looking down at her, a wicked smile on his face. "I am no better than a con man."

"You would kick me off my family's homestead and steal it for yourself." She moved toward the door.

He blocked her. "Like a crime boss. A Mafioso. A guerrilla fighter."

"Exactly like that." Her breath quickened.

"And does a fighter run away when his woman objects to his presence?"

"His w—"

She never finished. His mouth was on hers, and she forgot what they were arguing about and kissed him back. He was strong, his arm around her waist, holding her against him. Kissing her with a fury that weakened her knees.

When they came up for air, he looked at her, one eyebrow raised.

She leaned away from him and unbuttoned his shirt. Slowly.

* * * * *

HOURS LATER, SHE AWOKE TO THE SOUND OF RAIN pattering on the ramada over the front porch. Her cheek was pressed against his chest. She lifted her head. He had been looking at her. Watching her. She broke into a smile. "Hi."

He took her hand and kissed it, his mustache tickling her skin. "I dreamed of this."

"Me too."

He held her hand against his chest and stared into her eyes. "Just so you know, I did not intend for Roseanne to give me anything."

"Okay."

"Okay." He ran his finger over her lips. "Next time, we'll be at my house, where the bed is the size of a king from California."

"Next time," she whispered.

He gathered her in his arms.

She sighed. The last few hours had been heavenly. Although she had mixed feelings. The afternoon had been wonderful but also bittersweet. The thought of Mike flickered across her heart, and she squeezed her eyes shut.

Don't be crazy, she told herself. *He'd want you to be happy.*

It was a lie. Mike would probably want to kill Rafael.

And how would they move forward now?

As if reading her thoughts, he pulled her close. Through the rusty screens, the sound of rain dripping off the roof comforted her. She remembered that sound, and the scent of the desert, drenched.

He rolled on his side, wrapping her in an embrace, kissing her until she relaxed against him, her questions vanishing. She had missed the touch of a man, had thought she might never again experience that pleasure. Now, she felt reawakened, invigorated after the lonely slog of the last several years.

"Susan," his voice rumbled deep in his chest.

"Hmm?" She turned to him. He could be so tender yet so driven. She ran a finger over his full, straight eyebrows. His eyes weren't as dark as she had thought at first. Instead, the irises had bits of light in them. His mustache, neatly trimmed, was laced with silver.

He kissed her palm, his breath warm against her skin. "I don't want you to think I'm a gold digger."

She chuckled. "I don't really think that about you. I mean, I did, but I don't anymore."

"And I'm sorry you and Roseanne were enemies, but she was always good to me. In her own way."

She snuggled closer, her head on his shoulder. "I don't want to think about my sister right now."

"Nor do I. This complicates things, but I'm glad it happened." He placed his hand on her waist and ran it down her flank from her hip to the soft place behind her knee and then back again. Then he raised up on one elbow and brushed her hair from her brow. His kiss was like a promise, a surrender.

"Rafael?"

"Hmm?" His voice was gravelly, deep.

"This is crazy, isn't it?"

"Crazy good." He nuzzled her ear. "But I must go. I have to work tomorrow, not like some other people."

"I'll be working too. Planting flowers, buying appliances..."

"Susan. What am I going to do with you?"

With a kiss, she showed him.

Chapter Twenty-Five

After Rafael left, Sue slipped on a robe and sat on the front patio with Gypsy, not tired, not ready for sleep.

As much as it complicated everything, she was happier than she'd been in a long time. Even if Rafael was only making the best of an opportunity, because she was a woman and he had a reputation, still, she was happy. She had only ever loved Mike, and that was the way it would remain, but she was still young-ish, vibrant, and alive. And it felt good to respond as a woman again.

The afternoon storm had moved off, leaving the air cool and fresh with the scent of creosote and pine. Sue took a deep breath, filling her lungs with the fragrance of the damp red earth.

Incredible to think she'd just spent the last few hours in such intimacy with another man. She didn't want anything to dim her happiness, but it did strike her as sad that she was moving on. That she was pulling away from Mike, finding her way into the future without him.

She swallowed hard.

And yet, Rafael's attentions were a blessing. He made her feel alive. As if the horizon wasn't darkened by widowhood, grief, and loss.

It was a gift. She would take it as such.

* * * * *

RAFAEL SPED THROUGH THE FOREST, windows down, tires hissing on the wet pavement. He was the only one on the road, and he exulted in the movement of the Corvette in the curves, exulted over his hours with Susan, this magnificent woman who made him feel like a strong young bull.

He tried to work a few hours after arriving home since his firm was on deadline with a project in Flagstaff, but his thoughts kept drifting to the softness of her skin. Around midnight, he gave up and went to bed, where he fell asleep instantly.

Waking to the sound of his alarm going crazy, he cursed and switched it off.

He took his coffee out to the ramada and watched the branches of the tall pines sway in the gentle breeze. Texting Gabriela that he'd be in late, he sipped his coffee and gazed off across the landscape. Today might be the first time he'd enjoyed this view quite so much. Every part of him felt rested, languid. He didn't want to move, only wished to sit quietly and relive every minute of yesterday afternoon, starting with the moment he saw Sue kneeling at the feet of the Virgin.

He had to get to the office before too long, but the thought didn't appeal. Rafael wanted to jump in his truck and hurry down the hill to the Mesa and help her plant flowers.

Wait. What?

He narrowed his eyes.

The thought flitted across his mind that he could choose to do exactly that. Rather than fight with Susan and force her to sell the property, he could withdraw his interest, sign it over to her, and see what developed.

Rafael shook his head. Surely pigs would fly before he made such a sacrifice.

But he sat and enjoyed his coffee and the view for another thirty minutes, considering the impossibilities.

Chapter Twenty-Six

At daybreak, Sue walked with Gypsy out to the bunkhouse, one ear cocked for the sound of his truck coming up the driveway. She had no reason; it was very early, Monday, and he would be working, perhaps dropping by later to help her with the endless task of cleaning and clearing. But still, she listened.

Standing at the fence at the drop-off's edge, she stretched her arms out to the side, muscles rippling deliciously. She had slept like a teenager, like a woman satiated.

And she had no regrets, strangely enough. She'd half expected to awaken filled with remorse, but she was mature enough to put it in context. Rafael might have a reputation as the town's most eligible bachelor, but to her, he was just a friend. A very sexy, attentive friend. A business partner with benefits. Complicated, yes, but also delicious. She couldn't wait to see him again.

After breakfast, reluctant to be indoors, she returned to the flowerbed at the feet of the Virgin, shaded by the stately pine. After a few minutes of snuffling exploration, Gypsy stretched out on the grass nearby with a great sigh. The wind chimes jingled from an occasional breeze.

It had been years since Sue had felt such peacefulness, not since Mike decided to retire and then the diagnosis. Life had shot her out of a canon, but now—she shivered at the thought of what Rafael had done for her.

She finished her task, patting and shaping the good rich earth around salvia, sage, and marigolds.

Their lovemaking was probably just another fling for him, but she could have a fling too, and who better to have it with? At some point, she would have to get back into the dating world. Rafael would be an exceptional guide.

She looked forward to spending the next few days with him, working and playing together. For the next few weeks of their cease-fire, she would enjoy his company and not worry about the end of the month.

Was that even possible? She glanced at the statue as if looking for an answer. Mary's face was chipped. She'd have to fix that. Sue stood, brushed off her knees, and gathered her tools and the empty pots. What a glorious morning.

Inside the house, the rooms were emptier now, and in the early morning coolness, all the windows stood open, allowing the fresh air to flow through. The day stretched in front of her, and for the first time, she wasn't motivated to clean, sort, and organize. She retrieved her tablet from the kitchen and wandered from room to room, making notes about what tasks remained to be addressed and hoping for inspiration.

But she couldn't get interested. All she could think about was Rafael. His hands, his mouth, those searching eyes. She had slept with the enemy. But he didn't feel like an enemy, even though the proof of it surrounded her. Logic didn't help. Her thoughts were scrambled. Memories of their lovemaking crowded out all other possibilities.

She considered calling Carol or Katie, but they might deflate her balloon with sensible advice about being careful, making her push him away. She could call Vicky, but the hooting and snickering would be too much.

She spun around and went to her studio and placed a fresh canvas on the easel.

Uncapping her paints, she dabbed color on the canvas. Slowly at first, unaware of any goal, she simply followed her heart. From the palette to the canvas, she chose colors that sang, colors like sun and sky and the red earth of the desert. Dabbing and stroking, she didn't worry about form or structure, only color and mood and essence. Time passed, and her back and shoulders grew tired, but the process was joyful, so she kept on. When the sun was high overhead and Sue stood back to consider her work, she looked at her first abstract and realized she was in a new country.

Cleaning her brushes, she felt steady, grounded. It wasn't a landscape. Who would have expected this? Her mind felt refreshed, cleared of doubt and worry.

She heard the sound of truck tires crunching on the gravel through the open window.

Capping the last tube of paint and laughing to herself, she went to answer the door.

"We have to discuss this." He frowned fiercely.

"Yes, we do." She pulled him inside and closed the door. "There are implications."

He grabbed her around the waist. "We are not allies."

"Total enemies," she said, running her hands over his shoulders and backside. Pulling him to her.

He lowered his head and pressed his lips to hers. She opened to him, tasting him, losing herself. Breathless.

When the kiss ended, she took his hand and led him down the hall, past her new abstract, to her bedroom. Losing herself again in his embrace, savoring his attention. The man was an expert.

Afterward, Rafael gathered Sue to his chest and kissed the top of her head. "I was supposed to be at a meeting in Flagstaff today. I blew them off."

"You messed up my schedule too," she said. "I need to fix this place up so the other guy won't make me sell it."

He gazed into her eyes. "That is difficult for me to hear."

She ran a finger over his brow, tracing down to his cheek and jawbone. His beard was already emerging from his morning shave. She loved the stubbled look on him.

He took her face in his hands and kissed her slowly and sweetly. "When I saw you planting flowers, I felt regret. Because even if you don't believe me, I do know how much this place means to you."

"But you don't care."

He sighed. "I care. But it doesn't change anything."

"You haven't won yet," she said. "Don't get ahead of yourself."

He rolled on his side, running his fingertips across her skin. "I have an idea. Why don't we take some time off? A few days to enjoy each other's company, to stop this competition, to let our thoughts settle and figure out where we go from here."

"You want to extend our cease-fire."

"Yes! I'll have Gabriela rearrange my schedule. John and Matt can cover for me." He ran his fingers through her hair, massaging the nape of her neck. "I never take vacations. Let's give ourselves time to play."

"More picnics."

"Yes, but without the platonic pretense."

She traced his mouth. "I like that idea."

"Now I must go to the office and clear the decks." He sat up, his hand still on her hip. "It's so hard to leave you."

"You'll be back."

She walked him to the truck.

"I'll see you this evening. Let me bring dinner." He climbed into the truck, started it up, and rested his arm on the window edge.

She leaned in, giving him a kiss to remember. And then he drove away, and she knew that for all the fun and games, Rafael meant what he said. Because making love with him, spending languorous hours drifting in and out of sleep, waking and snacking and falling back into bed, changed nothing.

He was still after her land. But maybe they could continue the truce.

Until when? she wondered.

Shrugging, she went back inside. Life was too good right now. She was smart enough to enjoy it.

* * * * *

"DAMN, GIRL." AT THE DOWNTOWN GALLERY, Marissa studied Sue's joyful, post-sex painting.

It was Sue's first abstract, a riot of yellows, oranges, and greens, so full of orgasmic joy, she couldn't look at it without blushing.

Marissa held it up, studied it, set it on an easel, and walked away from it. She whirled, stared, stalked.

Sue began to worry. What had possessed her to bring the thing to Marissa in the first place? What incredible hubris. "I'll just wrap it back up," she said.

"Wait. Follow me." Marissa carried the painting to the front of the store and positioned it on an easel. "Go do something. Don't hover."

Sue sat behind the counter pretending to be working while Marissa greeted customers. They clustered in front of the landscape, holding hands, hugging, giggling.

Kissing.

Marissa sidled away from the crowd to the desk where Sue hid. "Are you seeing this?" She spoke behind her hand. "They love it."

"I am seeing this," Sue whispered.

The shop door opened, and a tall, familiar figure entered. "Hey, good lookin'."

"Hi, Jerry." Sue came out from behind the counter and gave him a hug.

"What've you been up to?"

"See for yourself," said Marissa.

Jerry looked from the painting to Sue and back. "That's yours?"

"I'm as surprised as you are."

Jerry went over and looked. When he came back, his smile could have blocked out the sun. "What're you calling it?"

"*Joy*," said Marissa. "Obviously."

Chapter Twenty-Seven

"Hey, handsome."

At the silky voice, Rafael spun around. Berkeley Novak had slipped under the caution tape and was mincing toward him in blue high-heeled sandals across the broken ground. He whipped off his hard hat and raced over to head her off.

After leaving Sue's that morning, he'd done a bit of work at the office, had lunch with a prospect, and now he was observing the initial phase of demolition of a creaky old two-story near the edge of downtown. The flatbed was in place, ready to offload the bulldozer. In the remaining hours of daylight, they should be able to get a good start.

"This is a construction zone, Berkeley." He gently grabbed her by the elbow and escorted her to the property's edge. "What can I do for you?"

She grinned, that beautiful uneven smile that always lit his flame, and he winced inwardly at his poor choice of words. The last person he'd expected to see at today's job was the curvaceous president of the local historical society. Today, she'd freed her hair from the typical messy bun. Honey-blond locks tumbled over her shoulders.

"Getting ready to smash something valuable?" With a secretive smile, she leaned nearer, cleavage on full display, her perfume intoxicating.

"Did you want to help?" he joked, masking his concern. There was no reason for her to be here. He had all the approvals, clearances, and permits. The two-story was coming down to be replaced by a sleek office complex.

"Just wanted to see how you were doing. You've been busy." Berkeley placed a hand on his chest and gazed up at him, batting her eyelashes. "Too busy to have dinner with me, I guess."

"Lots of work," he said, shifting slightly, wanting to escape her touch. There was a time it would have moved him. The two of them had had an off-and-on relationship for years, never anything serious.

Usually, her presence was compelling, and his mind filled with memories of what they had done for each other. In the past, one whiff of her perfume was enough to make him forget about work. But this morning was different. He felt nothing other than a gentle appreciation for the beautiful, smart woman standing in front of him. "Was there something you needed?" he asked.

She gave him a pretty frown. "Not if you're too busy."

"I don't mean to be rude, but work is demanding right now." His voice was tender. "What did you need, Berkeley?"

"Nothing." Her smile vanished. "Just checking on the work."

Rafael watched her huff back to her car, a stylish little two-door. Something was on her mind. Hopefully, it wouldn't be a problem.

* * * * *

JERRY STUCK HIS HANDS IN HIS POCKETS and rocked on his heels. "I'd like something like that in my office. Are you doing commissions?"

Sue still couldn't believe the reaction to her first abstract painting at the gallery that afternoon. "I don't know. It was kind of spontaneous."

Marissa said, "How about I call you when she has more available?"

Jerry handed her his card. "Looks like you've got an agent."

"Looks like." Sue felt off-balance, as if she were watching a movie of herself selling art in some magical future.

But the future was here.

With one last look at the abstract, Jerry left. Marissa wandered back to where a well-dressed, hipster couple stood at the easel. Their discussion turned animated, with the couple pleading and Marissa smiling kindly but shaking her head. Finally, she held up a hand, turned, and went back to where Sue waited behind the desk.

"They want to buy it. I told them eighteen fifty. Is that okay?"

"Eighteen dollars?"

"Eighteen hundred, goofball. But I could probably get more."

Sue's mouth fell open.

"Close that. You'll scare them away. Want to come say hello?"

Sue jumped up. "I would!"

Marissa introduced them as visitors from San Francisco. "I just love the light," said the woman. "It radiates beyond the canvas and fills the room. Don't you think so, Gil?"

"Absolutely," agreed the earnest young man. "We were in Bali last winter, and it reminds me of that. I don't know why."

"That's where we got engaged," said the woman. She held out her left hand to exhibit a blinding chunk of ice.

"Congratulations," said Sue.

Beaming, the couple paid and left with their prize.

"Here you go, less my commish." Marissa tore a check out of a three-ring business binder. "Weird how emotional people got about it. I think I should have charged more."

Sue stared at the check.

"Everything okay? I mean, it's a standard commission," said Marissa.

"I think I'm stunned stupid."

"You found your gear." Marissa put the checkbook in the drawer. "So, no more landscapes, agreed?"

Sue gave her a high five. "Agreed."

"And I was wondering," said Marissa, "if I might bring one of my classes out to the bunkhouse one of these days. How's the cleanup coming?"

"The whole front area is clear now," said Sue. "It's not pretty, but nobody's going to get hurt if they wanted to park and haul their stuff out to the edge of the property."

"I could bring a pop-up for shade," said Marissa. "Would you be interested in providing lunch? Nothing fancy, and I'd pay you."

Sue stared at the check in her hand. And Marissa wanted to start doing classes at the Mesa?

The dream was taking shape.

"I'm sure Franny would want to come," said Marissa. "She needs time away from Gene. And Flo. That helper of hers could drive her over here. Maybe we could talk him into posing in the nude."

Sue startled, remembering Rafael and their plans for the next few days. "Can I get a rain check?"

Marissa cocked her head. "Is that a blush? OMG, it's that guy, that developer! Are you guys a thing?"

"Am I that obvious?"

"I saw you dancing, remember? Looked pretty hot."

"We're just having fun," said Sue. "He's a nice guy."

Marissa's tone darkened. "You know he's a player, right?"

Sue nodded. "I'm just having fun. All this is weird and wonderful, especially at my age."

Marissa said, "What are you talking about? You're still young and beautiful."

"Not so young, but I feel like I look pretty good. I'm having a lot of fun, and I'm going to enjoy it as long as it lasts. Although I do feel a little guilty. And I wonder what my kids would think."

"They'd be happy for you," said Marissa. "My mother dates. I'm glad she's not alone."

"Rafael is good company. We're going to have fun for a few days and not worry about the property."

"And when you come back, you can paint about it!" said Marissa.

"So, how about the start of next week?"

"Sounds like a plan. I'll let everybody know."

"I'll call Flo," said Sue. "I've been meaning to check in with her anyway."

* * * * *

EARLIER THAT DAY, FLO HAD STRUGGLED through therapy while Eric offered encouragement. She appreciated his presence at her sessions, and anyway, she still couldn't drive. Her ankle was swollen but healing. Slowly.

Flo didn't enjoy exercising, but at her age, it was more important than ever. The therapist allowed Eric to observe so he could help her at home. That was how it was supposed to work, anyway.

But she was just so tired all the time.

Every day, Eric would make her a wonderful breakfast, and she'd shower and dress and go back to bed. She'd wake up to a delicious lunch on the patio, but soon after finishing the morning paper, she would find she could hardly keep her eyes open. She wondered if this was just a natural part of aging.

"I don't like it," she told Eric. "I feel like I'm sleeping away my life. I'll be dead soon enough. No need to rush it."

Eric told her not to worry. "It's probably a reaction to the injury. You'll be fine in another week."

She didn't want to think about being fine in another week, though, because what would keep Eric there after she no longer needed him to cook and clean for her? Maybe he'd be willing to stay on.

She wondered if she'd ever get back to her old life. She missed working. Rafael had been very understanding in having someone else take over her sales duties, but how long before someone younger took her place?

What would she do without her job?

She hated being old. Hated the accumulation of years gone by.

Flo yawned. She would be frustrated if she weren't too tired to care.

Chapter Twenty-Eight

Sue ran her fingers up the back of his neck and into his hair. "Is this too distracting?"

Rafael shifted his eyes from the road briefly. "Don't stop."

Earlier, Sue had loaded Gypsy and an overnight bag into Rafael's truck. Now they were on their way up the hill to spend the night. Sue felt like a teenager embarking on an illicit getaway, parents none the wiser. She felt light, free, and happy.

Rafael reached over and grasped her hand before downshifting into the curves, hurrying home. She leaned her head back against the seat, a happy captive being rushed back to his lair for seduction.

It was good to be healthy; it was good to be alive. A wave of gratitude washed over her.

"Did I tell you I sold a painting?" She couldn't wait any longer to break the news.

"Seriously? That's wonderful. I haven't seen it, have I?"

She chuckled. "I painted it after our first time together. It's very bright and happy."

"You are an artiste." He beamed at her. "You are on your way."

"That's what I think too." Flying up the mountain, she felt joy laced with the bittersweet sense of moving on.

Shake it off, she told herself. *He'd want you to be happy.*

And she was. She was as happy as she'd been in more than three years.

Rafael pressed the button to open the gate across his driveway. "You remember this from the service?"

"A little. That day was overwhelming."

"You will like my house. I'll give you a tour." And he did, from the bedrooms to the butler's pantry, from his office on the second floor to the basement.

She wandered around in awe, Gypsy's nails clicking on the cold tile. "This is a showplace."

"I am proud of it, yes."

"Did you build it?"

"I did. There is no other house like it."

"And the furniture. It's beautiful."

"Let me show you something." He took her through the kitchen and down a stairway to the basement. The house was built on a slope, with the basement's back wall against a hill and the front open to the view.

At the bottom of the stairs, he flicked a light and opened the door. Lining the walls were shelves of lumber, cabinetry hardware, and pieces of furniture in various stages of completion. A table and chairs, a writing desk, and a swing meant for a porch stood waiting for his attention.

She wandered from piece to piece, running her fingers over the smooth surfaces. "These are all yours? You did them?"

He nodded, one side of his mouth quirking upward, enjoying her surprise.

"And you call *me* an artiste? Rafael, these are exquisite."

"I'm pleased with them," he said. "Although there is always more to learn." He showed her around the shop, identifying each piece of equipment. "It is a hobby, a thing I do to relax."

"How did you get started?"

"My father taught me with hand tools. In our village, everyone respected him. And his work was everywhere." He tapped the table on which a lathe was mounted. "Of course, he had nothing like this. All his life, he had only primitive tools."

"And yet, he taught you."

"He did."

"Are your parents still—"

"No. Let's go upstairs." Rafael turned toward the door. "I have something for our little friend."

In the foyer, he opened a closet and retrieved a new dog bed. It was built to Gypsy's tiny proportion and looked like a wooden serving tray with handles carved into the sides.

"That's gorgeous. How thoughtful of you." Sue enticed Gypsy to try out the tartan-patterned cushion, and the little dog curled up on it without hesitation.

Rafael reached into a wine refrigerator at the bar and poured two glasses of Riesling.

She slid onto a bar stool. "Can I help?"

"You can keep me company while I prepare our dinner." Sue perched at the bar, sipping her wine while he prepared grilled salmon with lemon and dill, wild rice, and Caesar salad.

They carried their plates to the ramada at the edge of the property. Rafael tapped his phone, and music emanated from hidden speakers, a bossa nova selection that had her thinking of tropical beaches. A warm, light breeze wafted around them, carrying the bright fragrance of pine and the honey scent of manzanita.

"You were right. Your view is spectacular," she said. "You must love living here."

"I like the view, and I enjoy my shop."

Across the valley, the sun was setting in a riot of purples, golds, and yellows. "If I could paint that, I'd be famous."

"I think you will be anyway," he said.

She sipped her wine and fantasized about the two of them, famous in Sedona for their craftwork. "Do you ever think of retiring?"

"Never."

"Never?"

"My work is my life."

"But what if—"

"Susan." He reached for her hand and kissed it, his mustache tickling her skin. "I enjoy what I do. It's satisfying. I would be bored without it."

"But how would you know? Have you ever taken a vacation?"

"I have. They made me restless." He stood and gathered their dishes.

She followed him into the kitchen, Gypsy at her heels. As he rinsed their dishes, Sue drank in the look of him, his thoughtful profile, his relaxed shoulders. When she came up behind him and wrapped her arms around his middle, he turned and kissed her deeply, his lips promising everything.

Leading her upstairs, he slowly undressed her to music and candlelight, and she gave herself up to him.

In the middle of the night, she awakened. His breathing was gentle, steady, reassuring. He lay on his back, his arm across his belly. She snuggled close, her arm and leg thrown across him, his skin warm in the cool air of the night. He seemed like a brand-new person, not the territorial man who stalked over to her car when she arrived at the Mesa.

As the sun rose the next morning, she studied his face—the olive skin, the stubble on his jawline. Black mixed with silver, like his mustache. She touched his chin.

He awoke, grabbing her hand and startling them both. Laughing, he rolled over and gathered her in a bear hug, holding her so tightly she could barely breathe.

"I need air," she laughed.

"I can't believe you're here." He nuzzled her throat, his breath hot on her skin, his hands roaming.

She exhaled, the pain of the last few years fading, his touch restoring her to wholeness. They made love again, this time slowly. Tenderly.

He didn't feel like the enemy anymore. He felt like home.

When she awoke again, the aroma of coffee wafted up the stairs. She pulled on his robe and went to join him.

In the kitchen, he looked up, eyebrows raised. "Aren't you dressed yet?"

"I need caffeine," she said.

"Here." He poured her a mug. "Now go. Quickly. Lopez will be here in twenty minutes."

"Lopez—what?"

"Go. Dress warmly." Rafael made a shooing motion, and she hurried back up the stairs, perplexed. But the smile on his face promised an adventure.

Fifteen minutes later, a helicopter reverberated loudly against the house.

"Susan! Come quick."

She pulled on her sneakers and jogged down the stairs. A sightseeing helicopter had landed on the broad expanse of the hillside adjacent to the back lawn, its great whacking blades blasting the silence. Laughing, Rafael pulled open the passenger door and handed her up.

The pilot grinned behind her aviators, bright red lipstick and diamond earrings gleaming in the rising sunlight. Her dark brown hair was tied in a ponytail.

"Susan, this is Lopez." Rafael made the introductions as they donned headsets.

"¿Adónde vas?" the pilot asked.

"Your call."

The helicopter's engine increased in RPMs, and with a sickening lift of the tail, the bird rose and sailed over the cliff's edge. Sue gasped in delight, terrified and excited at the same time. Rafael reached for her hand as they carved downslope toward the canyon lands.

Lopez's voice came through the headsets as they flew over Sedona and the red rock country, "First time up?"

"I have been many times for my work," Rafael said. "And you?"

Sue bit her lip. "Once, in Hawaii, with my husband—"

The headsets fell silent. Sue looked out the window to the endless view below.

Later, when Lopez dropped them off, flying away with a little wave, Rafael pulled Sue into his arms. "I'm sorry."

"It's ancient history." They stood in the yard, her face pressed against his chest. When they broke apart, she said. "Who is Lopez?"

"A friend," he said. "We've known each other for years."

Sue cocked an eyebrow.

"It's not that," he said. "Well, it was. But it isn't anymore."

I'm glad, she thought, but didn't have the courage to say it.

Chapter Twenty-Nine

Rafael showed up at the Mesa house early the next morning, dressed for hauling and sorting, but Sue was in the kitchen, putting water bottles into a backpack.

He came up behind her, one arm encircling her waist. She smelled so good, like citrus and honey.

She stopped to lean back against him, a sigh escaping.

He turned her, seeking her mouth, forgetting everything but the taste and texture of the kiss. At this rate, he wondered how they would get anything done.

When they surfaced, she said, "We're taking a break from the cleanup. I want to show you the cave."

"Time is passing." He didn't like reminding her.

"This is important." She put two granola bars in the pack. "Have you ever been?"

"A long time ago."

"And how was that experience?" Grinning, she leaned back against the counter, arms folded. "You're not big on spirituality, are you?"

Ducking his head, Rafael went out the door, back to his truck to get his hat. Leaving Gypsy behind, Sue locked the door and led the way down into the canyon.

Rafael followed. He had no interest in this hole in the earth, but he went along with her plan since he was disrupting her life and it was the least he could do.

And in truth, the walk was a respite. Here were the smooth, burnished red limbs of the manzanita. A little farther, the whip-like spines of ocotillo bloomed tiny pink or red flowers in the springtime. And there, the scrubby creosote. Cupping the tip of a branch in both hands, she showed him how to huff breath on the leaves, and he was rewarded with the fragrance of desert rain.

They followed the creek bed at the bottom of the canyon, shaded by lush cottonwoods and paloverde trees, and the earth was fragrant and damp from yesterday's monsoon. The herbal fragrance of the desert filled his senses, and he inhaled deeply.

Turning from the path, Sue pushed aside the branches of a creosote bush, revealing a hidden walkway he would never have noticed on his own. The path led upward, and he found himself becoming curious, wondering why this place meant so much to her.

When they reached the top, she turned to him, her cheeks flushed and her eyes bright. "We're almost there."

He looked around. "All I see is a boulder. Where is this magical cave?"

"Follow me." She shimmied around the side of the boulder, and he followed, their fingers touching. A thornbush threatened, but they slipped past without being snagged. Stepping out of the thorn forest, he found himself at the mouth of a shallow cave. A paloverde tree protected them from the blazing sun.

Susan showed him where to sit, and he took up his position. It wasn't very comfortable, and a stone was digging into his ass. He fidgeted and shifted, finally settling, somewhat more comfortable. Across from him, she sat in the lotus position, which seemed quite astonishing. How limber and flexible she was. Then he began thinking other thoughts he shouldn't have, of course.

The cave wall was cool against his back. Rafael closed his eyes and tried to relax, given he would be here for the next little while. Besides, he was happy to be wherever she was.

Many of the women he dated were immersed in this rock-spirituality business, but he didn't fall for such schemes. He'd seen what happened to people who expected salvation from the clouds. Bored and antsy, he tried to think about nothing. But how? The very concept was a thought.

Rafael focused on his breathing, as he'd heard one should do. He inhaled boredom and exhaled boredom and wondered how long this would last. Across from him, Sue sat like a statue, serene as a sunset.

The only way to cope with this silliness was to stop fighting it, so he allowed himself to think, but only minor thoughts, such as a recent meal, but not a problem at work, such as how he would pay for the concrete work at the new Flagstaff mall. His financing was stretched pretty far at the moment, but there was a new bank in Scottsdale that had invited him to come in—

Stop.

He rolled his shoulders, shaking off the problems.

What could he think about that was pleasant and uncomplicated?

He took a couple of deep breaths and settled. Thought of blue water, soft sand beaches. Tropical rain forest. Green shadows. Jungle.

His family.

Rafael's eyes flew open. He didn't want to think of his parents. His brothers. All dead now.

The walls of the cave seemed nearer. He was achy and uncomfortable. In another thirty seconds, he would have to stand. To escape.

But there was the matter of his pride. So he allowed himself to think of Natalia and to wonder where she was and if she ever thought about him.

But it hurt to think of her, so he took another deep breath and cleared his mind for a tenth of a second...

...and he thought about his latest project, and he thought about financing it, and he thought about Flo's latest sales data, and her age and increasing frailty, and he thought about death and whatever happened to Roseanne, and what did a person have left if they were in their eighties and starting to forget things, and Flo looked more shrunken and bent lately.

Like his grandmother before they shot her.

His eyes flew open.

Rafael was freaking out. He had felt something here in this cave.

But that was stupid, like a nonsensical dream. His imagination had simply run wild.

He glanced up at Sue, surprised to see her looking concerned. "Are you all right?"

"Are you done?" he asked.

"I am. That was good. For me." She stood and stretched, looking as refreshed as if awakening from a night's sleep.

He got to his feet, his mind tortured, but his body was surprisingly loose after sitting on the cave floor for an hour.

Sue led them down the path, using a branch to brush away their footprints near the start of the hidden path. She tossed the branch aside and looked up at him, so serene, as if lit from within. He wondered if he kissed her now, would some of that light enter his body, give him some relief?

But he had to put an end to her expectations. And his own.

"Susan, I enjoyed your company and can see this is very meaningful for you."

"I'm glad. I wanted you to enjoy it." Standing in front of him, she took his hand.

"But it's *muy fácil.* Too simple. Life is so much more complicated, a struggle. A person must be clearheaded and logical. This isn't for me."

"If you feel that way, Rafael. I'm a little sorry, but okay."

He looked up at the trees overhead, their patterns shifting in the breeze. Such peace. He wished he could feel it. The memories were so close to the surface, even decades later. One could probably never leave them behind.

"What?" Sue whispered.

He shrugged. "My family was in church when the militia found us."

"Oh no." Sue put her arms around him. "I am so sorry."

He allowed himself to be held for a few seconds, then pulled away.

He needed to get out of there now. Quickly. She looked hurt when he drove away, but he had to leave before he felt anything more for her, putting himself in more danger than he could bear.

Back at his house, he parked the truck and took off on his motorcycle, which he hadn't ridden in months. It needed a run.

He needed a run.

He rode up the hill toward Flagstaff, rounding the curves a little too fast.

The memories roared back like a swarm of stinging bees.

He was ten years old, sitting in church with his mother. Out the window, militia pulled up in trucks armed with rifles. A woman screamed. Churchgoers jumped to their feet, wide-eyed and smelling of fear.

Men in ski masks and olive-green uniforms burst into the church, snarling commands. Rafael's neighbors and friends ran into each other, trying to get out the back, but men blocked that exit as well. Screaming filled his ears until it was drowned out by the staccato bursts of gunfire. With bullets ricocheting off the walls and his ears ringing, Rafael grabbed for his mother's arm as she flinched and fell to the floor. He scrambled after her, under the pew, hiding, his small hands wet with her blood. Curling into a fetal position, he pressed his face against her and prayed.

Eventually, the church fell silent except for the whimpering of a small child. "Mama," Rafael whispered, but the seeping red hole in her chest confirmed the horror.

Pressing his face against her bloody palm, he cursed God and reached for her bundle. Slipping in blood, he had run for the jungle.

Whipping through the curves, Rafael realized he was speeding dangerously. He eased off the throttle. What a joke it would be to splatter his guts at this point, driving an expensive motorcycle on a well-tended highway.

Would Susan understand? He had told no one the full story, not even John.

Rafael had wandered for days, terrified and hungry, when he came upon a band of soldiers who fed him and gave him his own rifle. Those young men with guns became his family. Everyone else was dead. His brother and father had been picked off in one assault on their small village. His sisters, another. He saw their little-girl shapes shoved into the dirt, relieved they hadn't survived to serve as playthings for their attackers.

For two years, the militia patrolled the hamlets, surviving on the gratitude of villagers, but when the soldiers began fighting with each other, Rafael headed north.

He was twelve when border guards discovered him in the back of a stakebed truck behind sacks of feed. The local policia kept him around for a while, running packets of coca between warring camps until they all went to prison. But not Rafael. Always keeping his nose to the wind, he sensed danger before it reached him.

At sixteen, having gotten as far north as Mexico, he was pulled from a railroad car and forced to work in the fields.

Now, reaching the top of the hill, he pulled over at a campground entrance, removed his glasses, and wiped his face on his shirt. He breathed hard, as if he'd just gone for a fast run.

At eighteen, he made it to Ciudad Juárez, then—glory be—across the border into El Paso and found work with a live-in crew at a sprawling mansion. The owner, an elderly woman of means, had once run an operation of her own out of Oaxaca. Now a respectable citizen of Los Estados Unidos, "Mrs. Smith" had debts to pay before she met her maker. She helped Rafael become a legal resident, enrolled him at the community college, and taught him how to use silverware properly.

No fool, he ran with it. At twenty-six, he graduated from Texas A&M with a master's in urban design. He'd found work at a firm in Albuquerque, fallen in love with one of the secretaries, and climbed the ladder of his career. Rafael had passions back then. He worked and played hard, amassing wealth and prestige. When Isabel became pregnant, he became frantic to build security for his wife and child. But his labors had the opposite effect.

Lonely, angry, and tired of feeling neglected, Isabel had taken their daughter and disappeared.

It was bad for a while. Brought back all his childhood terrors. He couldn't work. About drank himself to death before finally receiving a message from his wife. She wanted a divorce. And Natalia could one day decide if she wanted to see him or not.

As it turned out, not.

Rafael had learned his lesson. Everyone he loved left him, one way or the other. The cave experience brought it all back.

Better to keep Susan at arm's length.

She had texted him throughout the day, expressing concern and reassuring him, but he hadn't responded.

As he fell asleep that night, he wondered if he had matured enough to withstand another broken heart. Had age strengthened him or weakened him?

He thrashed and spun. Regardless of his feelings, they still had to resolve the property issue.

Rafael rolled over and stared into the darkness, missing her warmth, her kindness. He fell asleep, tormented by nightmares of bullets tearing into flesh.

Chapter Thirty

Sue didn't know where they were going, but after his moodiness yesterday, she didn't care. He sounded happier today, having awakened her before dawn with a phone call. Said he would arrive in thirty minutes and for her to be ready.

When he came through the door, he gave her a quick kiss and a hug. Following his lead, Sue acted as if the cave hadn't happened, grumbling good-naturedly at the early hour. If he wanted to move past it, whatever it was, she would do the same. He hurried her along, insisting she wore warm clothes. They fed Gypsy, locked up, and drove out of Sedona through the darkness toward the flatlands.

They arrived at a plateau lit by a line of what looked like bonfires.

"Balloons!" Sue turned to him with a big smile. "I've always wanted to ride in one."

"Get your sweater and let's go then."

As the giant orbs inflated, their colors were lit by the heaters and the rising sun. Nick, their gray-bearded pilot, helped them step over the edge of the basket. He wore a windbreaker and a watch cap, the latter bearing the insignia of conflict in the Persian Gulf.

Rafael's arm encircled her as they waited their turn, the other balloons lifting off like glowing jewels, rising up into the dawn sky with a roar of burners.

Nick said, "Hang on," and pulled an overhead lever. With a burst of flame from the burner, a bump, and a scrape, the balloon lifted off.

Sue gasped.

Beside her, Rafael was grinning. "Good so far?"

The balloon reached the plateau's edge, and the land fell away. They floated over a canyon, hundreds of feet below, now visible in the dawn. When the balloon reached altitude, the pilot cut the flame.

Sue marveled at the sensation of lightness, the silence, the cold air, and the view of the land slipping by beneath them. Her concern eased, replaced with a sense of peace. "It's so quiet."

"People are always surprised," said the pilot.

They fell silent as they floated toward the red rock formations, now lit crimson by the sunrise.

Sue felt Rafael watching her and turned. He was studying her with a little smile. She snuggled into his arms and touched her lips to his. Their kiss deepened.

The burner roared, interrupting them. Sue laughed around the kiss.

Nick grinned. "Sorry."

Warm in Rafael's embrace, they floated in companionable silence. Cirrus clouds streaked the sky, turning from navy to pink to gold. Forests appeared on the slopes, and the land sprawled away as they drifted on the slight breeze. If any activity in the world could erase the tension of the day before, this would be it. Sue squeezed Rafael's arm, and he leaned his head against hers. All was well.

Except nothing had changed. His demons, and the land, still stood between them. She would have to address this again and soon.

When the ride ended in a field, a van picked them up and returned them to the truck. They drove to a fancy breakfast place down by Oak Creek, with patio seating and a stonework fireplace. Across the way, pinnacles and spires glowed orange in the morning sun.

As they feasted on truffle eggs and mimosas, she tried to draw him out about yesterday, but he was skittish, so she dropped it. Instead, they relived the experience of floating over the land in the colorful, silent balloon.

Later, in his bed, they lay in contented silence, the windows open to the scented air and the calls of jays and ravens. He reached for her hand, kissed it, and held it against his chest. "I can't believe we're together."

"Roseanne did something right after all."

"I spent many years drinking too much. Suffering. Her friendship, such as it was, helped me survive. I might not be here if not for her."

Sue lifted her head. "I'm glad to know she did something good. What did she say to help you?"

He took a deep breath and slowly exhaled. "That I was full of shit and nobody would care if I died."

They looked at each other for two seconds and burst out laughing.

"Seriously? Oh, that is so Roseanne. How on earth was that helpful?"

"Because of her, I regained my perspective. And because of you, I have done one other thing as well." Propping himself on one elbow, he caressed her cheek. "I have located my daughter. Natalia. She's an attorney in Buenos Aires."

Sue's eyebrows rose. "That's fantastic."

"Yes, a big law firm, apparently. She's a partner."

"You must be very proud."

"I have missed a lot." He laid back against the pillow, staring at the ceiling. "She looked beautiful, strong like her mother."

"Rafael, I'm so happy for you. Did you send her a message?"

Rafael shook his head.

* * * * *

HE COULDN'T SAY MORE.

Natalia.

He had missed so much, drowning his sorrows in alcohol and work. Like those early days in the jungle, he had been on the run for his entire life. His daughter was nearly a middle-aged woman, and he was an old man.

He got up and walked across the room to his dresser, returning with a carved figurine the size of his thumb. He handed it to Sue.

She turned it over in her hand. "What is this?"

"Guatemalan jade," he said. "From my village."

"It looks like a saint or a prince," she said, fingering the intricate lines.

"It was my mother's. Somehow, I managed to hold on to it all these years."

"It's beautiful." She tried to give it back, but he refused.

"You will think of me when you see it. I will be in your head always."

"What are you saying?"

"Nothing. I don't know." Rafael pulled on a pair of shorts. "I'll be downstairs."

He left her in his bed, her look of concern an arrow through his heart.

Chapter Thirty-One

Flo sat in her favorite chair on the patio, watching the evening come on. She flexed her ankle. It didn't hurt. She hadn't had any pain meds since yesterday. Maybe it was healed?

She started to rise, to push herself carefully up using the chair arms, when Eric slid the screen open.

"What are you doing?" He rushed over and took her arm, bracing her as if she were completely decrepit.

"Checking my ankle." She withdrew her arm. "I'm fine. Don't worry so much."

"I don't want anything bad to happen to you."

"It won't."

"Are you hungry? Would you like me to fix you a snack?"

"Gosh, no. The way you're feeding me, I feel like a piglet." Sitting back down, Flo waved him away. "I'm just going to sit out here and be alone with my thoughts for a little while, if you don't mind."

He held up both hands. "Not a bit. Call if you need anything."

She listened for the door to slide shut. Thought about going for her phone and giving Sue a call. She was older; she'd understand and could help Flo decide whether she was overreacting. Feeling lonely and vulnerable in her elderhood, she might be losing her perspective.

Eric was kind and helpful and doting. Like the son she'd never had—okay, grandson, maybe.

Her one regret, if she believed in regrets, was that she was childless. She'd only been married a couple of years before Henry was killed in the mining accident, and in that brief period, the good Lord hadn't seen fit to bless them with babies. It wasn't her call, so no sense mulling over life's hard parts. Take your lumps and move on.

Flo heard the TV switch to the music channel she liked— golden oldies, familiar, nostalgic. How like Eric to do that. Almost instantly, the gloom receded.

No point in being morose. The sun had come up this morning in another pure-blue sky. She would do a little work from home and reach out to Rafael, whom she suspected was still miffed at her for siding with Sue.

But Sue was right to want to hang on to the Mesa house. Flo had loved the place ever since she first saw it, back in the seventies. She was a home seller at the time, and Sue's parents had been thinking of downsizing. The home was sprawling, decorated with iron and clay and the colors of the desert. Flo had considered buying it herself, but it was more property than she needed.

Sue's mother, God rest her soul, was a quietly sad woman, but the father seemed strong enough to handle Roseanne. Too bad he died young, when the girls were still in elementary school. He'd picked up meningitis, of all things.

Rafael was a fool to want to raze the place and let some soft-handed hedge fund manager build a monument to himself. There were more important things in life than money. She wished she could wave a magic wand and give Sue the money to buy Rafael's half. Once the house was fixed up, it would be a fine and sprawling abode. Sue would be happy there. Her family could visit, even stay for the summer. It was big enough to accommodate the whole lot. Sue had spoken of them, lighting up with joy at the mention of her grandchildren but becoming a bit more veiled when speaking of her son and daughter.

Flo was fine living alone, but she wondered how long she'd be able to stay in her house. It was too big for her, but she knew where everything was, and it was neat and clean.

Maybe she should look for something smaller. Sell this and move nearer town, where she could step outside and walk to a little corner shop for a cup of coffee and a cinnamon roll. Go to the movies without getting in the car. Order groceries delivered instead of hefting them herself.

Maybe someday, but until then, she could make a few changes. She'd already gotten rid of her throw rugs, and if necessary, her beloved Aubussons would have to go. Bare tiles from here on out. Clear the walkways. Donate the clutter.

The screen door slid open again. Eric appeared, holding a pot of tea and a plate of cookies.

Sighing, she watched as he poured.

Within fifteen minutes, she was so sleepy he had to help her to the living room sofa.

Yawning, she glanced at the clock on the mantel. It was barely five in the afternoon. Five! She'd been sleeping so much lately.

Maybe she was just getting old.

Chapter Thirty-Two

The evening light was so exquisite Sue wanted to paint a stained glass cathedral, but her mood had plummeted after Rafael dropped her off. The whole way down the hill, he'd been silent. Was he breaking off their relationship?

But what did they even have to break off? Two co-owners jockeying for position, each trying to manipulate the other over the land. And then, the magic of romance.

Which was, apparently, simple lust. For him, anyway. For her, she had begun to have feelings for the man, sympathy for his heartbreak, and hopefulness for reunification with his daughter. Joy at the sound of his truck in the driveway.

Maybe he had regrets about her. And maybe she wasn't built for a fling. If that's what this was.

She shouldn't be feeling this low. He wasn't anyone to her, and even if he was, people left. Children grew up and left you there alone. Husbands died.

Was that what it was—loneliness? A longing for community, for the communal feeling she desired for this house and garden? For the artists and classes and even wellness classes she envisioned here? A dream Rafael stood in the way of.

With their growing closeness, he had distracted her from that dream and the fact that his ambition stood in the way of it.

So, when he dropped her off and drove away, he not only left her lonely for him but for the community of friends that would never be.

Her phone buzzed. A text from Travis.

Dinner tonight?

Sue's spirits lifted. She hadn't heard from her son in weeks. His job sometimes took him out of reception range, but in this day and age, when cell towers were everywhere, that alone was frightening.

Travis always told her not to worry. As if that helped.

Pressing the phone icon, she called him right back. "Are you here? In Sedona?"

"I was in Phoenix and thought I'd drive up and surprise you."

"You definitely did that. Do you have a place to stay?"

"I'm at the Enchantment." Travis laughed, that deep chuckle so much like Mike's. "And I have a reservation for dinner at seven. Will that work?"

"Of course! Yes."

They talked a little longer before hanging up. Sue was thrilled to think she'd be seeing her boy. Like his father, Travis was quietly self-sufficient. He never spoke about any particular girl, traveled a lot for his work, and seemed happy not settling down.

In contrast to Katie's struggles, her son was thriving. At least she could take comfort in that.

Whatever it was he did for his work—and he was always a bit vague—it paid well, and he had behind-the-scenes political access. She always enjoyed his stories.

The prospect of his company and a gourmet meal at the Enchantment had her humming a happy tune as she went to take a shower.

At six-thirty, he drove up in a late-model BMW coupe, very sporty. Dressed in khakis and a button-down shirt rolled to the elbows, he looked so much like Mike she nearly wept, but when he gave her a long hug, all she felt was joy.

Soon they were seated at a window table looking out across the red rock expanse of Sedona, her heart near bursting with pride and happiness as she listened to his story.

When the server removed their appetizer plates, topped off their wine, then glided away, Travis lowered his voice dramatically. "And that's when I asked the senator if he was going to smoke that weed or play with it all night."

"You didn't."

"Take a look." Travis thumbed his phone until the senator's image appeared on the screen. The Senate Minority Leader, taking a toke.

Sue's eyes rounded. "Did he know you were filming him?"

"Mom. Give me some credit here." He put away his phone just as their dinners were delivered. "Now tell me about the property."

"I have a couple of friends helping me clean it up. We've filled a dozen dumpsters with junk."

"It looked pretty stark." Before leaving for dinner, Travis had walked the property. "A lot of work to make it into anything."

Was he trying to discourage her too? "It has tons of potential, though."

Travis eyed her over his prime rib. "Did I say something wrong?"

"I thought you understood. I'm planning to restore the house and preserve our family's heritage."

"I can't speak for Katie," he said, "but don't preserve it for me. The way I look at it, I have all those memories and heritage in here." He tapped his chest.

Discouraged, her shoulders slumped. Travis was a grown man now, with his own life and motivations, but she had hoped her children would want the property. Instead, they had no interest.

"It'll buy you a lot of security in your elder years, Mom. My recommendation is to sell it. That's all."

Sue looked down at the filet mignon cooling on her plate. "You sound like the other owner. Rafael."

"What do you know about him?"

"He's a local developer, so he only sees it from that perspective. Although he's already rolling in money."

"You could be too," said Travis. "You could live in Paris."

"I haven't thought about that in years."

When the kids were little, she had tried to get them interested in painting by hanging up pictures of the Eiffel Tower and farmers' markets in Paris. But Katie only wanted to mother her dolls, and Travis liked blowing things up.

Travis set down his fork. "I'm moving to Dubai in a couple months."

Anxiety surged through her. "Why so far?"

"It's the chance of a lifetime. One of Dad's old buddies invited me, and it pays like crazy. So I definitely don't need the money. And I'd like to see you indulge yourself, for once."

"I never went without. Your dad took very good care of us."

"Monetarily."

Sue bristled. "He couldn't be with us as much as he wanted. You know that. The government—"

"Yes, I know. And I appreciate how much you put up with. Dad was lucky to have you." He glanced at his watch. "I have a meeting in an hour."

"So late?"

"It's early where they are." Travis folded his napkin next to his plate and signaled to the waiter. "Mom, as far as the property goes, I'd like to meet this guy. Size him up."

"Why?"

"Maybe I can figure out an angle. It's what I do."

"Travis, what *do* you do?"

He smiled just like his dad.

"Oh no, you're not, are you?"

"Only on the paperwork end. Don't worry."

At the house, he walked her to the back door. She kissed his cheek. "Can you stop by for breakfast?"

"Briefly."

"I'll have Mr. Palacios here for you to interview. But no waterboarding, okay?"

"I promise."

Chapter Thirty-Three

The next morning, she opened the door to Rafael holding a bouquet of flowers.

"They're beautiful."

"As are you." Rafael took her in his arms. "When does your son arrive?"

"Any minute." Sue was relieved that he seemed back to his old self, lighter. Happy.

When their kiss ended, he looked around the bare living room. "You've been working."

Excited about Travis's visit, Sue had risen before dawn to sweep and mop. "These floors are original pavers brought from Mexico in the 1920s. Didn't they clean up nicely?"

Rafael sighed.

They both turned at the sound of a car in the driveway. When the door opened and Travis unfolded his long frame and stood, Sue beamed with pride.

After the hugging was finished, Travis eyed Rafael. The two men were about the same height, one dark-skinned, one white with blond hair. But they both had that air about them, Sue thought. Male posturing. They studied each other, neither smiling.

And then Rafael said something in Spanish, and Travis cracked a grin. They shook hands.

Sue brightened. "Anyone hungry for breakfast?" While she assembled a meal of scrambled eggs and bacon, Travis and Rafael discussed the current political situation in Central America, debating the merits and expected longevity of this politician and that regime.

When the eggs were ready, Travis jumped up to help serve. Setting the plates on the table, he said, "Mom tells me you two disagree over the property."

Rafael rose and brought over the coffee pot. "We'll work it out."

"I told her I think it's too much for her." Travis scooped a forkful of eggs. "I encouraged her to sell and chase after her dreams."

"This is my dream," said Sue.

"There are other properties just as nice," Rafael said. "I would like to show you one on the other side of the Mesa. It is smaller than this but with a beautiful view."

"I'm not interested in buying an alternate property."

"Not buy." Rafael set down his fork. "I will give it to you in exchange for this one."

"Do we have to discuss this now, in front of my son?"

Travis shrugged. "May as well, Mom."

"See? He agrees," said Rafael.

"He didn't say that."

"At least see it," said Travis. "Keep an open mind. You never know."

"Fine. For you, I will."

"Ouch," said Rafael.

When their meal ended, Travis helped clear the dishes. "I'm glad I was able to stop by. I'll call you when I get back to DC."

As he drove away, Sue and Rafael stood in the front yard like an old married couple, waving at the vanishing car.

"Is this a good time to see the property I mentioned?" asked Rafael.

"Let's get it over with."

"I appreciate your positive attitude. I'll wait out here."

* * * * *

As HE DROVE, RAFAEL WAS PREOCCUPIED, and not just with Susan's unhappiness. Travis was the approximate age of Natalia, reopening the hurt again. He wondered if she was happy, if she was married.

If he had grandchildren.

His daughter was hidden from him, as she had been when Isabel took her. The bile rose in his throat. He had been a shitty husband, but lifetime banishment was unfair.

He wondered, if he were to approach her after so much time, would she want anything to do with him? Would she even speak to him? Or would she think him a coward for staying away so long?

"Where is this property of yours?" Sue's voice brought him back.

"There are three." He turned off the highway down a residential road.

At the first home, in an older neighborhood, they got out and peered in the windows. It was a midcentury design, with lots of small rooms dividing up the space.

"I'd want to knock down some of the walls," she said.

Rafael's spirits lifted. "We could do that, no problem."

"But why bother when I already have the perfect house?"

He deflated. "I have more."

They returned to the truck.

"The next one is in a private community down this road."

The guard at the gatehouse waved as the transponder on his truck opened the gate. They drove into the neighborhood. The custom homes, mostly one-stories, sprawled over large lots decorated with saguaros, ocotillos, and bright yellow and pink lantana.

"What do you think so far?"

"It's fine."

"Is that all?"

It was one of the priciest gated communities in Sedona. He pulled up to a striking faux-adobe home with a beautifully wrought copper and turquoise front door. A rock waterfall adorned the walkway.

"Rafael..."

"You don't like it."

"There's no room to breathe. The houses on this street are practically on top of each other."

He had expected that. Compared to the Mesa, anything would seem close. "Let's look at the last one."

Passing one of the planet's most famous red rock formations, he turned left, drove into a country club neighborhood, and continued through winding lanes to the very outskirts of the community. There, a cement driveway looped through a small pine grove to a home overlooking the golf course and the pinnacles beyond. It was such a beautiful property, he would live there himself.

"It's quiet. It's private. The neighbors are far away," he pointed out.

Sue didn't answer.

"Look at the mature trees and the landscaping." He turned off the motor. "You have to admit it's beautiful."

"It's nice."

"I can show you the inside. It's a spectacular layout. You could turn any of five rooms into a studio for your paintings."

Sue stared at the entrance for a moment before shaking her head. "This was a mistake. I apologize for wasting your time."

"You don't even want to look?" He rested his arm on the truck's window sill. "Is something wrong with it?"

"The orientation is very nice, and I'm sure the inside is beautiful. But I don't want something new with no history or heritage. I want my family's land and house."

"What about your son? He wants you to sell."

"He's unsentimental. Like his father."

Rafael scowled. He was surrounded by blockheads. He put the truck in gear, backed out, and dropped her off at home. "I have appointments in Scottsdale for the next few days. I'll call you when I return."

He left her standing in the driveway.

* * * * *

AFTER HE LEFT, SUE PULLED OPEN THE SHED DOOR, its rusty hinges creaking. She felt bad about letting Rafael drag her around to see homes she would never live in. The fact was, she'd done it for Travis, wanting to make him happy, wanting to be a cheerful, resilient mother. But the minute the truck hit the highway, she'd wanted to turn around. She just hadn't had the guts to admit it to Rafael, who seemed so upbeat and optimistic at the thought he might be winning.

In the dimly lit shed, she unearthed her father's ancient toolbox. Flipping open the metal clasps, she lifted the lid. Claw hammer, check. Phillips and regular screwdriver, check. Assorted wrenches and pliers, all there. When was the last time her father had touched these tools?

Biting back the sentiment, she set off for the bunkhouse with Gypsy trotting alongside.

On the creaky wooden porch, she went to work where the door had been nailed shut. Hefting the big hammer, she fitted it around a nail head and levered it out of the wood. She extracted three more, then pushed open the door, stepping back to let dust and dead spiders rain down.

The bunkhouse contained a main room with a kitchen, dining table, and fireplace, two small bedrooms, and a tiny bathroom. The kitchen had a sink, a stove with an oven, and cabinets containing mismatched dishware and silverware. The place where a refrigerator once stood was empty.

Mouse droppings lay everywhere. She backed out. The building was nasty, but that could be remedied. She could clean it up and renovate it, install new appliances and plumbing fixtures, and rent it out as an artist's retreat. The money she brought in would help pay for the improvements.

The rumble of a truck interrupted her thoughts. Looping Gypsy's leash around her wrist, Sue went to see.

It was John in his bashed-up work truck. Spotting Sue, he lifted his chin in greeting.

"I wasn't expecting you," she said.

"I know. I had a few minutes, and Rafe said you had a couple stacks in the back for me."

Sue led him to the pile of furniture in the backyard. "All this."

"Goodwill?"

"Unless you want to take it home with you."

"No thanks."

She stared at him, a thought blooming in her mind. The bunkhouse needed rehabilitation. John was an expert craftsman.

"What?" He stopped in front of her, his eyes unreadable behind dark black sunglasses.

"What would you say to helping me fix up the bunkhouse?"

"Place is a wreck."

"It's solid, though. All it needs is some carpentry, plumbing, electrical. Then I could rent it out as a bed and breakfast. That little income stream could help me pay off your boss."

"It's not a bad idea."

"So you'll let me hire you?"

"Nope."

"Is it the money? I'll pay you what he does."

"Not the money." John hefted an ottoman into the truck. "Rafe's got plans for the place that don't involve me fixing up the bunkhouse."

Rafe's plans. What about hers? Sue's jaw clenched. "If you won't do it, can you recommend somebody?"

His silence served as the answer.

"Guess I'll have to find somebody myself."

"Look." John wiped his forearm across his brow. "I would, but he's my boss and my friend. It wouldn't be right."

"I understand," Sue said. "I should have taken that into consideration."

"Anything else, you call me, I'll help."

"You wouldn't happen to have a winning lottery ticket?"

John shook his head, one side of his mouth curving up.

Sue plopped down on a stack of boxes. "I am stuck."

"Right now you are," John said. "But Rafe says you're smart, so you'll figure out something."

"I'm about out of ideas."

"Thing is," said John, "he's hardheaded, and he's been eyeing this property for a while."

"I don't know why. At a certain point, how much money does a person need?"

"Not my call."

"Well, it's my land, and I'm not moving. Whether he likes it or not."

"He doesn't." John climbed into the truck, waving one arm out the window at her as the dust rose behind him.

She kicked a rock from the path. Rafael held all the cards. And he'd been eyeing the property for a while, had he?

Her doubts growing, she texted him a message.

Chapter Thirty-Four

Across the canyon, the horizon disappeared into a bank of purple-gray clouds. Sweat beaded along her hairline in the humid air. Rafael drank a beer and glared across the canyon, his boots resting on the bunkhouse railing. Their monthlong truce was ending, and she had summoned him because she was tired of feeling stuck.

"We need to wrap this up," she said. "I asked you to walk away because it's my family's land, not yours, but you said no. I offered to buy you out—"

"Which you cannot afford."

"Which you will not discount, so I have any hope of affording," she clarified. "And I can't find a donor interested in using it as a tax write-off."

"As an alternative," he said, "I have tried to convince you to sell and let me make you a rich woman, but you said no.

And I offered to buy *you* out by offering you three different properties, all of which you rejected."

A sudden gust of wind whirled around them, whipping her hair into her face. She hooked it back behind her ears and stared glumly at the coming storm.

"We're at an impasse, Rafael. I can't see a solution that will work for us, and I hate that this came between us. We're perfect friends in every other way, but the way things stand, I don't see how we can even continue that."

"Why go to extremes?" He held out his hands. "We can still find a way to resolve this."

"I don't know what else to do. Talking isn't helping. You won't give an inch." She stood.

"And now you are rejecting me?"

She shrugged. "There's no alternative. We're on opposite sides of this fight. I can't fight you and love you both."

He jumped up and reached for her, a silly grin splitting his face. "You love me?"

She stepped back. "Metaphorically speaking."

"You love me." He laughed and hugged her. "This is perfect. We will fight, and we will resolve this issue, and it will all be okay."

It was ridiculous. It was foolhardy. Yet just for a moment, she allowed herself to weaken, to stop fighting. To press her cheek against his chest, close her eyes, and fantasize about the possibilities.

Thunder rolled in the distance. A breeze lifted her hair.

"It's going to pour." She pulled away. "We need to get inside."

The sky darkened. All morning, the air had been heavy with moisture, steamy hot with the coming monsoons. Now, the wind picked up, and the smell of desert rain blew in. Across the canyon, a curtain of leaden gray approached. Lightning flashed, followed seconds later by the crack and boom of thunder. Rain began to fall, big fat drops that splatted and then drenched the ground.

Rafael grabbed her hand, and they ran to the house, laughter mixed with terror, Gypsy skittering alongside. They flung themselves through the door, dripping wet.

"That was crazy!" Sue gasped. "I thought we—"

Rafael stopped her words with a kiss, deep and heartfelt and tasting of rain. Good, clean desert rain. He tasted like a miracle. She slid her hands under his shirt, up his chest.

He sighed.

Against her better judgment, or perhaps with a sense of finality, she led him to the bedroom for their own afternoon lightning storm.

When the power went out, plunging the house into darkness, Rafael lit candles while Sue made a snack of grapes, cheese, and crackers. They ate in bed with the sheets pulled up, feeding each other and talking about their families. Sue spoke of Travis and his looming move to Dubai and of Katie and her demands that Sue live near the family to help with the children.

He spoke of his daughter and wanting to go to her in Buenos Aires.

"You should definitely try," Sue said. "Her mother kept the two of you apart. Natalia will understand."

He kissed Sue, his lips lingering on hers. "I don't know. I'm not sure I should even attempt this. What if all I do is upset her? I've been doing a lot of that lately."

"I think she would want to hear from you. She has nothing to lose."

Rafael listened, his eyes reflecting the candlelight as she spoke. For all the warmth in his touch, it felt like their last night together. He may have felt it, too, in the tenderness with which he fed her, kissed her, and touched her skin.

He brushed her hair back from her face and carried the food tray to the dresser. "I must leave," he said. "I have an early start in the morning..." His phone chimed with a text, and he read it, frowning. He looked down at her, his brows knitted.

"Rafael, what's wrong?" Sue pulled the sheet up to her throat.

He glared at her, eyes narrowed. "You are planning to picket my business? To say to the media that I am unethical?"

Sue groaned. Berkeley Novak. "That awful woman."

"What was your intention? To make me look bad to my clients?"

"I said it as a joke, weeks ago. I was frustrated. I didn't mean it."

He paced the room. "Not that I'm worried. My work speaks for itself."

"Come on, Rafael. I wasn't serious."

"According to Berkeley, you were very serious."

"She's a troublemaker. She wants you and is doing this to sabotage me."

"I have to leave." He pulled on his slacks.

She flung his shirt at him. "I can't believe you don't trust me."

"I don't trust anyone." Rafael pulled on his shoes and left.

Sue watched him splash through the rain puddles to the truck, slam the door, and back out. How could he be so upset over Novak's text?

How could he mistrust her to this extent, after they'd grown so close? Maybe he needed an out, an excuse, something he could tell himself, a reason to let her go. A way to extricate himself.

She flopped into a chair on the wet patio, not caring about the dampness. The air was rich with the fragrance of the soaking desert. An owl called out to its mate, who answered in kind. The last raindrops splashed off the roof.

There was no solution, and what might Rafael try now? He could take her to court, he could threaten her with endless litigation—not that he would, and she thought he wouldn't want to engage in warfare any more than she did.

But it could be ugly, and she didn't know what to do.

He'd left in anger, believing Novak's lie, believing Sue would stick a knife in his back. Maybe she didn't know Rafael as well as she'd thought.

She could give up, sell the place, take the money and live anywhere. Travis didn't want the land, and Katie was too wrapped up in her own problems to care. Her children were the legacy. The Mesa was just a place.

But not to her.

Here on the Mesa, Sue felt a sense of sanctuary. She had lived in dozens of locales but had never felt the sacred peace she felt on this stretch of red Arizona dirt. She hated the idea of it being cut up and sold.

Tipping her head back, she gazed up at the heavens. The clouds had parted, leaving diamond points in a black velvet sky. If Roseanne had intended to torture them both, she was making a good effort.

"You think you're so smart," Sue whispered, "but you are not going to win this time."

* * * * *

DRIVING HOME, RAFAEL WAS BESIDE HIMSELF. He hadn't expected Sue to go behind his back, to try to sabotage his business.

Berkeley Novak was unreliable, though.

But Sue had admitted it, calling it a joke. Maybe it was, but the thought had crossed her mind. What other strategies had she dreamed up to get her way?

And he had been on the verge of giving up his half, just to keep her happy. Thankfully, he hadn't confessed that to her. In a tender moment, it was on the tip of his tongue, but a lifetime of harsh experience held him back.

And it proved out. Now, they would have to go to the mat. What that involved, he didn't know, but he was bound and determined to extract half the value of the property for himself.

The streets were still flooded from the downpour. He drove rashly, throwing up water as he plowed through puddles on the way to his office.

He had beaten the militia as a boy. He could beat this problem too. All he needed to do was come up with the one shining option she could not refuse.

He turned into the parking lot. The rain was moving off,

the drops fewer on his windshield.

Until tonight, Rafael had begun to imagine a life with Susan. They would sell the Mesa and fund the rest of their wealthy, happy life. They could live in his house and travel the world, with John and Matt running things with his distant oversight. Never before had he entertained, even for a second, the idea of cutting back on work, but Susan had gotten into his head and given him ideas.

Into his heart.

And once again, it hurt. He had hoped to protect himself. He had failed.

At the office, John listened, his bald head glinting in the overhead lights. "I thought she was different."

"You and me both."

The two men sat silently, immersed in their own thoughts.

Rafael leaned back, his chair creaking. He rested one booted foot on a box. "I thought we could work out a solution, but it is impossible."

"Then let it go."

"I don't know if I can."

"She hasn't kicked you around enough yet?"

"Well." Yes, she had.

But John's perspective was warped. He had his own problems with women. Mostly, they were afraid of him. So he acted like he was fine living alone in his isolated cabin in the Arizona outback.

Rafael stared at the wall. Damn Roseanne. If only she had left it all to him. He and Sue would never have quarreled. The cursed Mesa property that stood in the way of their love—he blanched at the word, but it was the right one—he wished he had never heard of it.

But if it hadn't been for Roseanne's machinations, he would never have met Susan. He would have missed out on her warmth, her wit, her levelheadedness. She spoke honestly to him, without the pretense he was used to. Strong, lovely, and sexy. He had been wrong to take Novak's side.

John was right. He was in trouble.

But so was Susan. She was suffering as much as he. This torture had to come to an end in some way. He had no idea how.

Because he wanted them both—Susan and the land.

Chapter Thirty-Five

A few days later, Sue phoned his office. She hadn't been sleeping, she hadn't been eating, and depression was a consideration. But she had to move forward with her idea. "Don't tell him it's me," she said to Gabriela.

"Are you sure? He's been moping around here for days."

Poor baby, Sue thought with a grimace. Rafael was about to get a shot at fixing everything. If only he would go along with her new idea.

There was a moment of silence before Rafael barked a hello. When he realized who it was, his tone softened. "I've missed you."

The warmth in his voice reminded her of all their nights together, their afternoons watching the storms come in, their mornings rushing off to an adventure. Hiking, picnics, the balloon ride, the helicopter. Finding out about his family. Dining under the stars on his patio.

But the promise of the relationship was gone. "I have another proposal," she said. "Can I drop by your office?"

At first, he was flustered, but Rafael quickly pivoted. "Don't come here. Let's have dinner, my love. We must see each other at Paloma."

They agreed he would pick her up at seven. Sue set the phone on the kitchen counter, her hand shaking. At her feet, Gypsy whimpered. That was new. Ever since arriving in Sedona, the little animal had settled down. At first, Sue thought it was Roseanne, perversely. But in the weeks they'd been at the Mesa, Gypsy had transformed into a new dog. She never had accidents inside anymore and, despite her size, strutted around the property like a guard dog. And the two of them had bonded, tuned into each other's moods.

"You always know, don't you?" Sue picked her up and planted a kiss on her little head.

That evening, she dressed in a business outfit for dinner at Paloma. Her goal was to keep Rafael's mind on work, not romance. When he appeared at her door, his face radiated joy. As it did every time he looked at her, whether she wore a dressy outfit or filthy work clothes.

She would miss that.

"You look so beautiful." He came in for a kiss, but she turned her head, and it landed on her cheek.

Like siblings instead of lovers.

Undeterred, he handed her into his car, gallant to the last.

The hostess seated them, gave them each a menu, and departed. Rafael reached for Sue's hand. "I have missed you, Susan."

She focused on their hands, the warmth and strength of his. The silver bracelet, which he never removed. She slipped a finger between the metal and his skin. "Tell me about this."

"It is nothing. A memento." He let her go and reached for the menu.

Okay, then. She did the same, but the words meant nothing. Why was he so guarded, even after they'd been so close?

It didn't matter.

Because they had no future.

Rafael was staring out the window. When he turned back, she saw pain in his eyes.

Which he quickly masked with a deflection. "I spoke with Flo this morning. She is talking about taking a cruise with her attendant."

"With Eric? I don't think that's wise."

"Nor do I."

The server took their orders and slipped away.

They continued speaking of work and acquaintances, avoiding the tension Sue felt crackling through her veins. They pretended nothing was wrong, delaying the inevitable. But when dinner was over, Sue said, "Rafael."

"Yes, my love."

She winced a little at the endearment. How she wished she could hear it forever. And she would, but after tonight, only in her memories. "I want to tell you about my last proposal." She withdrew the canvas from its carrying case.

Determined to convince Rafael, she had drawn an illustration of the Mesa house as it might look after restoration. She had painted for hours, recreating the property as it was in the last century, but with a modern twist, showing what she could do with it if she had the chance. If they gave it up—both of them.

The corrals, bunkhouse, smithy, and stables were portrayed as studios, workplaces where artists could live and breathe their art. The courtyard at the front of the house was restored as a garden, with a vine-shaded ramada over the entry door.

Sue depicted well-dressed couples strolling through the gardens under twinkling lights, the expansive front yard decorated with native plants, fountains, and seating areas all the way to the bunkhouse. Waiters circulated with trays of beverages and appetizers prepared in the ranch house kitchen. She drew couples dancing and flirting, wandering hand-in-hand along the paths. She could see every detail, having already built the vision in her head. Sue painted a magical picture of what the Mesa could be if she were persuasive enough. If she were powerful enough. If she could move him, once and for all.

He studied the painting, his eyes moving from one spot to another as if taking in each detail. When he looked up, his face was tortured. "This is your original vision. The one you told me about at our first lunch."

"Right after Roseanne died. Yes." Under the tablecloth, Sue's hands shook. She clenched them into fists. "This is the optimal use for the property."

"That depends on one's objective."

"I'm asking you to walk away, and I will as well."

"From the land, my love?" Rafael handed back the painting. "Or from us?"

"I—we—" Sue swallowed. "I don't want to lose you."

Holding out his hands, he took both of hers. "We don't need to lose each other."

"So you'll relinquish your claim?"

He gave her hands a squeeze and shook his head. "I'm sorry."

"You have no right."

"That is incorrect, and this argument is tiresome."

"Rafael, you have all the money in the world! Why do you need more?"

He leaned forward. "You think I am a bad person, selfish. This is untrue, but I won't waste time trying to change your opinion."

Sue folded her napkin. "Roseanne must be laughing in hell."

They sat in silence for a few minutes. She looked out the window, racking her brain for another way to persuade him, feeling desperate.

"This is a complete mess." Sue saw no other option but to cart off what she could, make a digital album of the place, and sell it. "I'm exhausted. I'm out of ideas."

"There is one we haven't explored."

She looked up, hope and trepidation warring with each other. "What?"

"We could be married."

She choked on her water.

He frowned. "Why do you laugh?"

Sue waved him off, coughing. "How would that change anything? You'd still want to sell."

"But I am offering you half-interest in all my properties. No prenup. You would be fantastically rich."

"Rafael, I'm not doing a merger. If I ever got married again, it would be for love, not business."

He held out his hand.

She ignored it.

"I've hurt you," he said.

"Not at all." But he had. Deeply. "I've enjoyed your company. You are the most romantic of men. But this is it. Your proposing marriage to solidify a material gain—that's it."

"*Bella*, listen to me. You once suggested I retire and enjoy life. I have never stopped working, ever since I was a boy. But after we marry, we can buy a magnificent home together and travel all over the world. Does this idea appeal to you at all?"

"I've traveled enough. I want a home. A permanent one." They didn't even see eye-to-eye on their future plans.

He leaned forward. "We're so good together. You know this."

Her blood heated as she remembered their lovemaking. She had to look away.

"See?" he said. "You want it also."

"It doesn't matter what I want." She reached for her painting. "Please take me home."

He inclined his head, signed for the check, and delivered her to the front door. Wrapping her in an embrace, he held her, his warmth enveloping her. She longed for them to be together, but it couldn't happen.

He drove away, leaving her standing on the front porch, staring at his dust.

Chapter Thirty-Six

Sue wandered through the house, Gypsy clicking along behind her. At the end of the hall, she opened the door to her parents' room, now empty because she hadn't taken the time to move in. Maybe she never believed she would, doubting it would ever happen. So the room was cold, clean, and bare. Sue choked back the lump in her throat. She had never missed her mother and dad more than this moment when the entire homestead was slipping away.

The house would be razed. This was the last she'd see of it.

All because of Rafael.

She turned off the light and wandered to her old bedroom, now clear of the motorcycle, thanks to John. She had emptied the bookshelves her dad had built right into the wall. Sue ran her fingers over the surface, feeling the little dings and dents the wood had suffered over the years. She'd helped her father build the unit, six feet tall and eight across. They'd drilled holes and crafted pegs to anchor the shelves. Sue had stained the entire bookcase in a warm oak tint.

Now, it would go under the blade as well.

Tears prickled her eyes as she continued the tour. To Roseanne's bedroom, to the den, to the dining room and kitchen. Here stood a handcrafted kiva fireplace. There, an altar was built right into the wall to accommodate a statue of Jesus. The spot was vacant now, but she would have found a replacement if she were allowed to remain.

Bile rose in her throat. It wasn't fair. What Roseanne had done, pitting Sue against a greedy developer—whom she'd so badly underestimated!—was a crime. A crime against her family, against their history. It broke her heart.

It pissed her off.

And it served her right. She was the old fool who let another man into her heart. This was her punishment.

Mike had been the best. They'd had a whole lifetime together. What more did she want? What more could she expect? Rafael was the flashy lure, and she'd bit.

As he'd expected. As he had, no doubt, intended. Seduce the lonely widow and make a bundle off the land.

Furious, she paced the silent house, seeing her life in its entirety, the whole sixty-some years of it, corrupted by this foolish act. When one of Gypsy's toys happened to find itself in the path of Sue's ire, she hauled off and kicked it. The dog scurried for cover as the little stuffed bear flew up to the ceiling in a perfect arc, landing atop a floor lamp.

Sue was living there to prepare the handoff, that was all. Then she would go back to the vanilla world of Golden Era and try to make a future for herself. All because of Roseanne throwing a wrench into the machinery of her family history and screwing things up for her with that awesome man she cared for.

Had cared for.

Sue hardly realized she'd arrived in the bedroom that served as her studio, but seeing the blank canvas in front of her, a fire lit in her belly. Grabbing a number-four brush, she slashed three blazing swaths of harsh vermilion across the white expanse. Stepping back in surprise, she eyed the bright bands of color, made real as if her anger had taken on actual shape and hue. Returning to her work, she swiped colors over the red—burnt umber, deep yellow, harsh orange.

Rafael had tricked her in the beginning, gazing at her with naked admiration, showing her the delights of her body—oh, how she'd missed that!—and even hinting he loved her.

She dipped the brush tip into a pot of Mars Black and flung it at the red.

Rafael had been playing her, lying, acting out a part. In the end, it was only ever about the land and the deal, the money.

He conned her, and she fell for it. Just like Roseanne, bringing her here with the lure of the land. Just like her mother, who lied to Sue while giving away her savings.

With a guttural howl, Sue slashed bold strokes across the canvas, losing herself in color and motion, flinging paint without thinking, driven by pure anger. She flung drops of black across the red, then threw the brush across the room and smeared the paint with her bare hands.

Let it out, Marissa had said, and that's what Sue did. She let out her demons to scratch and burn. The shadows moved, and the light changed, and the paint kept flying. The only thing in her head was rage. Everything had been stolen from her, yet again. As she'd feared. As she'd expected.

She painted, and cursed, and cried, and painted some more. Night fell. The hours passed without her noticing.

By the time she came to her senses, dawn was breaking across the distant canyon lands. Her back ached, and her arms felt leaden with fatigue. At some point in her frenzy, she had switched on a lamp.

In her exhaustion, she had no sense of what she had created.

Now she looked, and her heart thudded. With its bands of demolition black and nuclear meltdown red and vomit orange, the painting was a firehose of grief and fury and— this realization made her smile—raw power.

It was an abomination.

It was brilliant.

Sue didn't care if it made people puke and rage. She loved it.

Lifting one tired arm, she extended her thumb and thrust her print onto the wet corner of the painting. Then she drew a tiny yellow star on top of her thumbprint.

Eventually, Sue would get over him, and Sedona, and her parents and Roseanne, and the lost promise of the Mesa, one way or another.

But now, all she wanted to do was sleep. She took Gypsy outside, waiting in the cool of dawn for the dog to finish her business.

It wasn't until noon that Sue awoke. Standing in front of the painting, her breath caught.

A primal scream captured in paint; it was raw, furious, and brutal. The paint wasn't applied so much as scorched onto the canvas, colors streaking every which way with predatory velocity. It was awful.

But it was cathartic.

Therapy was ugly. She would need a lot of therapy in the coming months to help her get over this last great chance at love.

And to resign herself to savoring what had been.

Chapter Thirty-Seven

Marissa stood in front of the canvas, one hand over her mouth.

"Well?" Sue felt embarrassed. She wished her friend would say something.

Shaking her head, her gait uncertain, Marissa stumbled out the back door to the bench in front of the Virgin.

Wind chimes tinkled in the pines. A road runner trotted hopefully after a baby lizard at the edge of the yard.

"You okay?" Sue sat down beside Marissa and gave her a sideways hug.

"Man, that was freaky. I don't know what happened. I took one look at that, and all of a sudden, these horrible memories of my childhood started coming back. All I felt was this overwhelming grief."

"I'm so sorry."

"It was so weird. I hadn't felt this way for years. I thought I was over it."

"Do you feel like talking about it?"

Eyes squeezed shut, Marissa dropped her head in her hands. "When I was eleven, my father beat my mother. It wasn't the first time, but it was the worst. He almost killed her. She finally, finally pressed charges, and he went to prison."

Sue rubbed her friend's back with gentle circles.

Marissa continued. "After Mom got out of the hospital, she was different. She couldn't take care of herself or me. We moved in with my aunt, but she had her own kids, and we were a burden to her. And she was pissed at Mom because she'd been warning her for years. So they had issues. Anyway, it was a horrible way to grow up. And then, when I was a teenager, I found a man just like Daddy and got my own beatings."

"That's heartbreaking," said Sue.

"So that's how me and Franny met. I went to a domestic violence shelter in Cottonwood, and she was there, helping. She still works there, although her husband doesn't like it."

"You two have been friends for a long time."

Marissa nodded. "She's like a second mother to me."

The two women sat quietly for a few minutes. Then Marissa said, "Looking at that painting, it all came back, and I felt like I wanted to die."

"I know," said Sue. "It's a monstrosity. I should burn it."

"Are you crazy?" Marissa stood, swiping away her tears. "I'm hanging it in my store. That sucker's gonna make us a mint."

After Marissa and the abomination had left, Sue painted another version of the Mesa, one that divided it in half. One that made her cry. But it would benefit the town and help her salvage this mess. Tomorrow she would meet with Flo and find out if such a division were even legal or possible. If it worked, it would kill her, but at least somebody would benefit.

Even if it wasn't her.

At the bakery the next morning, Flo eyed the painting. "You're getting better at landscapes."

"Not like it matters," Sue grumbled.

The server came by to take their orders. Sue chose tea and a cookie.

Flo ordered lemonade. "I don't trust tea anymore. It doesn't seem to agree with me."

"How so?"

"Puts me right to sleep." Flo gave a wry smile. "I know. You'd think the opposite, wouldn't you? But when you get old, everything changes. I never know what this old body's going to surprise me with."

Sue looked at her with concern. "But you're healthy, right?"

"Much as I can be, I guess." Flo studied the painting. "Your idea is a good one. It'll be good for Rafael and the shelter, I mean. Not so much for you."

"It's my only remaining option." Sue set the canvas aside. "Is it feasible?"

"It is," said Flo. "But I'm disappointed. I had hoped you two could come to an agreement."

"He offered to marry me."

"You turned him down?"

"I had to. He was only after my land."

"Do you really believe that?"

Sue shrugged.

"I am sorry to hear that, honey." Flo reached over and took Sue's hand. Gave it a squeeze. "But don't give up. Maybe that man'll pull his head out before it's too late."

"I think it's already too late."

The door opened with a little scrape, and an elderly gentleman came in. A straw fedora and spectator sunglasses topped a lean frame.

Flo broke into a big smile. "Afternoon, Albert."

"How's my desert rose?" The old gent leaned down and planted a kiss on Flo's cheek. "Getting hungry yet?"

"I will be soon." Flo introduced the two of them. "I sold Albert one of those new condos in town. We'll be enjoying happy hour on his patio later if you care to join us."

"I've got other plans, thanks."

"Pitching Mr. Palacios?" Flo nudged her with a gentle elbow. "Good luck. And if need be, I'll help you with the legal docs."

"That's very kind of you."

Flo winked. "He won't think so."

Leaving the bakery, Sue steeled her spine and headed for his office.

Gabriela looked up when Sue came through the door.

"Is he in?"

Attempting to cover her surprise, Gabriela headed down the hall to his office. When she returned, Rafael was right behind her.

"*Corazon,* you came." He kissed her on the cheek, one eye on the bundle under her arm. Sadness flickered in his gaze. "What do you have? Another presentation?"

She gripped the canvas, which was wrapped in butcher paper. "Can we speak privately?"

"Of course." He led the way down the hall and into his office. "Make yourself comfortable. Would you like something to drink?"

Sue placed the wrapped canvas on his desk. "No."

He turned at the sharpness in her tone. Reaching for her hands, he unclenched her fists. Her palms were gray, the creases black. "What happened here?"

"Nothing." Breaking free of his grasp, she unwrapped the canvas and propped it on his desk.

He peered at it, frowning. "This is what you would propose? You want me to get the front half, and you're giving the back to"—he squinted at the painting—"some charity? Who is the lucky one?"

"Doesn't matter."

"Cutting it in half—no. This will ruin the value of the property."

"You'll still get the front half."

"It isn't fair to you."

"That depends on what a person values."

"Susan, are you serious? Is this final?" He reached for her, but she held up a hand.

He walked over to his wall of windows. Facing the red rock formation, he remained silent as the minutes ticked away on the wall clock.

Fearing he'd throw another wrench, her stomach did a painful dip. This idea wasn't her choice, it was breaking her heart, and if he wanted to escalate, it would flat kill her. "This is my final offer, Rafael. If you don't accept it, we'll let the courts settle the matter. I'll argue that you conned Roseanne and that she wasn't in her right mind." She bit her lip. "I don't want to. It will destroy me."

"And me as well." He turned away from the window. "I accept your terms."

"You do?"

He inclined his head. "I will tell Flo and have her draw up the paperwork."

"She already knows."

"The two of you worked around me?"

"Out of necessity."

Rafael stared at the canvas. "I wasn't expecting this. I don't like it."

"I don't either."

"Is this final?" Rafael looked up at her, his face a mask of longing. "Will you remain here in Sedona, at least?"

"I'll be returning back to California."

Rafael gathered her in his arms, and she choked back a sob. For a moment, there was no sound, just his heartbeat against her ear. Regret nearly overwhelmed her.

"You know I wanted us to be together," he said. "We still could."

She closed her eyes, then broke away. "Too much water under the bridge, Rafael. I will always hate you a little."

"But you will always love me as well."

* * * * *

RAFAEL STOOD FROZEN, WATCHING HER WALK AWAY and trying to get through his head what had just happened.

Gabriela brought in a stack of papers for him to sign. "Remember, you have that meeting in an hour with the city manager in Flagstaff. You should probably get going."

"Tell him I can't make it."

"Do you want me to reschedule?"

"I don't care."

Gabriela slipped out, quietly closing the door behind her.

Rafael didn't notice. He should have been a little bit happy, at least. He had gotten half the land—the front half, the good half, which would bring in a lot of money.

He told himself that what he'd had with Sue was a fling, nothing more. It was what he did. Have fun, move on.

Outside his door, phones rang. Voices murmured. Commerce continued. Another afternoon passing as usual, in the normal pursuit of business.

He stared out the window. Breaking it off with Susan was for the best. It would interfere with his thoughts for a little while, but in a few days, he wouldn't even remember why he'd felt so distracted. Their entanglement had been the natural outcome of two attractive people forced into close proximity for a while. Animal magnetism, nothing more. Hadn't he been drawn to beautiful women before? In some cases, even mooned over them—privately, of course, not that they would ever know. Even, in one or two cases, deeply regretted the loss of their company. But in the end, it was correct.

He had dodged a bullet. He told himself it was a relief. That he loved his life and had everything ticking along just as he wanted it. Fortunately for him, Susan would pack up and head back to California, and he could return to his routine.

Which he loved.

Usually.

Shoving paperwork into his briefcase, he snapped it closed, wrenched open his door, and stomped out of the office. Four-wheeling in his truck, taking a forest trail, Rafael vented his frustration on the road, gunning the motor through the curves, flying over the ridged washboard.

When he skidded to a stop in John's front yard, the big man was standing on the porch. "Saw your dust. Want a beer?"

It wasn't yet noon, but Rafael took the frosty bottle from him. They flopped into the rocking chairs on John's sprawling porch. Rafael told him the news.

"Probably better this way," said John.

Rafael glowered at the red earth.

John laughed. "Old Roseanne is having her fun, isn't she? Stuck it to you both."

"One would draw that conclusion." Rafael sipped his beer. Truly, Roseanne was having the last laugh. "Of course, she is dead, and we are alive. It doesn't seem that she would have wanted it that way."

"Don't sell her short. Those long days she was hangin' on, holdin' off the Grim Reaper, she was figuring out your number."

"I will never understand."

"Women. Don't even try." John reached out his beer bottle and clinked the glass against Rafael's. "I have a personal rule, old buddy. Three dates. That's the max.

Where it redlines, you know? In the future, you might consider it."

Rafael grumbled into his beer. He continued to be surprised at the degree to which he had been misled. Susan apparently didn't really love him, or she would have gone along with his plans. She could have been happy with any of a dozen alternative homesites. Instead, she rejected them and him.

When Sue had contacted him with her final offer, he was delighted, thinking it portended a future for the two of them. What a shock. But that was his mistake and simply a barometer of how far out of line he'd allow his emotions to go.

He shouldn't be surprised. In this way, she was consistent with the women he'd known. Why he had fallen for her, he couldn't even remember. Those glacial eyes and silver hair. She was a human iceberg. Their attraction, however strong, would have flamed out over time.

They always did.

Anyway, at least the matter of the property would be settled.

As John said, he simply needed to keep his guard up. He was right to be alone all these years, and he would return to that state. Alone and independent, master of his own destiny.

In the end, they had hugged, and he had watched her walk away. The memory of her lovely form retreating brought a lump to his throat. Angry again, he was tempted to fling the empty bottle across the yard.

"Dude." John cleared his throat. "You want a fresh one?"

Rafael held up his empty bottle. "I may need the whole case."

Chapter Thirty-Eight

The sound of furious knocking woke her, first on the front door of the house, and then inside her skull. Pulling a pillow over her head, Sue tried to ignore the racket.

The hammering got louder. Gypsy barked and galloped from room to room, her claws sliding against the tiles.

Also, she probably had to go out.

Grumbling, Sue dragged herself from the bed to the front door.

"Holy crap." Marissa stood on the porch, frowning. Behind her, Franny looked worried.

"What do you want?" Sue hung on the door, nauseated.

"Are you sick?" asked Marissa.

"I'm fine. I'm just processing things."

"You don't look fine." Marissa's head-to-toe scrutiny stopped at Sue's feet.

Which were covered with dried mud.

From her conversation in the backyard last night.

With the statue.

Actually, less a conversation than a vile string of curses hurled at a cement block.

Marissa looked back up at Sue's face. "Why haven't you answered your phone? I've been calling and texting."

Gypsy bolted past them, out the front door. The smell of dog poop lingered in the air.

"Ugh." Marissa pushed past Sue. "What the heck's going on?"

"Nothing." Sue shuffled after her. The last time she'd left the house, it was three days ago when she and Franny visited the women's shelter in Cottonwood.

Tucked behind a row of oleanders in a rundown commercial area, the shelter office looked like a boarded-up storefront. Franny had called ahead, and the director, Emile, a short man with blue eyes and an earnest smile, had unlocked the door and let them in.

The large empty room echoed with their footsteps. A desk stood in the corner, two folding chairs at its front. Taking a seat behind the desk, Emile leaned forward, arms folded. "You are looking well," he said to Franny. "How is life going for you?"

To Sue's surprise, the older woman blushed. "I'm managing."

"You said something about a donation?" Emile spoke with a soft voice and a vaguely-European accent.

"My friend's wondering if you want her house." Franny gestured at Sue.

Sue gulped and nodded. "I am. I have a place that might serve your families' needs." With a quivering voice, she described the property. When she brought out the painting of the mesa house, Emile's hand covered his mouth.

He looked up. "Are you serious?"

"Completely."

His eyes darted from the two women to the canvas and back to Sue. "I suspect this is a big sacrifice."

"It's for a good cause," she said. "The house has four bedrooms, three baths, and a big kitchen. Plenty of room for families."

"I don't know what to say." The director held the painting out in front of him.

"There's a backyard, with grass and shade," said Franny. "And it's protected by a cliff wall. There's only one way in and out."

"If that's not a problem." Sue was imagining fire regulations and other restrictions.

"It's perfect. So peaceful. Our families will benefit greatly." The director took off his wire-rimmed glasses and rubbed his eyes. "You cannot imagine how much this will help."

Sue swallowed past the lump in her throat. "What's the next step?"

"We have an attorney. Well, he's the local mechanic, but he has a law degree and does pro bono work for us. I'll have him get in touch with you."

"Okay." Sue stood up. It was almost too difficult. Her body weighed a ton.

Emile set the painting on his desk. "May I give you a hug?"

"Me, too," said Franny. The three of them had clung to each other, Sue biting back tears.

Now, slumped in a kitchen chair, watching as Franny and Marissa cleaned things up, her stomach turned over. All she wanted was to close the door and go back to bed.

After taking Franny home, she'd fallen into a dark pit. Hadn't left the house in days, let her phone die, didn't eat. If it weren't for Gypsy needing attention, she wouldn't have gotten out of bed at all.

Franny swept a pile of poop into the trash. Sue looked away in shame. The little dog stood by her ankle, the hair on the back of her neck raised as if she were a police K-9, or a wolf. Seeing Gypsy trying to protect her, Sue almost wanted to smile.

And then the dark curtain fell again. Saying goodbye to Rafael had brought back all the grief of losing Mike.

At first, life without her husband had seemed almost impossible. Even getting up out of bed in the morning felt like an Olympic feat. But she had kept at it, moving into the new phase of her life, even if it was somewhat mechanical. At least she was functioning. A stretch of weeks would go by, during which she'd act like a normal person, going through the routines of a day, but then from out of nowhere, grief would rise up and slam into her like a rogue wave, knocking her senseless. Especially in the late afternoons, when the light faded and night crept in.

But eventually, she'd adapted to being alone.

Mostly.

People didn't talk about it, but the second-worst part about losing your beloved spouse was having to continue on into the unknowable future alone.

For a few weeks, working and playing alongside Rafael, Sue had been distracted from that reality, maybe even thinking she'd found a good man to accompany her on that path. In a tender moment, Rafael confessed he'd considered cutting back on work, looking for his daughter, maybe even doing something good for his village in Guatemala. She fell under his spell, imagining a life where they pursued their goals together.

But that would never happen, not with him, anyway. They were done. It had been a fantastic month but it was over. Rafael had chosen the land over her. For all the romance and fun, nothing could compare to a multimillion-dollar payday.

Sue felt as if Rafael had torn her heart out, ripped it in two, and handed it back. Against all expectation, she had fallen in love. It wasn't just a word thrown out randomly at the bunkhouse on a stormy evening. She had fallen in love with his kindness, and humor, and industry. With his vulnerability, the way he kept himself apart to avoid pain.

Like her.

It was a different kind of love than with Mike. He had been her youthful sweetheart, the man she adored before she knew what she wanted. But now she was a fully-grown woman, old enough to know she couldn't fix what was broken in Rafael.

"It's okay to be sad," said Franny.

"Come on." Marissa took her by the arm. "We'll make breakfast while you shower."

"I'd rather go back to bed."

"Go get cleaned up. You'll feel better."

Shuffling blindly down the hall, Sue wasn't sure she wanted to feel better. Or if it was possible.

And then her friends insisted on a field trip to the Pit House.

Wearing a hat pulled down low and a pair of industrial-grade sunglasses, Sue wobbled, unsteady, near the four-century-old ruins. The structure stood just outside of town on national park land, basically a metal roof over what remained of a mud foundation. The ruins were particularly unimpressive when viewed through the lens of a hangover.

"Why did you bring me here?"

"Because you need perspective." Marissa rested her hands on the pipe railing that protected the site.

"You think that's what I need?"

"Think of what was happening here, four hundred years ago. Before airplanes, and cars, and even roads," said Marissa. "Think how quiet it must have been."

"How difficult," said Franny. "How hard their lives were."

Sue leaned on the railing, the metal cold under her elbows. "It never ends, does it?"

"That's what I mean," said Marissa. "Because we're not the only ones. Life is a struggle, but so what? It's that way for everybody."

"Like at the shelter," said Franny. "Life goes on. People help each other, and you keep chugging along."

Sue glanced at her friends. Franny was older than she, almost elderly. Marissa was young, about the age of Travis and Katie. Yet the two of them seemed so settled. Maybe it was the fact of their earlier struggles, but for whatever reason, now they were content.

"Breathe," said Franny.

Sue filled her lungs. Her head felt like a miner was in there with a pickaxe.

Marissa took off down the trail. "Follow me."

Groaning, Sue hiked after them. Leaving the pit house, they followed a path winding upward, past signs identifying native plants and their importance to the original peoples. The pathway ended at a cliff, bounded by a double set of safety rails. Far below, aquamarine water glimmered in a stream-fed volcanic lake. Remnants of cliff dwellings clung to the upper edges of the caldera.

"Montezuma Well," said Marissa. "Isn't it amazing to think they lived here?"

"So beautiful. Look at the color of that water," said Franny.

"I need to get out of the sun," said Sue.

They left the caldera for a rock staircase leading down into a shaded canyon where the air temperature dropped ten degrees. At the foot of the stairs, the path continued alongside a creek. It was an oasis in the heat of summer. The women perched on a stone wall, shaded by the trees and serenaded by birdsong. In the background, the creek gurgled and splashed.

Sue couldn't enjoy it. Her stomach was churning from too much alcohol, and her brain was fried from lack of sleep. She stared at the ground. "I feel so stupid."

"You took a chance," said Marissa. "That was brave."

"I should have known better. I feel like a patsy."

"Don't go down that rabbit hole," said Franny. "There's such a thing as being too careful, especially when you get older. It limits you. Fear builds on fear and pretty soon, you're afraid to leave the house."

"I know," said Sue. "You're right."

Franny stood and dusted off her backside. "I hate to break things up, but Gene will be wondering where I am."

After they dropped Sue off, she shuffled down the hallway to her bed, sick with fatigue. She barely had time to slip off her shoes before she fell into a deep sleep, dreaming of hiking and cliffs and stream-fed gardens.

When she awoke, hours later, she felt more like herself. Funny how therapeutic sleep was, she thought. How the mind and body worked together. And thank goodness for her friends.

And family. She needed to get in touch with her daughter.

Katie answered on the first ring. "I've been worried about you."

"Why?"

"Last time we talked, you sounded sad," said Katie.

"So did you."

"Mom, though, I fixed everything. Remember I wanted to go to that conference? Well, I did. I went. Jason did fine with the kids. The three of them had a blast, and so did I."

"Katie, I'm proud of you."

"I think I needed to get out of my own way," her daughter said.

"Tell me about it." Putting one foot up on a chair, Sue took a breath and explained her decision to donate the house to the shelter. "So I hope you're not bummed out, but I'll be returning to Visalia."

"Main thing is, you'll have company," said Katie. "Lots of people there your age."

"You're okay with me not moving into the casita?"

"I forgot to tell you! We rented it out to a college student in exchange for a little housekeeping and babysitting."

"You really are doing well, honey."

"And you," said Katie. "I talked to Travis right after he went to see you. He told me about that developer. Way to go, Mom."

"Oh. It's nothing." Sue blinked at the ceiling. "He's nobody."

"Travis said it looked like you guys were really close. Maybe it was wishful thinking."

"I still love your father."

"But he'd want you to be happy. We all do."

"Thanks, honey. I love you."

"Love you too, Mom."

After they hung up, Sue sat back, processing what Katie had said. Not only was she free to sell the property without guilt, but the kids were cool with her seeing another man.

The only problem was, that man was in the past.

Shoving back the chair, Sue wandered from room to room, remembering the little skirmishes she and Rafael had had, and the kiss, and then everything that followed. The balloon ride, the cave experience. Going up in the helicopter, and down into the basement where he showed her his carpentry. Learning about his family.

She stopped in her tracks. That poor man. What he must have suffered in his youth. And then to have his wife take their daughter away from him, forever.

Sighing, Sue went into the kitchen and poured a glass of wine in a plastic cup. She would go to the bunkhouse and toast one of her last sunsets here in this magical place, freezing her memories forever. Remembering her dreams of the mesa house.

And of Rafael.

On impulse, she grabbed the whole bottle.

Then, remembering the night she'd cursed the statue, Sue put it back. Instead of the bunkhouse, she went out the back door and sat on the bench at feet of the Virgin of Guadalupe.

Some of the flowers remained, although most had been hurled across the yard, some into the trees. That night, furious at her life, Sue had flung a streak of curses at the statue. Impervious, Mary had continued to smile vacantly, which made Sue even madder. She had wanted to take a shovel to the vapid figurine, but that would have required her to enter the shed in the dark, when black widows ran the place.

She hadn't been *that* drunk. The statue remained unharmed.

Now, Mary smiled benevolently down at her. Apparently, they were still friends after all the abuse. At the base of the statue, a red tea rose struggled, clinging to life. Feeling remorseful, Sue dropped to her knees to repack the soil, but what she really needed was more plants. And fertilizer.

"Stay," she told Gypsy, who was busy chomping on a clump of grass.

When Sue came back out of the house, she was carrying the bronze urn. Grabbing a hand shovel, she began to work the ash into the soil. "You have a second chance to do something productive," she told Roseanne. "Try to make it nice for the shelter families, okay?"

Gypsy stuck her nose under Sue's hand.

"I know," she said. "I sound like an insane person. It runs in the family." She stood up and brushed off her knees. With a final look back, she pointed her finger at the flowerbed. "I'll be checking on you. So, behave."

Chapter Thirty-Nine

Rafael did not like the solution, not one bit. But he was sick of dealing with the Mesa. He wanted to sell it, take his cut, and move on.

Like a shark, always moving in order to breathe.

And, of course, there was the fact he had promised Sue. Who was no happier than he about their arrangement.

Flo had called to say the paperwork was completed. She'd brought together Rafael and the director of the women's shelter, and both parties had agreed to the particulars of the division. The front half of the parcel would go to Rafael, the house and back half, to the shelter. A temporary fence would be strung across the two halves, followed by an eight-foot wall and a planting of cactus and oleanders. Palacios Construction would lay fresh gravel on the dirt driveway and wall it off for private access. A new driveway would be constructed where pine trees and manzanita currently grew. This new drive would serve the front house.

When the last document was signed and notarized, Rafael stood to leave, faking good cheer as all parties shook hands. Once the door locked behind him, though, he trudged to his car, the heat beating on his shoulders. The interior of the Corvette felt like an oven. Driving back to Sedona, heat refraction radiated over the baked highway, and dried grasses and weeds crumpled in the sun. In the far distance, too far away to expect any relief, clouds formed on the horizon, promising no rain this afternoon.

Only the burning, baking blue sky.

He idled through town, through the crowds that surged across the road regardless of traffic or the risk of heatstroke. These days, the tourist season never seemed to end.

Deciding to go straight home, Rafael slowly followed a beer truck through the curves. He considered turning on the radio but didn't have the energy to bother.

It was finished.

He thought he'd felt bad when Sue walked out his office door, agreeing with a final hug on the property division and the implied understanding it was the last he would ever see of her. But that was nothing compared to the bleakness he felt now.

He had gotten what he wanted, though.

Hadn't he?

The beer truck slowed to let a couple of bicyclists skirt the narrow shoulder before it rumbled onward. Rafael followed, tapping his fingers on the steering wheel, trying to rein in his impatience.

What would his future look like now without Susan in it?

Staring at the truck's bumper, he trundled up the mountain to his isolated lair.

Chapter Forty

A few days later, Marissa and Franny appeared for one last afternoon of painting. They'd picked up Flo on the way and now stood chatting about the division of the property.

"You're doing a good thing," said Flo.

"Rafael thinks I'm crazy."

"Actually, I think he saw the wisdom of it," said Flo.

Sue's stomach churned at the thought.

Franny nodded. "We're always short of beds. This will help."

Standing in front of her easel, Sue shrugged. "It felt good to do it. I mean, since I really don't have another choice. And the place seemed well-run. Very discreet."

"They have to be."

Returning to her easel, Sue flailed. Having promised Marissa she would try again, she still hated what she was painting, another landscape of the red rocks across the canyon. And she couldn't get it right.

"You clearly have the skills," Marissa said. "You just have to stick with it."

Sue didn't see the point. She couldn't find her groove. Bored with landscapes but not depressed or angry enough to do a slash-and-dab abstract, she was foundering artistically. In desperation, she had invited her friends to the Mesa today.

Dipping a brush, Franny leaned to the side and gently bumped shoulders with Sue. "You're my hero. The women coming through that shelter need a break. And Emile is as good and ethical as the day is long."

"I had no idea it was there," said Sue. "Did you see all the locks on that place?"

"Emile's careful. He's got a black belt in karate, and keeps a gun in his desk."

"One must be careful, but to what degree?" Flo sat on a nearby folding chair, a stylish sun hat shading her face. "That is the whole question."

* * * * *

THE WOMEN TURNED TO HER.

"Did something happen?" asked Sue.

Flo's sunglasses hid her eyes. "Just that I've been a fool."

"What are you talking about?" asked Franny.

Flo examined her manicure. The polish was chipped and faded. She balled her hands in her lap. "Eric was stealing from me."

The three women stopped in mid-brushstroke.

From the very beginning, Flo knew it was too good to be true. There was a man in her house, an attractive, capable young man with shaggy golden-brown hair, broad shoulders, and muscular thighs. Which she had been able to see in some detail through his gym shorts.

Not that she had been looking. For Pete's sake, he was barely thirty, if that.

While she sat at the dining room table like a queen, reading the paper and enjoying a cup of coffee—which he'd made—this god-like young man was doing her housework. If she wasn't paying him so well, she would feel guilty. Flo had always done her own housework, but Eric was there and willing.

After finishing the living room, he shut off the vacuum cleaner. Wrapping the cord, he looked at her with that cute grin and asked if she wanted more tea.

"You could top it off," Flo said.

He came up behind, leaning over her shoulder to refill her cup. She could smell his cologne, something young and vibrant. If she were fifty years younger...

Though Flo never really saw herself as an old woman. She was always surprised when she looked in the mirror. More often, she thought of herself as still in her forties or fifties, at the peak of her beauty.

Eric was smooth. He was fastidious about his grooming, spoke with diplomacy or humor as the circumstances required, and performed household duties as if it were an honor.

And the man could cook. Last night, he had prepared seared ahi on a bed of rice accompanied by teriyaki-flavored green beans with water chestnuts. The night before that, it was lobster tacos.

Returning from the kitchen, he had sat across from her, looking so earnest. "Florence, there's something I want to ask you. Absolutely no pressure. Don't feel as if you have to say yes."

Her heart melted. "What is it, Eric?"

He hesitated, then looked up. "May I play your piano?"

Flo placed a hand over her heart. She hadn't been able to play since her arthritis kicked in, and oh, how she missed it. "Please," she said. "Feel free."

He lifted the cover of the baby grand, pulled out the seat, and tried a few notes, warming up with a little ditty.

And then he cut loose.

Eric played classical, he played jazz, he played pop, he played an old country western tune that brought tears to her eyes.

As Flo listened to the notes pour out of her beloved old piano, she felt her life force returning. Her pulse quickened, and her senses took in every note with deep appreciation.

There was nothing the man couldn't do.

But Flo was eighty-five, and when her eyes drooped, she begged off and went to lay down for a few minutes.

The last thing she heard before drifting off was the squeak of her office door. That sound didn't fit, but as tired as she was, it was the last thing she registered before slipping off to dreamland.

But in the morning, for all her grogginess, she remembered.

"I got suspicious," she explained to the women. "It wasn't just that incident. I realized how much I'd been sleeping, and it didn't seem right. I wondered if he was drugging me and why. The only reason would be from wanting to steal from me. Sure enough, things were missing from my jewelry box. And I may be old and forgetful, but I know what I have and where I keep it, and it was gone."

"How did you catch him?" Marissa stood, paintbrush in hand, listening.

"Last Saturday afternoon when he brought my meds, I spit them out when he wasn't looking. Then I pretended to be asleep, waited fifteen minutes, and followed him." Flo lifted her chin. "I went out the back slider and snuck around to the garage's side door. He was getting ready to load Henry's tools into the trunk of his car."

"What'd he say?"

"Not a thing," Flo said. "He bolted when he heard me cock that old shotgun. I called the locksmith and changed all the locks. Doubt I'll be hearing from young Eric again."

"You need to report him," said Sue. "Otherwise, he'll just keep doing it."

"I know." Flo removed her sunglasses and polished them on her blouse. "It was a real come-to-Jesus moment. I was delusional. Why didn't you girls set me straight?"

"You seemed so happy with him," Marissa said.

"Oh, honey." Flo chuckled. "You thought I was enamored?"

"Well, sort of."

"You must have thought me an old fool."

Marissa's eyes widened. "You're not old. I mean, you're not a fool either. Oh, man. Just shut me up." She covered her face with a hand.

"I am old," said Flo, "and I have no problem with that. I also don't regret having a young Adonis running around my house, waiting on me hand and foot. I am bothered that he got away with my jewelry."

"Was it worth a lot?" asked Franny.

Flo put her glasses back on. "I have insurance. I just hate being conned."

"I'm always reading about how elderly people get ripped off," said Marissa. "It's a shame."

"Honey, a person can be stupid at any age. Stupidity is not the province of the old."

Sue dipped her brush into a plodding dull brown. "Will you be able to manage?"

"I'm getting by," said Flo. "It's not easy, but I take my time, and if it doesn't get done, it doesn't get done. But this has given me pause. I have to think about the future."

"Don't we all," said Sue.

Chapter Forty-One

Watching them disappear down the driveway, Sue bit her lip. When would she see them again?

Count your blessings, she told herself. *You're healthy. You're loved. The Mesa is going to a worthy cause.*

Sue stood in the driveway for a long time after they left. She was alone, but not lonely.

Her children and grands loved her, and so did her friends, including people she'd met in their many moves from base to base. Mike's remaining family, those cousins and other relatives scattered around the country, had always been friendly to her. In Visalia, despite her grief, she'd made a few friends.

Besides, her situation was nothing special. People died every day. All around her, widows went about their lives looking as if nothing had happened. They laughed, they shopped, they danced. They got their cars serviced. Life went on.

And it would for her too.

Perhaps the best blessing was that she'd been lucky enough to fall in love with a man who'd awakened her in every way. Love, at this stage of her life. Who would have guessed? Rafael was a good man, burdened with his own demons. She couldn't help him, and he couldn't help himself. Roseanne had placed them in an impossible situation, and he did what he had to do.

As would she.

She went back into the house, her footsteps echoing in the silence.

The thought of his touch, of snuggling in bed with him, even just slumbering beside him, the joy of working together, their picnics—the loss of all of it would leave a gaping hole in her heart. She would miss him every day for the rest of her life.

But she had moved on before, and she would now.

She padded down the hall to her studio, Gypsy's nails clicking on the tile floor behind her, and pulled out a new canvas. She sat in a chair and stared at it. For no good reason, she thought of the day she and Rafael floated in the balloon, the sweet silence broken only by the roar of the heater. They drifted silently over Arizona's red and green tablelands, and her heart had filled with the view of the land she loved so much. Where her roots were.

As Sue applied brush to canvas, she thought of how much she would miss Vicky and Flo, Marissa and Franny. In just a short time, they'd grown close. Marissa was like one of her kids but also a mentor to Sue as an artist. Franny intrigued her with her oddball marriage, and Vicky with her bawdy laugh and indomitable spirit. And Flo. Sue would always wonder how she was doing and worry about her.

Her brush seemed to move on its own, and unusual creatures took shape on the white surface. They were women in all sizes. Scrawny, fat, tall, short, some with wings. Some had flowing hair, some short... One was bald. One had silver hair. They floated across the canvas as if flying in loose formation, like a flock of nonchalant ducks. The background colors were yellow and blue, with dots of planets and a crescent moon with a face.

Hours later, she finished with her thumbprint and star in the upper right corner. Her back ached, but her heart was full. She called to Gypsy and went to make dinner.

In the morning, she was finishing her first cup of coffee, standing in front of her painting and marveling over how odd and wonderful it was, when John arrived in his big pickup truck.

Surprised, she opened the door.

He hooked a thumb in the direction of his truck. "Brought you something. Come see."

She set down her coffee and trotted after him. Sue stepped back in shock when he unfurled a blue tarp from a tall object in the truck bed. "Is that her bike?"

"Got it in one," John smirked.

Under the tarp stood Roseanne's 1990 Harley Sportster. The sky-blue frame and teardrop gas tank, vintage-style headlamp, and two-person seat had been completely refurbished. John attached a ramp to the tailgate and rolled the bike to the ground. Even though she'd never been a motorcycle person, the beauty of the machine stole her breath.

John nodded at her reaction. "It's a good bike."

"You fixed it."

"Restored it. Crime the way she let it go."

"What's it doing here?"

"I'm giving it back."

She reached for the handlebar, ran her finger over the smooth blue metal of the gas tank, the soft leather of the seat. Somebody had loved this machine.

"I never drove one." She looked up at him. "I don't know anything about motorcycles."

"I can teach you."

"I don't have much time."

"Then we best get started."

Chapter Forty-Two

Vicky was showing jewelry to a pretty young woman the next morning when Sue arrived at the shop, so she planted herself in an easy chair near the candelabra and waited.

Yesterday had been a blast.

At first, she tried to tell John she didn't want the motorcycle. Then she told him the truth: she was afraid.

"Riding a bike is simple, and this one's small. You're Roseanne's size; well, originally. Anyway," he said, "I can teach you in five minutes, but then you have to practice. You got a nice long driveway for that. Just stay out of the ruts."

"I'm leaving in a few days."

"Take it with you."

He showed her the particulars and then put her on the bike. "Ease out the clutch," he said. "Little bit of gas, little bit of clutch, stay in low gear, use the brakes. I'll be right with you."

And he was. That brusque bear of a man trotted alongside her like she was a child on her first attempt without training wheels.

Once, anyway, up and back. Out to the street and then back to the house. For one brief moment, she thought she might hit the throttle or forget how to brake, but she cruised slowly and carefully up and down the driveway a dozen times before John gave the "throat cut" gesture.

"You've got it, no problem." He helped her set the kickstand and climb off.

She took a minute to look at the man. He was frightening, really, with that big body, dark glasses, and bald head with a bandanna tied over it. Bare, muscular arms. He could pick up that motorcycle and fling it if he wanted to.

He saw her studying him. "What?"

"Why are you being so nice?"

"I got enough bikes."

"That's not what I mean, John." She folded her arms. "All this time, you've acted like you hated me—"

John smirked at the ground, shaking his head.

"You did! And now that I'm leaving. Wait. It's because I'm leaving," said Sue. "You're glad I'll be out of here."

"Wrong." He pointed a beefy finger at her. "You were good for him, and he knew it."

Sue had her doubts, but the afternoon had been too much fun to dwell on them. It was a thrill to learn to ride the motorcycle, and in a small way, she felt like she was burying the hatchet with John *and* Roseanne. John had given her that.

As he was leaving, she hugged him. "You're a good person."

"Wouldn't go that far." He patted her awkwardly on the back and drove away.

Now in the consignment shop, the sale completed, Vicky turned to Sue. "I have a bad feeling about why you're here."

"Well, you're wrong." Sue held out a small bundle tied up in a scarf. "I brought you something."

Vicky unwrapped a rose-gold deco-style bracelet featuring a single black opal set between six diamonds. "Holy crap," she said. "Where did you find this?"

"Laying around the house."

"You want me to appraise it?" Vicky held up the bracelet. "Tell you right now, I'd ballpark it at five to six K."

"Whatever," said Sue. "I'm donating it to the art students' charity fund. You can keep the commission."

"Are you serious?" Vicky examined the stones. "I'm surprised Roseanne didn't sell it."

"She didn't know about it." Sue had found a secret cache of jewelry in the primary bathroom, behind a loose piece of wallboard that fell away from underneath the sink. "It belonged to my aunt."

"Just that piece, all by itself?" asked Vicky.

"A few others." In addition to the bracelet, the dusty cloth bag held three necklaces, six rings, and two sets of earrings, the latter made of gold and precious stones. Every item looked very old and very valuable.

Oh, well, Sue thought. *Too late now.*

Vicky looked up. "Hey, guess who was in here yesterday? Patsy McClanahan."

"Who?"

"The chick you know as Berkeley Novak. She wanted to hock some trashy old silverware, but I couldn't help her. She was pretty pissed off when she left."

Sue made a face. "She tried to make Rafael hate me," she said.

"Figures."

"Didn't matter anyway," said Sue. "We're done."

"So, no Mrs. Palacios for you?"

"Uh-uh."

"What now?"

"I'm moving back to California, to the house my husband and I bought just before he died."

"I'm sorry," said Vicky. "Rafael's been solo too long. He'll never settle down."

"No," said Sue. "His business will always be his priority."

Vicky finished examining the bracelet. "You'll be fine, though. You're tough."

"I know. I've surprised myself. This is the first time I've ever lived alone."

"Seriously?"

"Yeah, and I loved it. Loved living here. I wish it could have worked out, but it didn't."

Vicky wheeled around the counter, parked in front of Sue, and with great difficulty, struggled to a standing position. The two women hugged.

"Don't be a stranger," Vicky said.

"I won't."

A few minutes later, Sue hauled her latest painting into Marissa's gallery. The younger woman gasped, then laughed out loud. "Oh my gosh, they're us, aren't they?"

"I think so," said Sue. "I'm as surprised as you are."

"I love it," said Marissa. "It just makes me so happy, and it'll sell in a heartbeat."

"I'm not sure I want to sell it." Those were her friends in the picture. She couldn't imagine not seeing them every day. "Maybe I'll keep this one."

"You can paint more." Marissa elbowed her gently. "This one goes in the front window. Wait and watch."

As soon as the canvas was settled on an easel facing outward, two women stopped on the sidewalk to look. Another three joined them. The group stood in front of the painting, smiling and nodding.

"I thought of the title," said Sue. "*Friends for Life.*"

"That'll work," said Marissa.

Lost in thought, Sue drove back to the Mesa house, sad to leave her friends, her mind churning. So much so that she barely registered Rafael's work truck sitting in her driveway.

Chapter Forty-Three

Rafael stood at the edge of the property, near the bunkhouse, gazing at the red rock formations across the canyon.

He had lied to her when he said this view was nothing special. In fact, no sight was more compelling, not even from his own house.

Regrettably, the Mesa would be sold. In fact, it was already spoken for. His buyers were eager to start, although they wanted the whole lot. They were annoyed that the land would be divided and made dismissive comments about the old house, calling it an eyesore.

Rafael kept his mouth shut and accepted their deposit.

A car door slammed. He turned to see Gypsy racing up the path toward him, her little legs a blur.

"What is this!" He bent to scoop up the little dog, letting her kiss his chin. Tucking her against his chest, he walked slowly to where Sue waited, leaning against her SUV, arms folded.

"Can I help you?" he asked, the corner of his mouth turning up.

She didn't smile. "What are you doing here?"

"Susan." He reached for her.

She stepped back. "Don't."

His hand dropped. "I had to see you. To ask if you are okay." He cleared his throat. "To ask if you will always hate me."

"I don't hate you, Rafael." She shrugged. "I'm just very disappointed at how it all turned out."

This time when he reached for her, she let herself be drawn into his embrace. Sighing, she wrapped her arms around him. He rested his chin against her head and held her close.

They stood there for a long time, wordless. When he lifted her chin, she opened to him, and their kiss was deep, rich, and heartbreaking.

"I can't believe you're going," he said.

She looked like she wanted to say something but bit it back. "The movers are coming tomorrow morning," she said, "and I still have a lot to do."

"I understand." He caressed her cheek with the back of his fingers.

Her eyes closed.

"I wish it hadn't turned out like this," he said.

"But it did." She took a long, slow look at the property, then at him. He felt small under the gaze of eyes as blue and cold as glacial ice.

"I have to go," she said.

"Adios, *Corazon*."

Calling the dog, she turned on her heel and walked to the house, leaving him standing alone in her front yard.

* * * * *

CLOSING THE DOOR, SUE COLLAPSED AGAINST IT, stunned at her resolve. For one brief moment, caught in the sweet depth of his eyes, she had wanted to throw everything away. To beg him to consider a future together, however it worked out.

But she would always resent him. Rafael was the reason the Mesa would be cut in two like Solomon's infant. Flo had acted as her legal representative, obtaining all the necessary documents and signatures and generally cleaning up the loose ends so the property could be divided. A chain-link fence would be strung between the two halves.

With this solution, the Mesa would survive. As for Sue, she would limp away to the Central Valley to remake her life. She had lied to Rafael; nothing remained to be done. Everything was ready for the movers. All the shelves were empty, all the closets and cabinets were cleared. She had donated everything that the women's shelter couldn't use. Her new bed and other furniture would be shipped to the Visalia house.

"I'm doing the right thing," she mumbled, pushing off from the door. Outside, Rafael's truck started up. Peering through the kitchen window, she watched him go, her heart deflating like a sad old balloon. She gripped the edge of the sink, willing herself not to run after him, not to beg him to come back.

But their love had been corrupted. A life together was now impossible.

As Sue walked around the almost empty house one last time, grief flattened her. She would never forgive him for ruining her chances of living here or loving him. What a selfish decision, based entirely on his fear of poverty.

A sad smile crept across her lips. She had assumed he came from wealth, but as she learned about his difficult beginnings, she realized everything he had, he had earned. She admired that about him, but no matter how rich he became, he would never feel safe. She couldn't save him.

Rafael was sticking safely to a particular groove, following a pattern that worked well enough. A pattern that he would repeat until he died.

For one brief stretch, she had imagined them living together here, both excited about their work, turning the Mesa into a busy little community supporting artists and craftsmen.

He loved me, she thought. *I know this was true. But he gave me up for money.*

"His loss," she said, trying to be brave. All that remained was for her to get in the car and drive to Visalia. Sedona would remain in the rearview mirror. She would never return.

Chapter Forty-Four

The moving van parked out front. When the two men knocked on the door, Sue directed them to load her mother's bedroom furniture, some pieces from the living room and den, and the kitchen table and chairs, all mementos of her childhood.

There wasn't much. It only took an hour to load. The movers had another household to pick up and unload. They would arrive in Visalia tomorrow afternoon.

Once there, she would carry on and make a good, strong life for herself. Unfortunately, she didn't feel strong or brave walking around the house, merely sad. Worse than sad—grief-stricken. Because, she realized as she ran her fingertips over the fireplace mantle her father had built with his own hands, she wasn't just losing Rafael and the house. She was losing the last evidence of her family's existence.

Sue straightened her shoulders. Foolish to dwell. Minutes from now, she'd lock the door and drop the keys with Flo. Tonight, she'd sleep in a hotel room. Tomorrow morning, her new old life would begin.

Travis and Katie had given her a gift—that of acceptance. Whereas Sue had worried she made their childhood too difficult, Travis insisted their constant moving from base to base and Mike's demanding nature had made them strong. He was thriving, and Katie had found her way at last.

Sue wished she could keep the Mesa. She wished she could keep the man. But if she had to go on alone, without either of them, she would be all right.

The moving van started up, a blast of sound shattering her thoughts. Soon, she would be back in Visalia. Once there, she would get busy with committee work. Make more of an effort this time to settle in, to get to know people.

The air brakes released with a great whoosh. The motor strained as the truck started to move.

She checked the faucets one last time. Glimpsed the bright sun reflecting off a car across the canyon, by the rock formations. She never had gotten over there, and now she never would.

Straightening her shoulders again, she reached for her keys. Time to load Gypsy in the crate for the long drive back. Everything would work out.

The Visalia house would ground her. It would anchor her.

Sue pulled her suitcase to the front door.

Stopped.

The Visalia house would hold her down. Trap her in Mike's world, in the past.

But Sue didn't have to live in the past. She could make a community anywhere. The actual physical location didn't matter. The community was within her.

Dropping her purse, she ran out to stop the moving truck.

Chapter Forty-Five

Three months later, Rafael was in hell. It was just one damn thing after another. First, they took out a gas line and almost blew up the city. Who knew it would be there?

Susan might have known, but she was gone, and every time he thought of her, he found himself stuck, trapped, frozen in place. He wished she hadn't left, but what was done was done. She'd made her decision. He would respect that. Everything else he'd screwed up, but at least he could do that right. Respect her wishes and leave her alone.

Rafael stomped around the property, continually having to stop the earthmovers from wrecking some remnant of her family history—a bit of statuary or a slab of cement bearing child-sized hand prints and a date. When this happened, he would rush forward, dig the item out of the ground, put it in his truck, and haul it to his house. His collection was growing, as was consternation over what the hell he thought he was going to do with it.

Cursing, he rushed across the dirt to get the heavy equipment operator back in line. Rafael usually used his own crew, but they were busy putting up another condominium complex, something he had no interest in.

This Mesa property was going to kill him. The people he found to work with had no feeling for the land at all. So far, he had done little more than scrape off the topsoil and pound stakes. Eventually, it would be a breathtaking parcel, even with the old house at the back end.

After a draining legal battle, he'd won a ruling from the city planning commission that the rear house had no right to a pathway to the canyon, something Flo had scribbled into the plans without his knowing. The director of the women's shelter had put up an epic fight, represented by a bulldog-jawed lawyer covered in prison tattoos. The shelter lost, but only after costing Palacios a ton of money.

He had agreed to build a privacy wall between the properties, which would destroy any chance of a view from the back house, but that wasn't his concern.

The bunkhouse was gone, which would shame him had he not rescued most of the furnishings, now stored in his cabinetry workshop, crowding him out. Some day he would have to contact her and resolve that.

A rumble interrupted his thoughts, and he ran screaming across the property to grab yet another artifact: a faded pink tricycle, bent and twisted. He carried it to his truck.

In the parking lot, he groaned at the sight of Berkeley Novak's coupe. The historical society had changed their minds about wanting the property. Now, they were surprised and furious that he and Susan had moved so quickly.

Greedy bastards. It had all turned to shit. He was ashamed of the warzone the Mesa had become. His clients were no better. The couple buying his property were selfish pigs who constantly argued with each other and with him, as if he were a third person in their dysfunctional marriage. He would make a bundle from this property, but he would have earned it. The whole business sickened him. And he was no closer to leaving for Buenos Aires. He still hadn't contacted his daughter. Still hadn't worked up the nerve.

Then it turned out the bunkhouse had some historical artifacts underneath and around the foundation, so the department of archaeology at ASU had people going over it with picks and shovels and toothbrushes.

As he turned his back on Berkeley Novak, his buyer waddled toward him. The man had been fussing about the accuracy of the property line and the previously agreed-upon height of the dividing wall.

Rafael ducked around a clump of bushes, slunk down the slope to the streambed, and trotted west. There was only one place he could hide.

Ten minutes later, spotting the hidden walkway to the cave, he glanced around to make sure he hadn't been followed. Then he dragged the tangle of brush aside, slipped through, and pulled the vegetation closed behind him. At the top of the path, he flopped down on the red earth, his back resting against the cool, soft wall of the cave.

Susan had been the smart one, relinquishing her hold on this mess and letting him enjoy the fruits of his blind ambition. A hundred times a day, he considered letting her have the whole damned thing. He would have less material wealth, but perhaps he would also have had her. But it was too late now. The property was scraped, and the bunkhouse was gone.

Closing his eyes, Rafael regretted everything.

Chapter Forty-Six

Sue could hardly contain herself. Everything was ready, the gallery quiet. No sound except the beating of her heart, the thrum of blood racing through her veins.

A few days ago, she'd already felt like the luckiest woman in the world. Her cozy two-bedroom cottage in the California seaside town of Carlsbad was decorated with mementos from the Mesa House. Katie and her family lived a half-hour away, far enough to have lots of contact but not so close that her daughter took advantage. Travis was already in Dubai, but he was proud she'd resolved the standoff with Rafael. Whom he thought highly of, in case she wanted to know.

And tonight the local gallery would feature her works in an exclusive showing.

Sitting in her living room, looking out over the rooftops sloping downward toward the Pacific Ocean, Sue felt as if she had dreamed up an entire new existence. A new life, rising from the ashes of the old. Every morning, she and Gypsy walked on the beach. After breakfast, Sue would head for the spare bedroom to paint. Abstract, landscape, even a few tentative forays into portraiture. She had found her creative gear, and a gallery that appreciated her work.

In the evening, she'd prepare a healthy meal, after which she'd read or get caught up with email and phone calls. Her neighbors were friendly and often sat on their front porches, waving when she passed.

And of course, Sue had the joy of living near Katie's family. Already, Sophia and Ethan had claimed their territory within the cottage.

All in all, Sue had settled into her new home without too much trouble, having learned the art of adaptation. How different her life was now, compared to marriage and motherhood. Some days, she felt bereft, untethered. The grief would return, but it wasn't for Mike, specifically. More about the whole rotten deal of mortality, as Flo had put it.

On other mornings, Sue awoke with a sense of possibility, and at those times she would skip the walk and hurry to her bedroom studio to paint. She almost felt like a young woman again, although her heart would never heal completely.

Sue wondered constantly about Rafael. What he would be doing at that precise moment? How was the Mesa coming along? Were his clients settling down or still giving him grief?

She thought he would love this view.

But it hurt too much to ponder, so she stayed busy and tried not to think of him.

One day, three weeks after moving to Carlsbad, Sue and Katie met for lunch at a quaint little bistro in the village. Afterward, they wandered around, ducking into a toy shop, a chocolatier, a book store.

"Everything in Carlsbad is expensive," said Katie, "but you sure do get quality."

Sue nodded, her mouth full of handcrafted chocolate candy.

After that, they meandered into shops and galleries. One in particular drew her attention. It was more like Marissa's place in Sedona, classy without being uptight.

A curvy, middle-aged woman with honey-blonde hair waved to them from the desk, diamonds flashing at her wrist. "Good afternoon," she called out. "Are you here for the class?"

"We could be." Katie elbowed Sue.

"I'm Cynthia." The woman handed them flyers describing the classes. "Owner and instructor. You should come."

Now, three months and many classes later, Cynthia had already sold seven of Sue's pieces. That alone was exciting, but tonight was the culmination of a dream, a fantasy she never expected to come true.

When the featured artist canceled at the last minute, Cynthia asked Sue to step in. Heart in her throat, she had agreed. Tonight, the showing was dedicated solely to her work. It would be her California debut.

Now, she wandered around the silent room, telling herself to breathe. The staff had draped the front windows to hide her works until the doors opened. Drawn by the hype and the gallery's reputation, a line had formed on the sidewalk. A caterer stood ready with a plate of appetizers while the wine server poured flutes of champagne.

Heels clicking, Cynthia walked to the front doors. Turning, she raised one eyebrow at Sue, who took a deep breath, nodded, and forced a smile.

"Three, two, one," said Cynthia. The helpers pulled a cord, and the drapes fell to the floor. With a click, they swung the gallery doors open.

The crowd surged forward, chattering and laughing, drifting off to explore the artworks. Sue broke into a broad grin. It was really happening.

She was an artist.

Even though her knees were knocking in the minutes leading up to the opening, the fear went away as visitors reacted to her pieces. The wine server, a handsome man with a little silver ponytail, circulated among the crowd offering flutes of champagne.

Sue had recently created a series depicting female artists working in Sedona. In one, three women painted Bell Rock from their campsite next to a creek. In another, they worked from atop a fire lookout tower with a monsoon approaching. In a third, they drank wine while cleaning their brushes at a location that looked very much like the bunkhouse porch.

The series didn't have a formal name, but buyers referred to it as *The Girlfriends*. It was popular, it was beloved, and it made Sue a boatload of money, but it also carried an undertone of sadness.

Sue stood in the middle of a crowd, answering questions, laughing, and posing for pictures with Cynthia. A couple of local reporters interviewed her, holding their phones toward her, recording her responses.

She had so much fun telling them what inspired this painting, what inspired that. *The Girlfriends* series was the most popular by far. She didn't have anything as grotesque as the rage painting, but all of her paintings were popular. People stood in front of them, laughing and kissing or folding their arms and glaring at each other. An emotional seesaw for Sue to watch. She wanted to yell, "It's just a painting!" But maybe they were more than that.

Every single one of her paintings sold, and the mailing list was growing for notification of future availability.

Finally, the crowd dissipated. Cynthia eased the last few clients toward the door and locked it after them. Dimming the lights, the two women flopped into chairs in the manager's office.

Cynthia raised her glass. "You're on your way."

Sue laughed. How exciting to have realized her dream, to envision a career fired by passion, one that would carry her into the far future. She was an artist. She had arrived.

"I'm still kind of stunned," she admitted.

"You'll get used to it," said Cynthia. "Do you think you'll want to do it again in the spring?"

"I've been painting up a storm," said Sue. "I think I'll be ready."

"What I had in mind was—" A light rapping interrupted them. Someone was tapping on the glass out front. Cynthia twisted in her chair. "Can't they see we're closed?"

The tapping continued. Sue stood. "Somebody probably left their phone."

Groaning, Cynthia put her shoes back on. The two of them made their way down the darkened hallway to the dimly lit gallery. They paused in the shadows to study the person outside the store. A man. Dark hair, fierce mustache.

Sue inhaled. Held it. Tried to calm her pounding heart.

"Whatever that man wants," Cynthia said with a grin, "I'd be inclined to give him."

"He's a friend," said Sue. "From Sedona."

"Lucky you." Crossing the floor, Cynthia turned the lock and held open the door.

Rafael looked past her, his eyes fixing on Sue. "Am I too late?"

* * * * *

SUE AWOKE IN THE DARK OF HER BEDROOM. Beside her, Rafael lay on his side, his arm heavy across her rib cage, snoring softly. A big smile crept across her face.

As they made love, he'd gazed at her as if she were so precious, he couldn't risk closing his eyes and finding her gone.

In the dark room, she wished she could see his face; those deep-set eyes, full eyebrows, and mustache shot through with silver, but the candles had winked out long ago.

He'd found her.

Oh, she wasn't hiding. They'd had to communicate by text and email over the past few months for business reasons, both of them happy to avoid the phone. She hadn't wanted to hear his voice because it reminded her of too much she had lost.

But now he was back.

Wasn't he?

His breathing changed. His arm tightened, pulling her closer. "Stop thinking," he whispered against her temple.

She snuggled against him and fell back asleep.

In the morning, seated at her little breakfast nook with a view of the Pacific Ocean, they ate blueberry pancakes and got caught up.

"Flo and Vicky told me to say hello," he said. "Flo's back at the office. She's dating that guy, the old man. And Gabriela and Matt moved in together."

"And John?"

"He growled hello."

"He's a good man."

"He is a pain in the ass."

She poked at her food, not wanting to spoil the atmosphere, but she had to know. "How is the property going?"

"Horrible." He set down his fork and knife. "I think I made a big mistake."

"You think?"

"It's bad." He shook his head and gazed out the window. "My clients are pigs, your shelter guy is dangerous, and the antiquities people from the university are threatening to file an injunction."

"For what?"

"Desecration of Native lands." He pushed his plate away. "The worst part isn't the fighting and the arguing and the fussing and demands they all keep making. The worst part is none of it had to happen. It was all a matter of greed. Mine."

She reached for his hand. "You're not greedy, Rafael. You're anxious."

He rubbed his forehead. "You know me."

"What are you going to do?"

"What I am doing now. I told them I had business in California and sent the workers home. I hired a guard and told everybody to stay the hell off the property until I returned. And now I am ignoring my messages." He held up his phone. "I'm sure there are many."

She should have felt relief that she, at least, didn't have to endure what he was going through. But mostly, what she felt was regret for all of it.

"But Natalia has responded to my emails," he said, suddenly animated. "I am flying to Buenos Aires to meet my child." His voice faltered on the last few words. He pushed back his chair and walked to the living room, where he stopped in front of the window.

She followed, wrapping her arms around him from behind.

He layered his arms over hers. "She was glad to hear from me." He cleared his throat. "Very happy, in fact. We made plans immediately."

"Is she married? Are you a grandfather?"

"Come." He pulled her down on the couch with him. They sat holding hands as he described his daughter. Divorced with no children, she lived near her mother and stepfather in a suburb outside the city. Natalia loved her work as a land use attorney—

"The apple doesn't fall far from the tree," said Sue.

Rafael's mouth formed a straight line. "As many years as I have been away from her, I felt I could understand her," he said. "And I sensed that, although she was happy to hear from me, something else in her life is of concern. A burden. I will learn more when I see her."

He leaned back, gathering Sue to his side. She leaned her head on his shoulder, and he stroked her hair as they sat silently, thinking their own thoughts.

He turned, cradled her face in his hands, and kissed her deeply. "I am unhappy without you," he said. "I wish I hadn't screwed this all up. I am so sorry about your land." He rested his forehead against hers. "I wish there was some way to fix it."

"Me too. It's messed up. But it hurts too much for me to think about it. As much as I love having you here, it does bring it all back."

"Susan, I would give anything to start over with you. Is there any chance?"

"I live here now."

"How can you live without the red rocks?"

"I have all my life. Besides, the ocean gives me peace."

"I would move." He held her close, his voice reverberating in his chest. "I would sell everything, walk away from my business, to be with you."

"I love you too." Shocked, she looked up at him. If the words had surprised her, his smile didn't.

"I told you," he said, grinning like a loon. "I have loved you since you first stepped foot on your land, looking so formidable with those eyes." He kissed one and then the other. "So tough and so little."

"Mike used to call me 'small but mighty,'" she said.

Rafael raised an eyebrow.

She shook her head. "Don't be sad for me. Mike and I had so many good years together. He gave me my children. I miss him every day, but we're okay, and I believe he knows this."

"Susan, I mean it. I would move here if you would have me. Or if you like, we could live in Paris. You could paint."

"I can paint here. I'm becoming established. Would you really move to be with me? Anywhere?"

He exhaled slowly. "Anywhere."

She kissed him, long and slow. When they finally broke apart, she smiled so big it hurt. "Let me think about it."

Chapter Forty-Seven

When she came out of the shower, he was in the living room, talking loudly on the phone. Arguing. Angry.

Pulling the towel up, she stepped closer to listen.

"I don't care," he said. "Just do it. Play the old woman card, Flo. You know you can. They'll believe you." Rafael listened. Sighed. "I will. I promise. Just make this happen. Thank you." He hung up.

Sue ducked away and went back to dressing as if she'd heard nothing. It sounded like another of his business deals. Slipping in a pair of earrings, she wondered if he'd meant it, that he would sell all his properties and retire. Could he really? His drive to amass wealth was all-encompassing.

What could cause her to agree to change her life again? She'd been through so much lately she had whiplash.

Dressed, she found him in the living room, glowering at his phone and texting madly. When he saw her, he tossed the phone down. "Please sit with me. I have something to ask you."

Mystified, she sat.

"This is a beautiful place." He took her hand. "Do you love living here, or would you rather go home?"

"I am home."

"What I mean is, would you ever consider moving back to Sedona?"

She glanced at her watch. "Cynthia's expecting us at the gallery."

"Susan." Gently, he took her by the shoulders.

She looked away. She didn't want to hurt him, but she didn't plan to uproot her life again. And if she had to be in that close proximity to her beloved Mesa while someone else owned it, the answer was no. She would never go back. Not even to visit.

But there was no sense ruining the moment.

They had plans to stop at the gallery that morning, after which they'd enjoy the pipe organ at Balboa Park, followed by lunch at a seafood restaurant at the harbor.

Rafael's phone beeped. He picked it up and responded, jabbing the keys with an index finger. "Sorry. It's urgent." He set it down. "As I was saying—"

His phone beeped again. Apologizing, he grabbed it. "It's a business matter, very urgent. Almost finished."

"I'm fine." Sue got up and went to rinse their breakfast dishes. In fact, she wasn't fine. Despite his talk about being together, he would never stop working, would never put their relationship first.

His phone rang, and she heard him answer. Work, and the making of money, would always come first. She couldn't believe him when he spoke of strolling with her into the sunset. But she loved him anyway. And now he would break her heart all over again.

"*Corazon.*" Rafael came striding into the kitchen, arms wide, phone in one hand. His face looked joyful. He said to the caller, "She's here with me. Do you mind if I put you on speaker?"

Waving Sue over, he placed the phone on the kitchen table. "Go ahead."

"Well, hello, dear."

"Flo!" Sue grinned at the phone. The two of them hadn't spoken since Sedona. "How *are* you?"

"Perfectly well. Loving my life again," Flo said. "I'll get right to the point. You need to pack your bags and come home."

"Pardon?" Sue raised an eyebrow at Rafael.

"That man of yours has been busy," said Flo. "And because of the crackpot scheme he hatched, I'll probably lose my license, but it'll be worth it."

"What are you talking about?"

"I asked her to manufacture an oversight," said Rafael.

"What he means," said Flo, "is that I played the forgetful old bag and told the escrow people that I failed to obtain the necessary signatures on a whole bunch of binding docs and that you changed your mind about the sale and were pulling the property."

"You *what?*"

"It might not have worked, but Rafael's buyer jumped on it. He needed an excuse to back out."

Rafael grinned at the phone. "I told you."

"You did, and I admit, I was skeptical. But the moment we told him about my mistake, he and his wife started fighting again. She wanted to sue us, but he bribed her with the idea of an even better property." Flo chuckled. "Twenty bucks says they get a Vegas divorce on the way home."

"Was the prison lawyer a hard sell?"

"A perfect gentleman," said Flo. "He and the director, both. The problem was, I felt bad. They needed this house. Lots of families need a place to hide, unfortunately. So I told them we'd do a swap."

"Oh no." Rafael grimaced. "What are we swapping?"

"You know that little house you own in Cottonwood?"

Rafael's eyes widened. "The one on Verde Avenue? No."

"I figured with six bedrooms and four baths, it would be more useful to them than the Mesa. And it's closer to their office."

"That little house, as you call it, is worth a lot."

"But it's a very worthy cause, right, Sue?"

"Very." She looked up at Rafael, beaming.

With one arm, he reached for her. Pulled her in for a hug. "Good work, Flo. Thank you for making it happen."

With assurances they'd see each other soon, Rafael hung up.

Hope rose in Sue's chest. The Mesa property was theirs again. But still half Rafael's. "What happens now?" she asked.

"We unwind it," he said. "Return the deposits, reverse the donation. It's all going back to being a deserted piece of land. Unless somebody wanted to move back and live in that decrepit old shack."

She laughed. "You and Florence. What a team."

"Do you have a tablet?"

"Like, a computer?"

"Paper and pen. I know you have them."

She brought them over.

Rafael scribbled furiously on the lined yellow paper. With a flourish, he ripped off the sheet and handed it to Sue.

She read the words. Looked up, dumbfounded. "What is this?"

"A quit-claim. I am releasing my half of the property to you. You now own the Mesa one hundred percent."

"Is this legal?"

"Flo will help us make it so."

"You're giving up your half?" She gripped the arms of her chair, afraid if she didn't, she'd turn cartwheels across the room.

"It was never mine in the first place." He shrugged. "The hell with Roseanne."

Sue studied the paper. "Maybe she knew what she was doing."

"We will never know."

Sue held up the paper and ripped it in half. Then tore it again.

"I don't understand," Rafael said. "You don't want it?"

"It's moot," she said. "If we get married."

Chapter Forty-Eight

*L*ast night was a miracle, Sue thought. She and Rafael had enjoyed a romantic dinner at a restaurant overlooking the ocean, laughing and talking about their plans.

When dessert came, Rafael reached inside the breast pocket of his jacket for a black velvet box.

Then home to celebrate.

They lay with their limbs entwined for a long while afterward, her head on his shoulder. Every few minutes, she held out her hand to catch a bit of ambient lighting in the many facets of the large diamond.

"Susan, my soon-to-be wife, I wish I could invite you to come with me to Argentina." When he spoke, his voice rumbled against her ear.

"You want to see her alone this first time. I understand."

He kissed her forehead. "I don't know how long I'll be away."

"I'll be here. And then we'll go home."

"Yes." He gathered her against him. "And then we'll go home."

Chapter Forty-Nine

When they arrived at Katie's house in San Diego the next morning, her daughter spotted the new ring right away. Sue had been fearful of her reaction, but Katie couldn't stop beaming. "I'm glad you're happy," she whispered as she hugged Sue. "Dad would want that."

Jason stepped forward, his hand out to shake with Rafael. The two men warmed to each other immediately.

Ethan and Sophia barreled in from down the hall, flinging themselves into Sue's arms and chattering as only an eight- and ten-year-old could do. Noticing Rafael, they grew shy.

"Children, this is my—this is Rafael," Sue stammered.

"He's going to be your new grandpa," said Jason.

The little ones' faces fell.

"Oh no," said Katie. "Don't say that."

"Let's not jump to that place just yet," said Rafael. He dropped to one knee. "I hope you'll allow me to be a part of your family, to keep your grandmother company and make her happy."

Ethan studied Rafael. Then he nodded solemnly. "Then Grammie won't be by herself."

Sue bit her lip.

Sophia, peeking out from behind Katie, nodded.

"Good," said Rafael. "Thank you for making me feel welcome." He stood, reaching for Sue's hand and giving it a squeeze.

Sue felt her heart cracking in all new places. He was trying hard to fit in, and the family was willing to let him, but the memory of Mike hovered over them. Sue met her daughter's pointed gaze and quickly looked away, eyes stinging.

Because life was for the living, but you carried your memories with you forever, and it sharpened the sense of loss. But also of gratitude.

The children leaned against their mother, studying the stranger until it was time to take their seats.

"We need to have breakfast," said Jason. "I'm coaching Ethan's baseball team this morning, and we don't have a lot of time."

Rafael glanced at his watch. "We'll have to leave soon as well."

"Nervous?" Sue asked.

Rafael heaved a sigh. "Very."

She gave his waist a squeeze. "Then let's eat and get you on your way."

Chapter Fifty

Hair and makeup, check," said Katie. "Nails, check. Necklace, perfect. Are you ready for the dress?"

"Give me a minute." Sue had chosen springtime for the wedding, both for the weather and the spirit of renewal. The guest suite at Rafael's home served as the bride's dressing room today.

Outside, wind chimes jingled in the pines, and a wedding arch had been set up at the edge of the property overlooking the valley. A string quartet played classical music under an arbor twined with honeysuckle.

Standing beside Sue, Katie gave her a hug. "I can hardly believe this."

Earlier, Marissa and Vicky had helped her get ready. While Vicky did her makeup, Marissa put the finishing touches on her hair, which she wore in a French braid adorned with tiny flowers and pearls. Turning away from the mirror, Sue had held up her champagne flute. "Before we go out there, I want to say how much I appreciate all of you. How much I love you," she nodded to Katie, who blinked rapidly, "and I am so grateful to have all of you in my life."

"We're glad you're back," said Marissa.

"Looking forward to getting you in some trouble," said Vicky. She cocked her head at a distant rumble. "Is that the Rev?"

A motorcycle rumbled up, and the women gathered around the window. Some of the guests Sue knew— Gabriela and Matt were there, along with Flo, Franny, and John. Some were from Rafael's circle, people he'd worked with.

To Sue's great delight, his daughter, Natalia, a petite, ebony-haired beauty, had been able to break away from her law practice and fly north to attend the wedding. She stood chatting with John and Travis, both resplendent in gray morning suits. Sophia and Ethan ran around the yard, supervised by their father. Gabriela and Matt, Flo, Franny, and a handful of the locals from Roseanne's funeral were there.

Earlier, Rafael had introduced Natalia to everyone in attendance, beaming with pride at his beautiful and accomplished daughter. When he had traveled to Buenos Aires, Rafael was anxious that she would be distant toward him. Instead, she greeted him at the airport with a warm, tearful hug. In her early thirties, Natalia was single and childless, but by all accounts, she was happy and successful.

She had a good relationship with her mother and stepfather, who lived near her.

"I saw her," he said one evening as they sat at the edge of the Mesa, watching a storm move across the distant landscape. "Natalia's mother."

Sue set down her glass of port. "Tell me."

"We met at a park. Her hair was long and completely silver. She was much older. Well, we both are. So much time has passed." He looked down at his hands. "She embraced me."

Sue felt her throat close.

Rafael looked up at her, his eyes welling. "Christ." He rubbed his face.

"It was rough?"

"I asked her forgiveness. She asked mine." He looked away, nodding. "It was good."

Sue had leaned her head on his shoulder. They sat quietly for a long time, watching the night come on.

Katie's voice broke into her thoughts. "We should get moving," she said.

Sue tore herself away from the window.

Vicky held out a blue velvet box. "I brought you something old."

Opening the box, Sue gasped. "My mother's earrings." Sue reached for them, her fingers trembling. "I thought they were long gone."

"Couldn't sell 'em," said Vicky. "Nobody wanted them."

"Right." Sue gave her a wry smile. The earrings, pearl and diamonds set in gold, were probably the most valuable jewelry her mother had owned.

Katie held out the dress. It was blue satin, knee-length, with a princess neckline and a nipped-in waist.

In front of the mirror, stepping into the dress, Sue bit her lip. Memories of Mike flooded her chest.

"You look beautiful, Mom." Katie zipped her up. Wrapping her in a hug from behind, Katie rested her chin on Sue's shoulder. Together, they gazed into the mirror, knowing each other's thoughts.

Outside, the quartet played a prelude to the main event. The achingly sweet strains of the violin reached them through the bedroom window. Sue inhaled deeply, her emotions all over the place. The past was never really past, and she would always carry Mike in her heart, but her life was about to begin again, thanks to that good man waiting outside.

Better than ever.

"Okay. Let's go."

The women filed out to the living room, where Travis stood waiting. He broke into a broad grin. "You look awesome, Mom."

"So do you." She kissed his cheek and reached for Katie. "So do both of you."

"Come on. Your guy is waiting." Travis offered her his arm. With the other, Sue linked to Katie's, and the three of them stepped out into the spring sunshine.

Epilogue

The early summer breeze swept across the Mesa, threatening to blow Rafael's blueprints from the picnic table. He and John had moved it from the backyard to the edge of the property. Now it stood under a makeshift ramada.

Sue handed Rafael another chunk of wood from what was left of the bunkhouse. Although she'd been furious to learn he'd razed the structure, it created an opportunity.

He anchored the corners of the blueprints, and the three of them leaned forward to study the plans. A gust blew a strand of Sue's hair into her face, and she hooked it behind her ear. On her left hand, the emerald-cut solitaire caught the late-morning sun and threatened to blind her. She looked up at her husband and caught him grinning.

"I'm glad you love it."

"I love you," she said.

Rafael hugged her, his eyes crinkling in a joyful smile.

John shook his head. "If you two could break away for a minute." He tapped the blueprint with one finger. "You should rebuild the bunkhouse right over the old slab. There's already gas and electric."

Rafael nodded. "That location will allow for front and back courtyards, as well as access to the secondary parking area."

"And a side driveway for catering vans and delivery trucks," said Sue.

"Big plans, Mrs. Palacios."

"Yes." Sue grinned up at her husband. The blueprints were the start of a new life for the Mesa. One he'd promised her on their honeymoon in Paris.

They'd been walking the Champs-Élysées, pausing on the bridge overlooking the river, a cool breeze brushing their faces, when he'd apologized for everything that had happened under her sister's watch.

"I saw Roseanne decline for years, and the property along with it," he admitted. "I tried to talk her into clearing it, and at times she would let me remove some small thing. But I had no serious impact, and I gave up. I should not have."

"It wasn't your problem to solve," Sue had said.

"But I want to make it up to you." Rafael turned her to face him. "Tell me again about your dreams."

Feeling his warm embrace and gazing into his dark eyes, she shivered. They had barely made it out of the hotel room by noon, and if it were up to her, she'd go back there now. But she was nearly as excited about her plans for the Mesa.

"You already know." She thought of their first lunch right after Roseanne died.

"You wanted a place where artists could gather." He fixed his gaze on her as he began speaking. "You want to foster creativity and wellness. Small groups inspiring each other. Motivating each other. Providing company and support."

He remembered. He had listened.

Overwhelmed, she snuggled against his chest.

His voice rumbled in her ear. "I will build it for you."

They had celebrated for days, sharing exquisite meals and long walks along the Seine, talking about their plans and their future. Rafael planned to sell his house in the mountains, although he had no intentions of giving up Palacios Development.

Now, she awoke every morning to his embrace in the Mesa house bedroom where her parents used to sleep. The house was undergoing rehab, with new plumbing and electrical, a carpentry shop in the back, and a garden center around the Virgin of Guadalupe, now sporting a riot of colorful flowers.

Studying the blueprints, Sue looked up at Rafael and John. "I want to host events," she said. "Baby showers. Weddings."

"In the new bunkhouse," Rafael tapped the diagram. "You will need a larger kitchen here, but we can build it to resemble the original structure."

"Can you do that, John?" When the big man didn't answer, Sue looked up. "John?"

John's eyes were fixed on a person, a woman, picking her way toward them over the rocky ground. She was tall and wore a floppy sun hat over long, blond-gray hair pulled into a ponytail.

"Hello?" The woman's voice reached them, strong for such a thin frame.

She looked familiar. Sue stepped forward. "Can I help you with something?"

"Yes, excuse me, sorry to intrude." She had an East Coast accent, very proper, with rounded vowels and a clipped cadence. Lifting her chin at John, she said. "I was looking for the contractor. I assume that would be you?"

John folded his arms across his chest.

"You see, I have a project that needs to be done at my home. I noted the name of your business on your vehicle and inquired about you."

Sue remembered. "You're Celeste Waterbury. We met at the charity dance last summer."

"Yes, that's right." Celeste gazed around the property. "You've been busy."

"I could give you a tour," said Sue.

"I'd like that. At some point." She looked back at John. "Are you available for hire?"

"Could be. I work for this guy." John hooked a thumb over his shoulder.

Rafael grinned. "Don't let me stop you, amigo."

"Yeah then," said John. "What do you need?"

"A meditation room," Celeste said. "With proper acoustics, and possibly, a water feature. A subtle fountain, perhaps. Can you do that?"

"Easy," said John.

Sue cut a look at Rafael. He caught her eye and turned away, hiding a smile.

Celeste tapped her phone. "Excellent. How is next Wednesday, in the morning?"

"I got time now." John hitched his tool belt. "Let's go take a look."

The End

Author Note and Acknowledgements

I hope you enjoyed *Starting Over in Sedona*. If you'd like to see more about me or my other books, or receive my empowering and uplifting monthly newsletter, please visit AnyShinyThing.com.

I first discovered Sedona years ago when a family member was married there. I had no idea what to expect (too busy working to do the research, I guess) and we arrived at night. The next morning, when I threw open the doors of my balcony room, I was stunned. Across the canyon stood red rock formations, dotted with sparkling white snow and set against a backdrop of robin's-egg-blue sky. I was enthralled.

Since then, of course, Sedona has become quite a bit busier, regrettably! But I still love the idea of it, and visit whenever I can.

In creating this series, my vision was to portray a community of people who are united by their love for art, creativity, and the red rock country.

Thanks so much to my team, the people who helped produce this novel: pre-publication readers Leslie James, Debbie Vannimwegen, Nanci Sheeran, Sandy Nachlinger, Cathy Nieswonger, Heather Wood, Joanne Hardy, and Linda Robinson. Also, many thanks to my editor Michelle Rascon, and cover designer Damonza,com. I am grateful for your help.

PS: Ratings help authors stay afloat. It only takes a minute, and I'd be very grateful! Go here to leave stars or a review: https://mybook.to/SedonaOne

Made in the USA
Las Vegas, NV
11 February 2025

17981755R00215